GNA: INITIATE

By Rob Steele

*To Mom & Dad
Look! I did it again!*

PublishAmerica
Baltimore

© 2006 by Rob Steele.

All rights reserved. No part of this book may be reproduced, stored in a retrieval system or transmitted in any form or by any means without the prior written permission of the publishers, except by a reviewer who may quote brief passages in a review to be printed in a newspaper, magazine or journal.

First printing

At the specific preference of the author, PublishAmerica allowed this work to remain exactly as the author intended, verbatim, without editorial input.

All characters appearing in this work are fictitious. Any resemblance to real persons, living or dead, is purely coincidental.

ISBN: 1-4241-4202-4
PUBLISHED BY PUBLISHAMERICA, LLLP
www.publishamerica.com
Baltimore

Printed in the United States of America

Dedication

For Frank, Lorraine, Dianne, Alyx, Myndi,

Acknowledgements

I would also really like to thank EVERYONE at PublishAmerica for being so helpful with everything they do.

I would like to thank Stanley "Big Rob" Robinson for agreeing to be in the book.

And I'd like to really thank my wife, Dianne, for putting up with me on this. (It was in our vows… love, honor, cherish, put up with.)

PROLOGUE

It was supposed to be a simple job. One of the easier jobs he'd ever done. Ok, it was an easy job on a *military base*.

But it was all so easy. What could possibly go wrong? They had gotten the forged IDs.

They had gotten the truck, the people, the map, the location of the armory—all those weapons would make big money on the black-market. They even lined up several buyers.

They got in the gate. They got to the armory. They even got the first pallet of weapons loaded. Mostly RPGs—Rocket Propelled Grenades.

Then *they* had appeared. Literally out of nowhere!

There were only four of *them*, and twenty of his group. All of his were armed and trained. They should have had no problem. Just four people in weird outfits. *They picked a hell of a time for a Candid Camera bit*, he thought. *This should not be a problem. Only one of them is armed...* at least visibly.

The interior of the armory, more of a big warehouse, really, was empty save for the crates of weapons. The only problem was the only exit, the loading dock, was blocked off by the truck.

Not a problem. Twenty to four were good odds. Until the one in the middle wearing a half-red and half-blue bodysuit, split color-wise down the middle, burst into flames sending fireballs into half of his men.

One of the others, in a pinkish bodysuit (spandex?) jumped from the other side of the armory and in one bound landed on top of two of his men, knocking them into a stack of crates and relative state of unconsciousness.

One in gray seemed to float above the ground. The gray one outstretched his arms and the rest of his men seemed to fly into the wall behind them.

The armed one of the four unslung a large rifle from her back and pointed it at him. He saw four red lines stretching from the rifle to various points on him at about the same time his pistols on both hips, rifle strap and sheathed knife on his bandoleer were shot off in what appeared to be only one shot clattering to the floor behind him, except the knife, of course, which simply fell with a clang in front of him.

The flaming one in the middle suddenly turned blue and a white mist permeated the side of the armory with his men that were on fire. Once touched by the mist, they were encased in… *ice?* Going from one temperature extreme to the other instantly.

He fell over, partly in shock, partly because he'd been shot in the chest. It may have hit the knife but it still hurt! It was all over. That quickly. Less than fifteen seconds. The plans he'd been making for months were all foiled in less than fifteen seconds.

He started in shock at the quartet and mumbled something about the best-laid plans of mice and men when he noticed a small white mouse sitting on his leg.

"Never underestimate us mice," it said.

His jaw fell. The mouse and the four vanished. Not so much as a puff of smoke.

Their disappearance coincided with the opening of other, previously hidden doors of the armory and the influx of troops all over the room, all with weapons at the ready.

Not that there was anyone to oppose them.

PART I
INITIATION

1
THE LAST THREE

Ranj Serikahn had had enough of his cubical.

His girlfriend of six years had told him the previous night saying she *just wants to be friends*. This, of course, after catching her with... *him*.

His boss was apparently out of coffee again and on a rampage—demanding reports that no one had ever heard of, and wanting them now!

The last straw had been that idiot on his way in to the office after lunch. *Go back to the sand you terrorist bastard!* He'd heard this all before—especially after 9-11.

Yes, he was of Middle Eastern descent. Yes, he vaguely resembled some of the suspected terrorists on *CNN*—tall, thin, slight beard and moustache. Yes, he was a Muslim.

But he was born in South Carolina. He was an American, just like that moron who insulted him this morning. That jerk had looked younger than Ranj. At least, he'd looked younger than Ranj felt. Shouldn't that mean he'd been an American longer than that idiot outside the office? And just being a Muslim doesn't make you a terrorist.

Working in a bank for almost ten years, in the same cubicle, for almost the same pay, the girlfriend situation, the boss, and that racist moron had been enough. With a building this size, Ranj thought there was only one thing to do.

Besides, he's always wondered what it would be like to fly.

* * *

He'd never had this much attention before. It made him a bit nervous, standing on the ledge of the seventh and top floor of the bank building. There were seven police cars surrounding the building, all with the lights flashing.

Ranj liked the view. Actually he'd come up here often, just never actually walked out on the ledge. Two cops were on the roof with him. There were three, but the third took Ranj's boss back inside after threatening to fire Ranj if he jumped.

That cinches it, he thought, *my boss really is an idiot.*

The other cops had tried to talk him out of jumping, but he was not interested in anything they had to say.

They had found his ex-girlfriend earlier. She tried to explain why she broke up with him and that it was stupid to jump off a building.

He didn't care about what she had said either. This was it. It was time to go. The last minute attention had been nice. If it had come earlier he might have stayed. But it was too late now.

"Ranj," a soft voice said from behind him. He was standing on the ledge, but facing the door to the lower floors, back to the street. The two cops seemed a bit startled that someone else was on the roof as well since they were both facing this newcomer.

A small, light-skinned woman appeared near the door, wearing a light blue... cloak with a hood? *Odd thing to wear in July*, he thought. He couldn't make out much of her figure but her face, which was mostly shielded but the hood, was familiar. So was her voice.

"Ranj," she said again, "I think I have a better offer for you."

"Gigi?" Ranj asked, feeling quite confounded. *I haven't seen her since high school.* "You picked a hell of a time to show up." He glanced over his shoulder at the ground, seven stories down. It made him a bit dizzy at this angle and he staggered a bit.

"Ranj," she continued, "you have a lot more to live for than you know about. I was coming here to offer you a considerably better life than what you have now. You are one of the few people on the planet that I am supposed to... *initiate*."

After her last word, Ranj felt... strange. His body seemed to quiver and sway. He almost lost his balance. He didn't want to jump backwards. He was intent on jumping, spreading his arms and making a general spectacle of himself.

He looked at Gigi with a perplexed expression. He felt as if his skin was sliding off the bone. Not painful, but definitely weird, as if his entire body had been dosed with Novocain. "What did you do to me?" he tried to ask. It came out a bit more like "Vat di ew do to muh?" Something had happened to his jaw. It felt... rubbery.

He turned back to the street and looked down. He noticed his right arm stretch a bit at the end of his turn. This was all too much. From the breakup to the racist bastard to... whatever this was, now was the time for it all to end. He'd had enough.

Ranj spread his arms, which went a bit wider than he thought was possible. He held his head up proudly, and jumped.

The first second was exhilarating. As the descent continued his life passed in front of his eyes—very quickly, and not all of it, but most of his life, including a striking image of Gigi in that blue cloak on the roof.

When he passed the second floor he had his first "second thoughts" on jumping. In the split second it took him to get to the first floor, his "second thoughts" were gone, replaced with a sense of euphoria. He was doing the right thing. He was convinced of it.

In the next split second, he hit the ground.

Then he bounced—

Six times.

* * *

Rich Walker was one of the happiest people on the planet. He stood on the second turnbuckle of the ring and hoisted his newly won championship belt over his head. He'd waited years for this moment.

Everyone in the crowd was on their feet. They were all chanting his name. Actually they were chanting "MAM-MOTH! MAM-MOTH!" Which was fine with him. That was the name he used in the ring.

He'd always been big. Even in high school. Too big really. He couldn't play basketball. He was too slow to get up and down the court. He couldn't play football; he'd probably kill someone.

Professional wrestling had been his calling. And now he'd finally made it to the top. World Heavyweight Champion in the ACW. Not the biggest pro-wrestling league, but far from the smallest. This should get him noticed by the big boys in the bigger leagues.

He soaked up the moment, letting the chant of his name reverberate through his entire body.

It took him almost ten minutes after the match to make his way to the locker room. He did check on his opponent, Christian Cross. He was afraid the finishing "power bomb" might have been a bit too hard. Chris winded, but other wise ok. Some officials and a medic wheeled him out on a stretcher anyway—just for show.

Chris was a good kid but his gimmick in the ring offended actual Christians. He wasn't the actual second coming. Actually it was an odd choice for a gimmick since Christian's real name was Stan Goldman. And, yes, he was Jewish.

Just looking at the two, Christian and Rich, one would have thought it obvious that Rich would win. Christian looked impressive at about 6'2, 245 muscular pounds. But Rich was almost 7'4 and close to 450.

Neither Rich nor Stan/Christian, who were actually good friends "off-stage", thought of wrestling as fake. Scripted was a better word. Yes, the winner was determined by scriptwriters. But it still hurt like hell when someone landed on you, connected on a dropkick, or picked you up and slammed you on the mat.

Not that anyone in this league *could* slam Rich. He was just too big, which is one of the reasons he was so surprised to see the lithe little person in his dressing room—a small woman in a light blue cloak with the hood up.

"Sorry little lady," he began; using his best cocky wrestler voice, the one he used on-stage, "I know you want to be with the champ, but I'm pretty sure I'd break you." He laughed in that annoying, on-stage wrestler laugh.

"You've gotten a little full of yourself haven't you Rich?" she replied in a light delicate tone. She looked up at him to reveal a rather pretty, pale face with large green eyes and lips that weren't very different in color from the rest of her face.

It took Rich a moment to make a connection, but when he did, he swooped his large arms down and picked up the wispy woman and gave her a big, but gentle, hug. "Gigi! My God! I haven't seen you in years! We're you out there tonight?"

"Yes," she wheezed. "You can put me down now."

He did and smiled. Gigi struggled for a moment to catch her breath before resuming her somewhat rigid stature. "Sorry," he mumbled looking temporarily abashed before resuming his excited, adrenaline fueled ecstasy.

"I finally got this damn thing!" he exclaimed like the excitable schoolboy she remembered, holding up the belt.

She remembered when he finally got a birthday present he'd been wanting for years. She didn't remember what it was, but she did remember him getting it taken away when he accidentally knocked down a small tree in his parent's front yard—and sent it flying through the new living room window. He was acting just like that now—the euphoric dance of the successful present recipient. She just hoped that she wouldn't be the tree that got knocked down.

"I need to talk to you Rich," she started. "It's actually very important."

Rich's eyes widened and he looked suddenly sober. "Someone died didn't they? I mean, other than Joahn and Eric. I already know about them." Joahn and Eric, mutual friend of Gigi and Rich had died—Joahn in a car wreck about five years ago, Eric more recently, but under unusual circumstances. But both had died since he had seen her last.

Gigi was a little relieved that he was off his elated kick, but a bit unhappy with herself that she had to bring him down. He *had* worked a long time for this. And now she had to take it away.

"No, Rich. No one died," she replied somberly. "But I do need to take you with me. I'm kind of... well, drafting you."

Rich's eyes widened even more and he began to perk up. "You're working with the W-W..."

"No no no," she interrupted with a delicate smirk. "Do I look like someone in professional wrestling?" she asked widening her arms, revealing a small but definitely feminine body in a skintight bodysuit that was slightly darker than her light blue cloak.

"Um, well, no. You don't. What's this all about Gi?" Rich was beginning to get frustrated. He just finally completed a life goal and been reunited with an old friend, but instead of being happy, he felt like going back to the ring to beat up anyone who even came close to the ring. Script be damned.

"I just want you to know," she started, somberly, "that I was hoping you wouldn't win that belt tonight." She gave him a very poignant look.

"Gi... you're not making sense. And I'm getting upset. What the hell are you talking about?!" Gigi knew that the giant man would never hurt her... unless he hugged her again. But that didn't make this any easier on her.

She looked up into his eyes with almost-tears in hers. "I'm sorry big guy." She hesitated briefly before she said, "Initiate."

* * *

Stanley Robinson sat in the studio and stared at the computer screen. The new editing program the recording label had bought wasn't working up to his specifications.

The recording session had gone wonderfully. But the mixing process was becoming very tedious. He wasn't a particularly big fan of George McCallum, but he was an up and coming new artist. George had gone home shortly after the session.

He was a good performer with a great voice, but his attitude was... well, George was becoming a primadonna. *If he keeps this up*, Stan thought, *he'll be a post-Madonna. 'Cause I'm gonna kill 'im.*

Stan loved working in the studio. The recording label was throwing a lot of money at him to produce this album. He had to get it done. Unfortunately the studio insisted on using this new software that, in turn, insisted on not listening to the simplest commands.

He lit another cigarette. The studio did have a strict no smoking policy, but at this point Stan didn't care. He was the only one there and it made him feel better... kinda. He stubbed it out after two drags and threw the pack at the monitor in frustration. He knew that was silly since the monitor just showed the errors in the file that had popped up. Everything was on the server... in the next room.

He looked long and hard at his lighter and contemplated setting the server on fire. Maybe they'd let him go back to the old software. Of course, he'd have to get McCallum back to re-record everything. No-win situation.

He started to light another cigarette when he felt a small breeze from the back of the room, which was very odd since the room was sealed and soundproof.

He turned his swivel chair around to find a small woman in a blue cloak standing against the back wall behind him. Startled, he dropped his (thankfully) unlit cigarette and stammered, "W-w-who are you and how the hell did you get in here?"

The only door was in front of him. She wasn't there before. No one came in the door. How did she get there? He did several 'double takes' looking from the door, which was still closed, to the small form in blue.

He picked up his dropped cigarette and started to light it. He was more startled that someone was in the studio than who it actually was. Not that he recognized her but he was pretty sure he could take her out... whoever she was.

The diminutive figure raised her head; her light skin and lips showing a wickedly playful smirk and shook a small finger at him. "You know smoking is still bad for you dear."

"Gigi? Girl, what the hell are you doin' here?" He dropped the still unlit cigarette again and crossed the room to give her a hug. As with most people, Stan dwarfed her. He was only about 6'1... but her 4'10 frame made most people feel tall. His ultra-dark complexion also stood out against her very pale skin. Anyone seeing them in their embrace would have thought they made an unusual couple, appearance wise.

"Uh, Stan, put me down." She had returned his embrace. After all, they were rather close back in the day. She was just getting a little winded with everyone wanting to give her bear hugs. What made her so huggable anyway? *Probably my size*, she thought.

After her return to the floor, she straightened her cloak and looked up at her old friend. "It is good to see you," she said, looking around the studio. "I guess you finally made it. This is what you said you'd always wanted to do."

"Yeah," he replied, sounding rather disheartened. "The actual work is wonderful. It's the people."

"I know the feeling," she said, thinking of her old job. A nuclear physicist turned... genetic stimulator? "I need to tell you something. And you're the only one I think I can really talk to about this."

"Um, sure Gi. Have a seat." Stan offered her a chair, another swivel model like his. He sat in his seat at the audio console. He wasn't sure if he was hiding it well or not but he was still very confused as to how she had gotten in the room. "What's up? I'm guessing you didn't just pop outta' nowhere to discus the weather."

She giggled a little. "No," she said, suddenly turning serious. "Something was kept from us when we were kids."

Stan arched an eyebrow, "What? You can teleport, right? That how you got in here?" he said in an only half-joking tone, looking at the still closed door.

"Me, no," she smirked again. "But that is how I got in here. We were experimented on."

"Pardon?"

"When we were young, we all basically had the same doctors right?" she explained. "We lived in a government town. Went to a government school. Parents all worked for the government. I know you used to watch the *X-Files*..."

Stan's eyes had gotten progressively bigger as she went on. "We've been altered at a genetic level," she continued. "Not *everyone* at the school mind you... but most of the people in our... class."

"The project was scrapped before we graduated, but we were still monitored. The genetic manipulation is dormant until activated by one of three methods. The first is a direct threat to the person altered. The second is flipping the switch in the lab. The third..." She hesitated and looked down. Stan was certain he heard a sob.

"G? You ok?" Stan moved a bit closer to comfort his friend. "What's wrong? I don't think I get all of what you're telling me."

"*I'm* the third method," she said, still sobbing. "I was keyed with the ability to activate everyone with a *special word*. If I say it around anyone of us who was altered, they activate."

"Um, G… this is a bit weird y'know?" Stan was now sitting beside her with an arm around her shoulder. "I mean, does this mean we've got, what, super powers? And I'm guessing something went wrong somewhere… otherwise, why the tears?" he asked, wiping another tear from her face.

"We weren't supposed to be activated," she looked up at him, still crying. "Ever."

"So what happened?"

"I think I killed Eric," she sniffled. "Again."

Noticeably stunned, he reflexively backed away from Gigi, rolling his chair back a bit before moving back to put his arm around her again.

Gigi and Eric had been a couple back in their early high school years, but they had gone their separate ways long before graduation. They were still close, but he didn't know if they had kept in touch after graduation. He'd heard Eric had died a couple days ago, but not that someone had killed him.

To find out Gigi had killed him… well, that would certainly explain why she was upset. "Uh, Gi," he started, uncertain of how to ask. "Ok, you know me. I'm blunt and I can*not* think of another way to ask this… what do you mean you killed Eric? I heard he died in some sort of accident."

Gigi had curled into an almost fetal ball against Stan, crying freely. She sniffled and looked up at her friend. She uncurled and tried to compose herself, failed, and leaned against him again.

"I ran into him few days ago," she began between sobs. "Actually I didn't know I ran into him. I was on vacation. I was in a building, I guess. I don't know the details," she sounded confused. Which made Stan feel a bit better since he *was* confused, about how Gigi had killed Eric, who genetically manipulated him, how she had gotten in the room, and why the equipment wouldn't hit the bass just right. The latter concern growing more and more distant.

"You don't know that you ran into him… and you killed him," he tried to sound confused, hoping she'd stop sobbing long enough to make enough sense for him to understand a little of what was going on.

"I was told."

"By who?"

"You'll get to meet him soon. I have to activate you now." He felt a small vibration from where her ear was against his chest. A communicator? "They want us to come back. I'm sorry Stan."

She looked up, kissed his cheek lightly and whispered in his ear, "Initiate."

2
HOMECOMING

Ranj Serikahn, Rich Walker and Stan Robinson lay unconscious, side-by-side in a mostly blank room, on the floor. It was hard to tell how large the room was since it was almost completely dark, except for what seemed like a spotlight on the middle of the room where the three lay. Beyond the light... blackness.

Which is exactly how they wanted it, being partial to the whole sci-fi / alien abduction look, for no particular reason.

Rich was the first to start moving, but they all regained consciousness about the same time, eventually sitting up. Ranj seemed to sit up too far and spent a moment trying to stabilize his motion. Stan, of course, was the first one to actually say anything.

"Rich?" he mumbled, looking up at the man who was still taller when sitting, "Ranj?" looking at the slightly wavering man on the other side.

Rich jumped to his feet, put his hands on his hips and said, in his best pro-wrestler voice, "I... AM... MAMMOTH!"

Ranj covered his mouth and tried not to laugh. Stan exhaled, "Man, knock that shit off! We had gym together remember? That and, well, you're white." Then he and Ranj burst out laughing.

Rich, for his part, held his pose for almost two seconds before realizing that he really had just made an ass of himself. "Stan? Man what the hell is going on here?" he asked and extended a hand to each of his friends, helping them up. "I just won the belt..." he trailed off and looked around the floor. His wrestling costume was still on, but "My belt is gone!"

"You wouldn't actually wear it in public would you?" Ranj asked.

"Well, no," he admitted. "But I did work my ass off for that thing."

"I have a feeling you wouldn't need it here," Stan said, looking around.

"You ever watch the X-Files?" he asked no one in particular.

"Yeah, all the time," Ranj replied. "I know when you die you're supposed to see a big light and everything. I had thought that's what this was. But you're right. It looks more X-Files or something."

Stan and Rich were visibly shaken by the comment. "Why would you think you were dead?" Stan asked.

Several expressions ran across Ranj's face: pain, embarrassment, shock, amusement, and probably a couple that don't really have names yet. "Well, I did just jump off a building."

Stan and Rich's eyebrows shot up before looking at each other, as if for confirmation of what they had just heard, before turning back realizing both had, indeed, heard correctly. "And…" they both said in an attempt to get their old friend to embellish.

"I bounced."

"Bounced?" came the stereo response.

"Yeah," Ranj replied sheepishly, "I think I bounced."

Stan looked confused and decided to walk to the edge of where the spotlight seemed to end. Rich simply stood there visibly trying to wrap the concept of bouncing around his brain. "Bounced?"

"Yeah, Gigi showed up just before I jumped…"

"Gigi?" both responded.

"Gigi. Eric's ex. Short girl. Went to school with us."

"She showed up just after I won the belt! Had this little blue cloak?"

"She popped up at the studio too."

Rich looked at Stan incredulously. "Gi knocked me out?"

Stan ignored the question and looked at Ranj to ask a possibly more important question. "Uh, Ranj, are your arms, uh, stretching?"

Ranj looked down at his arms, both at his side. "I think so." He flapped both arms up and down a couple times, which had the effect of turning his hands into something of a yo-yo.

He was simultaneously perplexed and horrified but his body's strange actions, but in a euphoric way. He began to giggle as he flung his arms out wide making a "T" with his body; only the top of the "T" was a bit longer than it should be. Then he brought his arms together to hug himself quickly.

His arms wrapped around his body twice.

"Dude, that is sooo wrong," Rich mumbled. He glanced at Stan, who seemed to be having trouble putting his eyes back in his head. (Metaphorically, not literally.)

Ranj began to laugh, not in a funny way, more of a funny-farm way. He fell to his knees still literally wrapped up in himself. He looked up at his friends. Despite his maniacal laughter, he had tears streaming down his face.

Stan and Rich knelt by Ranj and tried not to feel inept. Rich's expression of worry and puzzlement about what to do for Ranj was only met with Stan's wide-eyed shrug.

"TWO OUT OF THREE STABLE THROUGH PHASE ONE."

The mechanical voice startled all three. Rich reassumed his "Mammoth Persona" and tried to look into the darkness for something, anything. Stan also stood, but closer to Ranj, in a somewhat protective stance.

Nothing appeared. Nothing moved. If the darkness had any secrets, it was keeping them.

Mammoth glanced back at Stan, who shrugged again. He looked at Ranj, who was now curled up in an almost literal ball on the floor.

"REINITIALIZING SEQUENCE."

This was the last thing the three of them heard before passing out.

3
TAKE TWO

Rich Walker and Stanley Robinson lay unconscious, side-by-side in a mostly blank room, on the floor. It was hard to tell how large the room was since it was almost completely dark, except for what seemed like a spotlight on the middle of the room where the two lay. Beyond the light… blackness.

Rich was the first to start moving, but pair regained consciousness about the same time, eventually sitting up. Stan, of course, was the first one to actually say anything.

"Rich?" he mumbled.

Rich jumped to his feet, put his hands on his hips and said, in his best pro-wrestler voice, "I… AM…" he paused and looked confused, "experiencing deja-vu. How about you?"

"Kinda," he replied. "But I don't recall ever being abducted by aliens before." He stood and looked around the room. "It's a bit dark in here."

"I can't see anything beyond the…" Rich looked up, "what kind of spotlight is this? I've been in a few, y'know. And I've never seen one like this."

"Beats me, man. I do audio. Not video."

"Wanna see what's out there?" he asked, jerking a thumb toward one edge of the light.

"You lead the way big man," Stan replied with a grandiose gesture.

Rich reached the edge of the spotlight and paused. He reached his hand through the edge of the light. He harrumphed, feeling slightly foolish. A hand appeared about halfway down his arm and he nearly jumped out of his own skin. It was Stan's. "Easy big guy. It's just me," Stan said, stifling a laugh at his friend's expense. "And I doubt there's a force-field or anything."

"Yeah, I guess you're right."

There was a loud snap that made both of them jump. They looked for the source but both noticed the same thing. Small, transparent circles appeared at the edge of the light, all of them slightly moving, but all overlapping to one extent or another.

"Actually," a smug voice said from behind them, in the middle of the circle of light, "we developed a working force-field years ago."

The pair whipped around to face the voice, Rich slightly in front in a protective stance. In the middle of the circle was a woman with shoulder length reddish-brown hair and a cherubic face. She smirked at the pair.

"Joahn?!" they both exclaimed. Stan and Rich spent several stunned moments staring at her. She looked real enough. They did not recall ever seeing her in black jumpsuit before, but that was immaterial. This actually looked like Joahn.

"Y-y-you can't be real," Rich stammered.

Joahn took mock offense at the comment, placing her hands on her hips. "Oh, really?" she said with air of incredulousness that both members of her audience knew was false. She walked huffily over to them and swatted Rich on the chest (almost) playfully. "And why is that?"

Rich was too stunned to reply, so Stan did. "Um, because you died."

* * *

Stan had a sudden thought. He was afraid it might be a revelation. He looked up a Rich. Rich could tell he was scared. Stan looked at Joahn. "Uh, Jo," he started, feeling his eyes bug out of his head again. *Again?* "We're not dead are we?"

Joahn hunched her shoulders and began to laugh, "No silly. I have missed you Stan. Your sense of humor." She hugged him. Eventually he tried to hug her back, but was wary about doing so.

Breaking off from Stan, she hugged Rich. "Didn't want'cha to feel left out big guy!" Rich was equally hesitant about returning the affection, but did anyway.

She eventually stopped being "huggy" and turned to walk toward the opposite end of the circle. She stopped about halfway and turned equally as much and made a follow-me motion. "You coming?"

There was another loud snap. The circles disappeared, but another spotlight turned on, creating a "hallway" ending with a gray *Star Trek*-ish door. "This is just the staging area," Joahn explained. "I have a feeling you'll want to see the rest of the base."

Stan and Rich exchanged glances, shrugged, and followed their dead friend.

4
SOME EXPLANATION

The door slid open revealing an almost obnoxiously light yellow hallway stretching both left and right. Straight ahead was a large sign that looked more like a billboard. It read "HYDRA CORPORATION" in big letters with the slogan "Many Heads, One Goal" beneath. The slogan was slightly to the right to make room for, apparently, a corporate logo.

"They like to make sure we don't forget who we work for," Jo shrugged pointing a thumb at the sign.

"Uh, Jo," Stan started, still feeling weird about talking to someone whose funeral he had attended, "that logo looks a bit more like a Medusa than a Hydra."

As Jo turned her head, a shadow left the logo and darted down the hall, opposite of the way Jo was turning. Stan raised an eyebrow, then a hand to rub his temples. "Never mind," he said looking at the unhidden logo. "That is a hydra, alright." He glanced up at Rich, who looked down and made a subtle motion with his hand, palm down. Rich had seen it too, but they'd discuss it later.

Jo turned back around to face them with a smirk. "I know the staging area can be a bit disorientating, but really, Stan, you were the mythology nut."

"Sorry, Jo," he replied. "I guess I am a bit, um, disoriented." His eyes glanced up at Rich, who slightly shrugged.

"Well, gentlemen," she said moving between them and taking each one arm-in-arm with a big smile, "I think you should come with me. Time to get you guys briefed."

Rich, who was mentally trying his best not to think of the woman as some kind of zombie, looked down at her. "Hopefully you're meaning someone will tell us what's going on," he smirked, "and not give us some form of *wedgie*."

* * *

Joahn led them down the hall to the left. There was a long gap between the first door, the one they exited, and second door, the one they skipped. "Here we are," she announced when they reached the third door, which was almost connected to the second. Stan thought the second and third doors were more like regular "Trek" doors, unlike the first door, which would have been more "hangar-like".

As the third door, labeled "Brief", opened, the second door, mysteriously labeled "X", opened, revealing a diminutive woman in a blue cloak. "Extradition NOW!" the small woman said, grabbing Joahn by the arm and pulling her in the "X" room.

Joahn looked, understandably, surprised, but relented to the smaller woman. "Go on in guys," Joahn motioned to the "Brief" room. "I'll be right back."

"That was quick," Joahn said to someone as the "X" door shut, leaving the pair in the hall.

Rich looked at Stan and jerked a thumb at the "X" door. "Was that Gigi?"

"I think so," Stan replied.

"What's with the cape she was wearing?"

Stan looked up dubiously. "And what the hell makes you think I know?" He looked at the 'Brief' door. "Think we should go in?"

"Do we really have a choice?" the big man replied. "I want to know what the hell is going on. Jo said we'd get answers in there. We don't know where we are." He paused. "Do we?" Stan shook his head. "Ok, we don't know where we are… or how to get out of here. Options?"

Stan scratched the back of his head. "Knock on the door?"

At Stan's smartass reply, the door opened, revealing a rather large room. Again, like the walls in the hallway, the room was light yellow. The middle of the room contained a large wooden boardroom-type table. On the wall on the opposite end of the room hung a large screen. A lump in the ceiling was presumably a projector. The room had two occupants, both males with graying, short-cropped hair, one seated at the head of the table and the other to his right. The one on the right looked taller and 'better built' than the rather skinny man at the head of the table; but both were smaller than Stan, and, obviously, Rich.

Picard and Riker, Stan thought to himself. *Definitely a'* Trek *theme going on here.*

The two men rose at the other pair's entrance. The man at the head of the table smiled and waved them over. "Gentlemen," he said in an almost grandfatherly voice, "welcome to the Hydra Project."

The man at the head of the table met them toward the far end and extended a hand. "Mr. Stanley Alpheus Robinson," he said, shaking Stan's hand. "Mr. Richard Edward Walker," he said, shaking Rich's hand. "My name is Jim Yost, I'm the senior director here. This is my… second-in-command, Kent Edwards," he said indicating the other man.

Edwards not only did not shake either of their hands in greeting, he hadn't moved from his spot at the table. He gave only a cursory nod to each before sitting back in his chair.

Yost dropped his head and shook it slightly before turning again to Stan and Rich. "Sorry, he's been like that since the D-Rays lost the World Series."

Stan's eyes dropped to slits and raised an eyebrow. "Um, Mr. Yost, the D-Rays haven't even *been* to a World Series."

Yost just smiled. "Ah, you see my point." He returned to his seat and gestured at two chairs opposite Edwards. "Please, gentlemen, have a seat and I'll explain why we brought you here."

* * *

Stan and Rich took their seats; Stan closer to Yost as the next seat was obviously built for someone Rich's size. Edwards continued to stare through them. Stan was getting the impression that Edwards did not want them there.

"Gentlemen," Yost began," may I call you, um-" His eyes darted to a paper in front of him, "Stan and Rich, right?" he said, pointing to each correctly.

"I'm good with that," Stan replied nonchalantly. Rich just nodded and looked expectantly at their host.

Yost looked pleased. Edwards did not. Yost began again, "Gentlemen, do you remember a Doctor Anthony Forrest?"

"Vaguely," Rich replied similarly to Stan's "Kinda."

"I'll refresh your memories a bit," Yost said, when Edwards abruptly stood.

"I have better things to do, Jim," Edwards said, his voice sounding somewhere between gravelly and avalanchey. "You can handle this on your own." And, as abruptly as he stood up, he left the room with the other three watching.

Rich's head tilted back toward Yost. "GBS?"

Yost looked puzzled. "GBS?"

"Grumpy Bastard Syndrome," both replied having co-created the term to apply to an English teacher the two had shared.

Yost just laughed. "Yes, actually. I've been trying to diagnose that for years and I think you just hit it right on the head.

"Anyway," he continued, "Dr. Anthony Forrest used to work for us many years ago, but was released because we wouldn't fund his experiments in G-N-A. And, before you ask, I'll get to that in a minute.

"Forrest went into private practice in your hometown. We kept an eye on him, but, apparently not enough of one since he found subjects for his experiments. That would be, well, you."

Stan and Rich exchanged glances. "Us?" Stan asked, pointing a wiggling thumb between the two of them. "We're... experiments?"

"Not exactly experiments," Yost said, "but experimented on. Let me explain. Dr. Forrest was apparently successful in creating what he called G-N-A. I believe it stood for Genetic Nanotechnological Advancement.

"I'm not a scientist but I'll explain what I can." He gestured at the ceiling and the "lump" projector swiveled so the lens was pointing at the tabletop instead of the screen. A small humming sound began and a hologram of a DNA helix appeared between the tabletop and the projector. Stan and Rich exchanged glances, clearly impressed with the technology.

"Don't be too impressed with this stuff," Yost said with a smirk. "You'll see better later. Anyway, as you can see, regular DNA looks, well, like DNA."

"Ooh," Rich mumbled, "That's deep."

"Hey," Yost reprimanded jokingly, pointing at the giant. "I'm not an English major. I'm a scientist. Anyway, from what we have been able to figure out, the GNA project was nanotech that would attach to cells DNA and create, basically a third strand." As Yost said this, the hologram showed small dots creating a third line down the middle of the DNA twist creating almost a braid. "The idea was to create a superhuman."

Rich interrupted. "You keep saying you *believe* and you *think*. Why don't you *know*?"

Stan sat straighter in his chair. "I remember why," he said, apparently having a revelation. "He was the bastard who..." he trailed off, "killed Joahn?" He looked puzzled at Yost.

"In a sense," Yost replied, "you're right. We never got his full work and none of the GNA nano-bots were activated, except for two, and those are the two you've met. Joahn's ability manifested itself when Forrest's car ran headlong into hers. There was no body at the funeral not because it was burned beyond recognition, but because there was no body to be recovered."

Rich and Stan had yet to stop looking puzzled. Yost continued. "Joahn now has the ability to open portals in space and, basically, teleport. We had received a message from Forrest saying that something would happen that would change the face of the planet. To be honest, we thought he was nuts. Then Joahn appeared in our DC office. Poof! There she was.

"We've searched everything we could find at Forrest's house, office, storeroom… whatever, but we can't find the full, formula, for lack of a better term, to recreate his experiments. And since he died in the… accident, we can't ask him. But we did find a list of all the ones he experimented on and how to activate the nano-bots.

"One method of activation is to have something traumatic physically happen. The shock of hearing something bad happening wouldn't do it, but being in a car accident would trigger the sequence. Joahn's car wreck for example."

"Does this mean we can teleport, too?" Stan asked.

"Probably not," Yost replied, shaking his head slightly. "Forrest seems to have given everyone different powers. And he knew what powers they would be too. He knew Joahn would teleport when the car struck. He most likely somehow programmed the first jump to land in our boardroom."

"So," Rich started leadingly, "what can we do?"

"Rich," Yost began, stifling a laugh, "um, well, you're big and strong."

"Yeah, and…?"

"No," Yost said, "that's your… power."

Stan began to snicker. "Uh, dude," he began, addressing Yost, "he's always been big and strong." He turned to Rich, "You're what? Seven-five? Seven-six?"

"Seven-nine if you read my press packet," the giant replied with a smirk. "Why do I get the feeling I got jipped on this whole thing?"

"Not at all," Yost said, having taken a moment to compose himself. "You've always been big and strong, but not strong to this extent. We will be testing you later to see how much your strength has increased."

"And if I don't want to be tested," he asked menacingly.

Yost looked confused, "You mean you don't want to know?"

At those words, Rich seemed to deflate. "Good point."

"And what do I do?" Stan asked.

"To be honest, we're not sure." Yost seemed genuinely puzzled. "The file we found on you said 'amplify'. We're not sure what you're amplifying, sound? electricity? someone else's powers? We won't know until we run tests on you too? And, no, they won't be painful."

"I'm going to back up for a minute," Stan began, feeling a little 'jipped' on the powers as well, "you said we'd met two people who had been activated. Jo's one." He ticked off a finger with his hand. "Who's the other?"

"Ah, the memory thing again." Yost looked a bit distressed. "That happens sometimes. When activation occurs, there is some very short-term memory loss. Although," he reflected, "I think you saw her in the hall. Geraldine Wood? Used to be Davis."

I guess that was Gigi, Stan thought recalling the small, blue-cloaked woman in the "X" room. "Ms. Wood's power was always active apparently. According to the files, her ability is to activate the other experiments, namely, you, and to be able to find them anywhere on the globe. She visited both of you before activating you. And, with some of the developments we've discovered recently, we need all of the super-powered people we can find. There have been—"

A loud crash from the door interrupted him. All three turned to the door area. It would be improper to say turned to the door as the door itself was now on the opposite side of the room from where it was. And it was looking a bit crumpled as it leaned against the wall.

"YOST!" The voice was feminine, and definitely not happy. A woman strode into the room and stopped at the opposite end of the table from Yost. She slammed her (clawed?) hands on the table, which Rich felt would have flipped over if he had not been resting one arm on it. The woman was dressed in what looked like tight fitting (and well filled-out) pink-spandex with a "Catwoman" type mask, which she promptly ripped off and threw at Yost. "What the hell it this, Yost?!? Do I look like the kind of person who would wear *pink spandex*?!?"

Rich and Stan exchanged glances again as they recognized the not-so-much "Catwoman" as "Hello-Kitty Girl". Katerina Parker; one of the high school Goths. Her hair had not changed much since school. It was still mostly black in the back with a bright neon blue splash in the front. Her eyes were still dark from heavy mascara and her lips wore matching lipstick.

"Katerina," Yost began before realizing his mistake when she pointed a clawed finger at him and raised her eyebrows. No one ever calls her Katerina.

"Sorry," he apologized, holding his hands up from the table in mock-surrender. "Kat, the costume is just a prototype. I didn't make the color scheme, or the design. Its still bulletproof, water-resistant, flame-resistan—"

"I don't care!" Kat protested. "It's…"

"Friggin'…"

"PINK!!"

"Tell your 'design people'" she quoted the words with a pair of clawed fingers, "there is no way in hell I'm wearing this again! And if they have a problem with that…" she trailed off and glanced at the two newcomers as if seeing them there for the first time. "Rich? Stan? I guess Gi found you guys, too."

"Guess so," Stan quipped standing and moving to greet his old friend.

"You don't want to do that right now," she retorted holding up a pink gloved, clawed and bloodstained hand.

Yost visibly paled. "You didn't kill them, did you?" He sounded aghast.

"No, Yost," she replied rolling her eyes. "I just gave them a few scratches to remember us by," she said with a feral grin. She turned back to her friends. "I'll catch up with you guys later after I get cleaned up," she turned back to Yost, "and burn this costume. By the way, Yost, situation neutralized," she added before disappearing through the now permanently open door.

"I think she missed the flame resistant part," Yost quipped when Kat was, he hoped, out of earshot.

"Oh, she was always resourceful. She'll find a way." Rich rolled his eyes. "Well, she seems happy with her job."

Yost shrugged. "Ok, gentlemen, new subject, would you like to see what you're capable of?"

5
ABILITIES

"So how long is this supposed to take?" Stan asked impatiently. He'd been led from the briefing room down several halls and two elevators to what he'd been told was the testing room.

"We're getting there," came the reply from yet another old classmate, Jason Yook. Jason and Chris *'No-Not-That-One'* Rock were conducting the tests. Chris and Stan got along fine in school. Jason—not so much.

Becoming more convinced this was just a scheme of Jason's to keep him occupied; he decided to keep his conversation with Chris. "So Rocko, what can you do? I mean we all got powers now right?"

Chris's complexion grew darker; which usually meant he was upset since he was already several shades darker than Stan. "I got jipped." He hung his head and shook it briefly before looking at his old friend. "Me and Jace basically got the same power. Electrokenesis."

"Electro-ka-what?"

"Electrokenesis," Jason answered from his computer terminal, which was facing away from Stan. "Basically we can control anything electronic. I'm a bit better than Chris but he got an added gift."

Stan turned to Chris who shrugged and promptly began to shrink until he could no longer be seen. "He's good with nano-tech," Jason continued. "When I'm guessing you thought he was plugging more electrodes on the back of your head, he actually was inside you."

Chris immediately grew back to normal size and turned on Jason and shoved a finger in his face. "I am really sick of that joke! Every time someone makes that joke Dandy Sandy thinks he can hit on me! It's gotten a bit old!"

"Sandy came out of the closet?" Stan asked, hoping to diffuse the situation.

Both turned to him and replied together, "You didn't know?"

"Well, yeah," Stan quipped, "Not first hand, but I knew. I thought he was trying to keep it a secret though."

"His closet had a glass front," Jason said trying to make a joke, but judging from the reaction of his audience, failing miserably.

"A-hem." All three turned to see a rather tall man leaning against the doorway, which was about halfway between Stan and the electrokenetics. "So do we have anything yet?" he asked.

"Stan, have you met Randall O'Neal yet?" Chris asked. "He's one of the guys from ops. Keeps us running in the right direction and all that."

Stan sized-up the pale man in the doorway. "You'll forgive me if I don't get up or shake your hand or something. I'm kinda strapped to a chair." He looked down at his restraints again, tested them again, found they still didn't budge, and looked menacingly at Jason and Chris.

"I think we've got it figured out," Jason said. He looked at a piece of equipment on the wall to his right and a light on the panel changed from an up arrow to a down arrow. Stan might have wondered if that was part of Jason's ability if his chair hadn't abruptly turned 180-degrees to face the back wall, jostling him.

"You could warn me when you do things like that," Stan called out, trying to crane his neck to look behind him. He didn't get a verbal reply, but was satisfied with a slapping noise and Jason's muffled "Hey!" He thought it was nice to know Chris still had his back, in this case, literally.

"Ok, Stan, on that back wall is a target," Chris said. "I want you to yell at it."

Several things confused him about that statement. One: the back wall was about fifty meters away, which was farther than he thought it was when he was first brought into the room. Two: "You want me to... yell at it?" he asked skeptically.

"Yep. You have to think about breaking the target or else your GNA won't, um, turn on, for lack of a better term. Oh, wait a sec." Had Stan been facing the other direction, he would have seen Chris distributing industrial strength earplugs. After a few seconds he said "OK, YELL AT IT," not realizing he was, himself, yelling.

Stan scrunched his face in concentration. In the back of his mind, he knew this was just some stupid thing Jason had come up with. He never liked that guy. But he knew Chris still had his back, if nothing else, from the pop on the head he had just given Jason. He squinted at the target, which looked really small. He took a deep breath… and yelled.

He didn't hear anything come out of his mouth. Actually he didn't hear anything at all. He did see the target, and most of the back wall, explode outward revealing a mountainous terrain. This was the first clue he had as to where he actually was, somewhere with mountains. This was not what he was thinking about. *I just yelled the back wall off!* was his first thought. *I have a feeling I'll be spending a lot of time putting my eyes back in my head* was his second.

The chair slowly turned back around and he realized that his were not the only eyes that needed to be re-popped to their original position. Chris, Jason and Randy were all pop-eyed and slack jawed. Randy eventually looked at the electro-pair and said, "We're going to need a bigger target."

6
NICE CAR

Rich was bored. He'd done so many physicals in the past year it had become routine. The ACW required them every month. Ever since two of their wrestlers had died of suspicious causes, management had gotten a little paranoid. He'd done steroid tests weekly. Not that he used them, but he knew some of his colleagues did. He'd done drug tests. Again, he didn't use them.

Everything he was asked to do, he did. The treadmill, still not terribly fast but he could probably outrun anyone his size, not that there were many people his size. He lifted a dumbbell on a bench. It seemed a bit easier, but he thought that it might be his subconscious playing tricks on him.

Finally he was lead to a testing room. The first thing he saw was that the room was quite large and the far wall was covered with a tarp. The second thing he noticed were two more old schoolmates, Jason and Chris, huddled around a computer. He nonchalantly waved at them and mumbled a "Hi" but, as expected with those two near a computer, did not get a reaction.

Rich spent a few moments leaning against the door, waiting patiently to be noticed. He actually savored moments like this. It wasn't often the giant went unnoticed and he found he liked being invisible. Unfortunately the door slid open, pinching his arm. He mumbled something about knocking first without looking back to see whom it was.

"Sorry Mr. Walker," came the rather unexpected reply. Rich wasn't sure if he thought it was the reply that was unexpected, the formalness in the way it was said, or the complete lack of recognizing the voice, but he was sure something was unexpected about the whole situation. He moved aside letting the unknown voice through the door.

"Nah," he said, "my bad. It's what I get for leaning on a door." He noticed Jason and Chris were now looking at him and he felt a bit embarrassed. Here he was, a hulking giant of a man, complaining about getting pinched by a door he was ignorantly leaning against. In what felt like a desperate attempt to change the subject, he thrust out his hand to the newcomer. "Hi, I'm Rich."

"Greetings Rich," said the smaller man, "My name is Randall O'Neal. I'm one of the ops people. Most people call me Randy." Randy looked uncomfortable. *Probably used to being one of the taller people*, Rich thought.

"Well, Randy, what kind of tests do I get to do here? I'm probably not going to get much of an answer out of the compu-nerds," he said, jerking a thumb towards Jason and Chris, who had resumed their study of the computer monitor.

Randy donned a mischievous smile and touched his right hand to his ear. "Ok Pop. Middle of the room, if you don't mind," he seemed to say to no one. Rich's eyebrow rose inquiringly and slowly turned his head to the middle of the room, which was empty. He turned back to Randy, who, in turn, motioned he turn back to the middle of the room. Feeling almost completely out of sorts, Rich turned his head back to the center of the room, which was now filled with three cars. Rich rubbed his eyes and looked again. Indeed, there were three cars in the middle of the room: a small, yellow VW bug, a Cadillac... Tank, and a military looking troop truck with tank treads on the back.

"Where...?" he began.

"We have a teleporter," Randy shrugged with a smirk.

"A guy named 'pop'?"

"Girl, actually," Randy replied looking vaguely puzzled. "I thought you already saw Joahn?"

The gears of Rich's mind started clicking. Teleportation is how she survived the car wreck. Teleportation would also be how she got in the room with Stan when the door never opened. It might also explain how he got here in the first place. Even when he was wrestling it would usually take two or three people to pick him up. Teleporting would make it easier.

"Her, what? Codename? Is 'Pop'?"

"Why not?" he replied with another shrug. "She makes things pop up, pop out, pop in..." he stopped mid-explanation and looked up at the behemoth, "can you pop down? Oh well, I'm sure she could do that too. Anyway, most of the other names were taken."

"By who?"

"Comic book companies. Most of them trademarked all the really good names. I'm still sure we'll come up with something good for you later. Now," he gestured to the cars, "if you don't mind, let's get started on your GNA tests."

The two moved to the first car in the line, the Bug. "Don't worry about damaging them," Randy said. "They were all repossessed anyway. Yes, even the tank. Don't ask. I don't know that story."

"Uh huh," the giant mumbled, "So what do you want me to do?"

"Well," Chris began, startling Rich. *When did he get over here?* "We've pretty much figured out your power involves strength. The way to trigger your GNA is to think about what you want to do where your power is concerned. Your GNA starts up, and you can do it."

"You want me to pick up a car?" Rich asked skeptically. "I'm not *that* strong, guys."

"Actually we think you are," Randy replied.

"Try the Bug," Chris suggested.

Rich stood in front of the small yellow car and wrapped his arms around the hood, placing one hand on each door. He abruptly let go of the car and stood ramrod straight before turning on Chris, pointing a large finger in the face of his former schoolmate. "Ha, got it! This is a joke to make up for all those techno-geek cracks, isn't it?"

Chris covered his mouth to stifle a laugh. "No," Randy answered for him. "Yes, the position you were just in was a bit... odd. And we are filming this to study later. But we honestly think you are capable of this." Chris just shrugged, still trying not to laugh.

Leaning over the bug again, hands on the doors, Rich began to lift. *They think I can pick up a... whoa!* Not only did Rich pick up the car, but he almost suplexed it. He felt a bit foolish on several fronts. He had just errantly called out two people he thought were playing a joke on him. He was holding a compact car over his head. The car was not terribly heavy. *And,* he realized, *I might actually be a superhero. I don't look good in spandex.* He put the car down.

Randy and Chris looked impressed. Jason, who still hadn't moved from the computer, called out "Try the Caddy!"

Rich moved to the Cadillac. It was one similar to the one his grandparents used to drive. He looked at the car, measuring it in his head. Unsure of how to proceed, he looked to Randy. "So how do I lift this thing? Climb under it?"

Randy and Chris exchanged confused glances. "Uhhmmm," Chris stammered. "Didn't think about that part. Jace? Any ideas?" Jason, who still hadn't moved, didn't reply. Randy and Chris simply shrugged at the giant. "Uh, try improvising. We won't hold it against you."

"Gee, thanks," Rich quipped. "That was really helpful." He looked at the car. The windows were open. *Maybe if I do this...* he thought, sticking on arm through the open window, planting his hand on the middle of the ceiling of the car. He pushed slightly, and the whole roof of the car ripped off, shattering the front and rear windshields. He looked up, realizing that the ceiling of the room was higher than he expected. A few moments later the roof of the car landed on top of the Bug, breaking both of its windshields too.

Rich looked embarrassed. Randy looked impressed. Chris laughed out loud, no longer stifling his amusement. Jason, unsurprisingly, didn't move. "Um, do you still…" Rich began, pointing at the roofless car.

Randy shook his head and chuckled. "I think the Caddy is done. Why don't you just try *bench pressing* the tank?"

Rich nodded and climbed under the vehicle from the side. Realizing he would not get a good grip on anything that way he climbed out and climbed under from the back of the tank to get a better grip. He could get his arms around to the sides of the tank. He pushed. The tank lifted off the ground effortlessly. Rich just held it there for a moment before putting it down and climbing out. He wasn't even sweating. He looked expectantly at Randy and Chris, who simply looked at each other, smiling.

Jason finally said, from his computer, "Maybe we should try the sims instead."

7
A NEW NAME

Stan sat on the bed in his room. It was a nice room. Windows showing waves crashing on the shore of a beach he didn't know the name of. A bookshelf full of tech manuals. A chair. A television that got CNN, period. A closet full of clothes that fit him nicely but weren't exactly his style. His own bathroom.

He'd been there a week. Not in his room the whole time, of course. Every morning someone would show up and take him somewhere to be tested or trained. He went along with it not quite cheerfully, but not exactly resisting either.

Something was wrong but he couldn't quite put a finger on it.

He'd had a life, hadn't he? And some corporation just scooped him up, put him in, what amounts to, a cell, tested him repeatedly and trained him in forms of combat and on how to focus his 'sonic scream'.

Shouldn't he have had some say in what was happening? Isn't it the inalienable right of every person to have free will? And whenever he thought about such things, did he seem to lose any ability to voice these opinions? Why did his ability to voice these opinions dwindle to nothingness? Was someone messing with his head?

He held on to the thoughts. He went through the motions with every lab tech or trainer he was taken to. He was very obedient and even nice to some of the techs. He still had a problem with Jason, but that was expected. Who didn't have a problem with him?

But he kept his mouth shut to everyone regarding his concerns. Rich seemed to be going along with everything just fine. He hadn't even mentioned his championship belt since the staging room.

He had gotten to find out who some of the other GNAs were. Joahn, he found out from Rich, was a teleporter with the "codename" of Pop. Gigi was a locator and activator. She didn't get a codename, since, supposedly, she never went anywhere.

Chris due to his shrinking ability was codenamed Dot. Jason and his computer skills was Hack. And, apparently, they hung out with Steve Callahan. Steve's fingernails were apparently diamond hard, really sharp and could grow to sword length. He was named: Slash. So Hack, Dot and Slash were a clique. Appropriate somehow.

He'd only seen Kat once since the "Pink Costume Incident", but apparently she was now very much like her namesake, right down to the claws, and a tail that she usually kept tucked away somewhere.

Sandy Drose (Thermal) had, indeed, come out of the closet. The one time he had seen Kat was when Sandy was trying to talk her back into the pink costume because it looked "thoooo good awn her." Sandy's powers were complicated, something about being able to generate intense heat and intense cold.

Erica Danube, the rich-kid / library nut in school, was now the GNA telepath, codenamed Com.

Melanie Greene (Recoil) had some power having to do with targeting and telekinetic control of whatever she 'shot' from whatever 'gun'.

Matt Frasier (Breeze) had developed an ability to control wind. He was one of the two GNAs who could actually fly.

Rich and Stan were scheduled to meet with Randy today to discuss codenames. Rich's name should be relatively easy. Something big and impressive sounding.

Stan figured "Loud Shouting Guy" probably wouldn't work for him.

Eventually, after tai-kwan-do training, which Stan had always wanted to learn anyway, he and Rich met back at the "Briefing Room". As they entered the room, they noticed that Randy O'Neal was not the sole occupant. Jason Yook was there as well.

Rich and Stan exchanged glances. "Sorry," Stan began. "We'll come back." And the pair started to turn around.

"Guys," Randy called after them, "You're on time. I've just asked Jason to be here for legal purposes."

Rich and Stan exchanged looks again. "Legal purposes?" Rich asked.

Randy nodded. "I know, that sounds a bit weird. But we are working for a corporation. Lawyers are involved and we don't want to get sued for copyright infringement."

Rich and Stan, who had entered and sat in the same chairs as last time, with Randy and Jason taking the place of Jim Yost and Kent Edwards. "Copyright infringement?" Rich asked.

"Ok, big guy, I know you've heard about this. Y'know how that wrestling promoter copyrighted some wrestling names, and when the wrestlers moved to a different promotion they couldn't take their name with them?"

"The Dudley Boys sound better the Team 3D." Rich rolled his eyes in disgust. "I don't know that I've heard of such a big asshole as Vi—"

"Watch it!" Randy interrupted. "He's so lawsuit happy of late, let's not even mention his name. But you got my point. Team 3D is just as good at wrestling but just doesn't sound as good. But if they use the Dudley name, they'll get sued. We'd like to avoid that here."

Rich still looked disgusted but nodded. Stan also nodded his consent. "Good! Let's get started. Rich... big, strong... what comes to mind?"

"Uh, Mammoth? Been using it for years." Rich clearly thought this was a no-brainer.

Randy pursed his lips, grimaced, and finally shook his head. "That's probably not a good idea. I mean, seriously, the secret identity thing is to protect you from people who may call in the middle of the night wanting something, or may use your family to blackmail you into something. No, its best to have something different."

"Besides, DC Comics already has that one for a super-villain." The trio looked at Jason, who hadn't spoken since the whole thing began. "It may institute another lawsuit. Bad idea."

Stan noticed that Jason's eyes were slightly glowing blue. *Is he connected to a computer or something?* He also felt an urge to ask how someone would call Rich if Rich didn't even know where he was, much less a phone number. But that urge was suppressed so quickly he almost didn't notice it was there until it was gone.

"So I guess Superman is out too, eh?" Rich chuckled. "Um, hang on a minute, I'll come up with something."

Randy turned to Stan. "Any ideas for you?"

"Earsplitter?" Jason said mockingly. "Yeah, that's it! Earsplitter the Barbarian! We'll give him a big club with a speaker on the end."

Stan's eyes narrowed to slits and tried to stare a hole through Jason. "Oh, that's good, Jace. And the other end of the club can have a woofer, too." Stan was pretty sure he had spoken with enough sarcasm for most people in the room to get it, but if memory served, Jason wouldn't.

"Remix?" he asked Randy before turning to Jason, "unless that's already taken too?"

Jason's eyes lit up a bit brighter and he cocked an eyebrow. "Hmph, I've got nothing on that." He turned to Randy, the first time he seemed to have moved during the conversation. "I'm surprised it hasn't been taken yet."

"Ok, Stan," Randy smiled, "Remix it is." He turned back to Rich. "We're down to you now big guy."

Rich looked pained. Stan knew he was just thinking really hard, but it was still difficult to see his friend think without stifling a chuckle. He did smirk when Rich asked "Immense?"

Stan, Jason and Randy all exchanged glances before all turning to the big man and simultaneously saying "Porn star."

Rich just shrugged and glanced down before smiling, "Well…"

Randy shook a finger cutting him off, "I don't want to know that. We need a better name."

"We could name him after a mountain…" Stan suggested. "How about… ooh… Glacier? Big moving mountain?" He looked up at his friend expectantly. Rich seemed to be mulling the idea and looking positive about it. He finally nodded and looked at Jason, who, in turn, looked at Randy, pouted his bottom lip and shook his head.

"Glacier it is." Randy looked pleased. "Now, we need to get you guys to, um, wardrobe."

8
A NEW LOOK

"Don't be so jittery, guys, I do everyone's costume."

Stan felt vaguely uncomfortable. Rich was absolutely panic stricken. They still considered Sandy Drose a friend even though they hadn't seen him in years. They knew Sandy was homosexual even before he came out of the proverbial closet. Neither really had a problem with it... until now.

Actually it wasn't so much a problem, but a really uncomfortable feeling. There was something about standing in a room, naked, and being measured for a suit by someone they knew was *not* looking at them in *that* way.

But it was still an uncomfortable feeling.

Sandy stood after measuring Rich's inseam. Rich thought he had never been that uncomfortable before. "Ok, guys," Sandy said to the pair almost playfully. "Now bend over, I've got one more measurement to take."

Stan and Rich looked terrified. "I'm KID-DING," Sandy laughed. "God, you guys are really paranoid aren't you. Get dressed." He picked up a clipboard from his chair. "Look, if I wanted to do anything with you I would have tried before now."

Stan and Rich felt a bit relieved and hurriedly moved to get their clothes back on, pants first. "Hell, I had a great opportunity on that camping trip. Right, Big Guy?" Sandy smirked as he made some notations on the clipboard.

Rich turned beet red. Stan stopped midway through putting his shirt on and looked up at his friend. "Camping trip?"

"I AM *NOT* TALKING ABOUT THAT!"

Sandy laughed. Stan looked back and forth between the two before finally laughing along with Sandy. "So, Sand-man, just to change the subject to something *Gla-see-ur* is better suited to," taunting the big man with his new name, "what's this about you having hot *and* cold... uh... powers?"

Sandy looked up from his clipboard expectantly. "You really want to know?" he asked. "Most of us haven't really talked about what we can do. I'm glad someone *finally* wants to… 'cause this is soooo friggin' cool!"

He dropped the clipboard back on the chair and held up his hands, pointed at the ceiling, palms toward himself. His left hand burst into flames. His right turned to ice. His face was lit up like a kid on Christmas. "Isn't this cool?!?" He looked specifically at his left hand, "or is it hot? Check this out!" Suddenly his right hand burst into flames and his left became ice. Sandy switched them back and forth a few times.

Stan and Rich gazed at their friend, then at each other. "I think we got jipped," Rich quipped. "I was already big and strong. But that," he pointed at Sandy, "is awesome."

"I can fly too!"

"Fly?"

"Yeah, but not in here. Ceiling's a bit low." He extinguished one hand, thawed the other, and shrugged. "I'm not that great at controlling it yet… but, dudes. It is sooo cool.

"So, Stanley, you do sound?"

"Yeah, Chris was explaining it a big more to me yesterday. He says my GNA creates a vacuum around me sucking in all sound and then refocuses it into an…" he mentally searched for a term, "intensely focused sound wave. That's why it actually doesn't make any noise. The only thing that would hear the sound wave is the thing it hits. Right now I can only do it when I yell at something, but Rocko thinks I may be able to focus it with anything."

"Cool," Sandy looked impressed.

"I guess," Stan shrugged. "I can't fly though."

Sandy looked up at Rich. "I heard you picked up a tank."

"I don't think it was a tank. I think it was, like, one of those… troop carriers from World War Two or something."

"Rich, look at me," Sandy started. "I'm a scrawny little guy. Yeah, I can do the flame and ice thing, but I'll be damned if I could bench-press fifty pounds. My costume is even padded to make me look bigger. I'd love to be able to—" he broke off and looked up slightly, not a Rich, but at nothing in particular. "I hate it when she does that!" he murmured. "Dani wants to see you two in the briefing room."

"And you know this… how?" Rich asked.

Stan, already knowing the answer stated, "She's a telepath. She can send messages into people's heads. Probably read them too."

"Yep," Sandy confirmed. "You probably ought to go. She can get pissy sometimes." Then he winced in pain, grabbed his head and glanced up at the same nothingness as before. "Well, you can!" he seemed to say to no one in particular.

Rich and Stan laughed as they finished getting dressed and left.

"I'll have the uniforms tomorrow!" Sandy called after them.

In the hall, Stan couldn't resist the opportunity to taunt his friend. He smirked at Rich. "What camping trip?"

Rich didn't speak to him for the rest of the day.

INTERLUDE

The briefing room was dark and quiet. The one source of light, the GNA hologram rearranging itself on the table, was being studied.

"He clearly not stable."

"Is there a way to correct the problem?"

"Not that we can tell," said the third voice.

"Are the newcomers ready?" asked the first.

"Almost," answered the second, "they'll be outfitted tomorrow morning and be assigned to ACT 1 by noon. The operation should be completed by sixteen-hundred."

"Good," said the second as he switched off the GNA hologram and turned on the lights. "Do any of the others show any signs?"

"Not yet," said the third, "but it's only a matter of time." He took a slow drink of something from a square-shaped glass. "They all will eventually." He set the glass down. The ice in the glass made a tinkling sound.

The second winced. "We will deal with them eventually. But will they suffice until the current operation is completed?"

"Yes," answered the first, "they will do much better than the others."

"Then we should adjourn. This room will be used soon." The other two nodded in ascension.

In the three seats at the head of the table, three hazy holograms winked from existence.

9
42 + 8*6 = BAD

Every seat in the briefing room was filled by the time Stan and Rich arrived. Randy O'Neal was at the head of the table. To his immediate right, was Melanie. Around the table were Kat, Steve, Matt, Mel eventually ending with the two seats on Randy's left, apparently for Stan and Rich.

The room was heavy in its serious tone. Everyone looked tense. This added an anxious feeling to Stan and Rich, who were usually upbeat. As they took their seats, they looked to Randy. "Sorry we're late," Stan quipped, feeling as though everyone in the room was staring at him, which they were.

"This is your first briefing, gentlemen." Randy's tone was deadly serious, almost icy. "Tomorrow you have your first mission."

Stan and Rich exchanged looks. "Already?" asked Rich. "We haven't been here that long an-"

"This mission can not wait." Randy's tone was definitely icy. "When we get assignments, we do not question them. We follow orders. Period."

"And we've always got the job done so far," came a very high-pitched voice that Rich and Stan not only did not recognize, they couldn't locate its source.

"Remix, Glacier, I'd like you to meet Squeak." Randy gestured toward Kat, who opened her not quite clenched hand to reveal...

A small white mouse. "Remix," small bow, "Glacier," small bow, "nice to meet the two of you," said the mouse.

Well, it's about time, thought Stan, *my eyes hadn't popped out of my skull for at least a week now.* Before he could completely turn his head to him, Randy started, "Yes, Squeak is a mouse. He was the first experiment in GNA. It produced a super-intelligent mouse who now works for us as an intelligence agent."

"I'm a *damn good spy* thank you very much!" proclaimed Squeak. He looked to Remix and Glacier. "I think we'll work well together."

Remix... gotta get used to that. "As long as you don't try to open my head to figure out the answer to life the universe and everything, I think we'll do fine." He turned to O'Neal. "So what are we doing?"

O'Neal looked at Squeak.

"Tomorrow," began the mouse, "an Arian associated militia group in central Texas will be moving their arms shipment to Iowa. Our job will be to 'pop' in, take them out, preferably without killing them, but incapacitating them so the local authorities can handle them, and 'pop' out before anyone knows we were there.

"Pop, Com and Gi will be monitoring the situation from here with O'Neal. Recoil and Remix, you will be providing cover. Breeze, Glacier, Slash and Kat, your job is to take out the vehicles, primarily trucks. Without those they can't very well move the weaponry very well, can they? Just remember not to damage the weaponry. It wouldn't do any good to have the whole convoy explode. Just concentrate on the engines and tires.

"Don't worry everyone," Squeak continued, "this'll be a cakewalk."

Remix looked worried. *I'm taking command assignments from a mouse. What the hell have I gotten in to?*

* * *

The next day they all met in the staging area. All of them were wearing their costumes, including Rich and Stan.

"This thing itches," the giant complained while trying, in vain, to stretch the neck of his uniform out. "The mask doesn't feel right either."

"You'll get used to it Glacier," quipped Breeze, his gunmetal grey costume made him look vaguely like the underside of a fighter jet. "And you'll want to get used to using the codenames. It does take a while, but Randy gets really pissed when we don't."

"Uh, ok, um, Breeze? Right?"

Breeze snickered. "Yes. Let's go over all the names again. Make Randy happy." He pointed to his own chest, "Breeze."

"Kat." Her new costume was similar to her old one, only black.

"Slash." His costume was silver, and his fingernails were already grown to dagger length.

"Recoil." Her black, tight fitting costume almost matched Kat's, except for a red circle HUD target over the left eye of her skullcap/mask and the large rifle slung over her shoulder. As she said her name, she stared icily through Stan/Remix.

"Uh, Remix." He answered sheepishly. *What the hell did I do to Mel- no- her name is Recoil- what the hell did I do to Recoil?* He quickly reflected on his time with the Hydra Corporation and realized that she'd been pretty much like this the whole time.

He felt his face flush. Of course, no one saw it under the skullcap/mask. Everyone had one. Apparently it was bulletproof, but he had no intention of testing to find out. The cap, like the rest of his costume, was almost blood red with what looked almost like a black hole in the center.

"GLAY-SHE-UHR!" Rich was in full 'Mammoth' mode again. Hands on hips. Lots of posturing. Big goofy grin. This look went over well with his costume. White from feet to mid-chest changing into a mountainous peak with dark blue at the top. This caused a few laughs among the group. Even Rich laughed at himself. Always a good tension breaker, he thought.

Recoil didn't so much as flinch. She kept her icy glare on Remix, who decided not to notice.

The door to the staging area opened revealing the large empty, but now well lit room. The middle of the floor had a large red circle painted on it. The rest of the room was the same obnoxious light yellow as the rest of the complex. Opposite the door was a series of windows revealing what looked like a control room. Remix recognized Pop, Gi, Com and O'Neal. That particular group was in the center of what looked like a long, narrow, computer filled room. The other four were seated closest to the glass wall with monitors in front of them. Remix did not recognize them.

"Remix and Recoil, to the circle please." O'Neal's voice came over an unseen speaker. They had worked out a more detailed plan last night. Remix and Recoil would be popped in first on a building overlooking the militias compound so they could get a good read on how to cover everyone. They stepped into the circle.

Suddenly the yellow walls became sunshine, grass, hills and... height. Remix almost stumbled off the end of the roof he now found himself standing on. He was held back by Recoil's firm grasp on a handful of his costume. She quickly dragged him down to the roof. "Are you trying to get shot already? You need to stay down!" her voice was still icy.

"I told them you weren't ready yet," she muttered. "But no, 'the GNAMC has provided them with everything they need.'"

"The what?" Remix looked perplexed.

"Damn, they didn't tell you much did they? Look, worry about it later. You need to be looking for targets! We've got thirty seconds before they pop in!" Recoil unslung the large, powerful rifle from her shoulder and began scanning the ground with the scope.

Remix looked over the ledge, and down several floors, to the ground below. The complex looked like a prison. The building they were on was the tallest and attached to one of the outer walls of the rectangular complex. The wall was large and looked like concrete. It surrounded the entire base, which looked like a series of smaller concrete buildings. There were eight military transport-type trucks lined up in front of a large metal gate to their left. At either side of the gate were two guard towers, but at this distance it was hard to tell if they were manned or not.

"Mel, shit! Sorry, Recoil, is there anyone in those towers?" Recoil simply turned the rifle in the direction of the tower. Remix saw her trigger finger twitch twice and the gun made two very small 'puff' noises.

"Not anymore. Good call."

Remix's was visibly shaken. It was finally sinking in that this was not the cakewalk Squeak had talked about. There were guys down there with guns who would have no problem killing him just like Recoil had just killed the guards in the towers.

"They're just tranquilizers. We try not to kill."

OK, Remix amended; *there are guys down there with guns who would have no problem shooting him just like Recoil had just tranqed the guards in the towers.* It didn't make him feel much better.

"Ten seconds." Her words snapped him out of his reverie and he began to scan the ground again. There were certainly enough people to choose from as targets.

A sudden thought came to him. *What happens when I scream at a person?* The thought didn't have much time to have any effect as something caught his eye. There was one truck in the line, number three from the door, which had a long shadow. At this time of day there shouldn't be long shadows, but that was not what caught his attention about it. It was that the shadow suddenly left the truck and attached itself to a nearby building.

* * *

Glacier, Kat, Breeze and Slash materialized next to the fourth truck in the line. This, of course, startled most of the people in the area, all of whom were to be considered hostile. Kat immediately started toward the gate, slashing tires with her claws on the way. Slash mirrored her movements toward the rear of the line. Breeze created a tornado-like wind that knocked most of the non-GNA enhanced people down or against a wall and kept them from shooting the group.

Glacier, still somewhat recovering from the transport, raised one of his large hands and brought it crashing down on the front of the closest transport. The truck's hood crumpled to the ground; presumably the engine of the truck had crumpled as well since its compartment was now about six inches thick.

Cool, he thought, bringing a feral smile to his face as he leaped toward the third truck in line. He wasn't sure his stunt would work but he did, in fact, clear the cargo section of truck three and landed on the hood with a resounding crunch.

There were two things he did not count on though. The first was being shot at by the people on the other side of the truck not affected by Breeze's wind. The other was the impact he made on the truck would flip it over his own head and land upside-down on truck two, which promptly exploded. Glacier was pelted with a considerable amount of shrapnel and, despite the armored costume, passed out. The last thing he saw was Kat being thrown into one of the concrete walls near the gate.

Breeze was almost bisected by shrapnel from the explosion, leaving Slash the only member of the groundside group able to finish the job. Slash noticed several of the troops falling, presumably from Recoil's shooting and the back two trucks' engines appeared liquefied, presumably from Remix yelling at them.

He managed to pierce the engine block of truck five before men with guns surrounded him. He knew what would happen to him if he killed anyone. He'd done it before, accidentally, of course. But the repercussions were not something he liked to think about. He hung his head and retracted his claws.

* * *

"THIS IS SO COMPLETELY FUBAR!" Recoil felt herself shout, pouring as many shots out as she could. She couldn't hear it, of course, since she was next to Remix's sound vacuum. She managed to take out about half of the men surrounding Slash before her own location was pinpointed.

She saw three rocket-propelled grenades were fired at her from three different ground locations. *No, not like this*, she thought and promptly fired three shots of her own to intercept them. She saw she was successful as they exploded well short of their target. Unfortunately, there was a fourth.

* * *

Remix, for his part, did an admirable job. It was just not the job he was supposed to do. He decided the best thing for him to do was help take out the trucks. He did not want to be responsible for whatever happened when his sonic blasts hit flesh and bone. He managed to liquefy the engines of the back two trucks when the front three trucks exploded.

He couldn't see Glacier for the smoke. He did see Breeze take a large piece of shrapnel and fall. He also saw Kat leave an impression on the wall near the gate, where she still 'hung', imprinted into the wall in an almost cartoon-ish fashion.

Wrong! The word ran rampant through his head. *Wrong! Wrong! This is wrong! Don't panic. Don't panic.* Of course, he knew the instant one started thinking 'don't panic' was when one was usually panicking. He froze. He couldn't move. Two members of the ground group looked dead. One he couldn't see. And one had just been surrounded. He heard the repeated 'puffing' of Recoil's gun and realized that his power had turned off.

He also noticed four RPG's fired at the rooftop. Three exploded before they got there. One didn't.

* * *

Remix opened his eyes. He was lying on a table in an almost all white room. There was medical equipment beeping somewhere. The ringing in his head made it hard to figure out where it was coming from. He tried to sit up, and failed. He tried simply to prop himself up on his elbows, and was mildly successful.

He noticed several things immediately. One was that his uniform shirt and helmet had been removed. Another was that he was covered in electrodes connected to a large, medical-looking computer to his left, obviously the source of the beeping.

The third thing was Randall O'Neal standing at the end of his bed holding a chart in his crossed arms. O'Neal scowled at Remix. "I don't think that went too well, do you?"

10
WHAT?

Stan sat at a table by himself in the cafeteria. He felt claustrophobic and nauseous. The claustrophobia came from the almost ever-present yellow walls. The nausea from what had happened. O'Neal had sent him to the cafeteria to get something to eat after his debriefing. "It will make you feel better," he had said. But eating was not what would help this feeling.

O'Neal, he couldn't think of his as 'just Randy' anymore, had explained what happened. The whole thing was just a training exercise. The group was just popped a few floors down to a holographic chamber. All the feelings were imaginary, the wind, the sun, just telepathic illusions supplied by Com/Dani. The whole thing was just a set-up to see how Glacier and Remix would respond to that type of situation. The others knew going in, but saying something would ruin the experiment.

He looked up at a table on the other side of the room. Rich was telling the story of how he finally won one of his wrestling belts. Kat, Matt, Steve and even O'Neal seemed amused by the giant's storytelling. Mel was, not surprisingly, absent.

Everyone was actually fine, physically. They even seemed to be in good spirits. *Except poor little shell-shocked Remix.* The others had invited him to join them. He just couldn't bring himself to do it. He knew it would probably do him some good, but sometimes he liked to 'wallow in his own misery'. He stood slowly, trying not to attract any attention, and left. Glacier noticed his friend leave but let him go. He knew Stan well enough to give him some space.

* * *

Stan remembered running down a hill when he was in elementary school. His arms outstretched, pretending to be *Superman*, or the *Human Torch*, or *Captain Marvel.* He'd always been fascinated with superheroes. He collected comic books for years before finally giving up on them. Not because he didn't believe anymore, it just got too expensive.

He'd occasionally wondered about his own mental health. *Should I believe in this comic book stuff?* Sometimes he believed it too much, and that worried him. He'd always wanted to believe he would make a great superhero. It was his oldest dream and wildest fantasy.

And now, here he was. An actual superhero. *No*, he thought, *superpowered, but not a hero*. His fantasy finally came true and it had turned into a nightmare. He had the ability, or so he thought, to stop his friends from getting hurt. He could have liquefied the 'bad guys.' Then maybe they wouldn't have died. Not that they really did, it was a simulation. But he still remembered the feeling. He had let them down. Horribly. And there was nothing he could do to take it back.

"Seven," a voice said to his left startling him out of his wallowing. He turned to see Melanie leaning against an open doorway. Her tanned face scowling at him. She was still in costume, minus the helmet and rifle. Judging from the appearance of the room behind her, this was the door to her room.

"Excuse me?"

"That's the seventh lap you've made of this level."

He looked puzzled. "You're counting my laps?" She responded with a huff and leaned back, letting the door close, with her still on the inside.

"No." He knocked on the door. "What the hell did I do?" he tried to call through the door, knowing it was soundproofed. "What is wrong with you?" he called as he began pounding on the door. "Why have..." he began when the door opened.

"Absolutely clueless."

"What?" he cried, tilting his head and cocking an eyebrow at her. "What the hell are you talking about?"

She grabbed him by the collar and pulled him into the room, the door closing behind them. "You really don't have a clue do you?"

"Look," he sighed, "I pretty sure you know I've already had a really shitty day, but"

"And now," she interrupted, "you're having a pity Stanley party. You're big superhero fantasy all shattered. Poor baby!"

Stan backed into the door. "Uh, are you telepa..."

"Clueless," she accused again. "Ok, elementary school, right? Who played superheroes With you most often?"

"Uh..." he thought a moment. "Steve?"

She shut her eyes and shook her head. "Who helped you with your French so Ma*dame Seurpuss* wouldn't flunk you?"

"Uh, you." That one he knew. He believed he was slowly catching on, and feeling like a complete ass for missing it.

"Who downloaded and taught you how to use the computer mixer for your audio stuff?"

"That was illegally downloaded wasn't it?" Her icy stare told him that was the completely wrong thing to say. "Uh, you... Mel. I've, uh, caught on."

"No Stan, you haven't." She turned and flopped down into the room's only chair. He sat on the edge of the bed. "When I was six years old I saw this boy. He was so cute, with these little cornrows on his head and a *Battlestar Galactica* tee shirt. Back then, hell, I don't know if I turned on too early or what but I fell in love with the little bastard!

"I spent so much time trying to get his attention," she exasperated. "Teaching him French without getting Frenched. Getting him, yes, *illegal*, gifts. Hell, playing the *Invisible Girl* to his *Human Torch*. Of course, retrospectively, that was probably not the best idea."

Stan was stunned. He wanted to say something, but what can you say to something like this? Here was a girl he had known... forever, who knew him inside and out, and had, apparently, been infatuated with him for, well, ever, and he completely missed it. He'd always considered her a friend, but it never occurred to him that she would be interested in him like that. Or that he should be interested in her that way.

Of course, looking at her now, he realized something that most people probably already knew about her. She was gorgeous. The zipper of her uniform was down enough to give an ample cleavage shot. And he'd never noticed before. *Today is getting worse*, he thought, *first I screwed up and everyone died. Now I screwed up and realized I've missed this for years.*

"Then you had to go do that to Eric!" she exclaimed. Before the conversation, Stan wasn't sure there was much of a difference between being stunned and shocked. Now he knew. "How could you do that to him!?"

"You knew?" he asked weakly.

"Of course I knew!" she cried. "How could I not know? You and Eric were almost brothers. He and Gigi were 'Most Likely to Get Married' in the yearbook. That would make you doing her incestual, y'know?"

He had felt guilt about it for years but tried to keep it repressed. It was just the one time, not that many people believed that. They were both drunk; both there. Gigi asked if black guys were really 'hung better', and it went from there. They probably wouldn't even have remembered it if Eric hadn't been the one to wake them up.

"I'm here. Waiting for you all these years," she stood and pushed him off the bed and toward the door. "And you go and basically screw your sister! That damn near killed Eric! Who was my friend too, by the way!"

She eventually shoved him through the door. "He was never the same after that! I was never the same after that! You're a complete bastard! And," she unzipped the rest of her top revealing probably the best looking breasts Stan had ever seen, "these could have been yours! But you screwed that up years ago!"

The door hissed shut.

Stan stared at the door, jaw quivering slightly. He wasn't sure how long he was staring at the door before O'Neal walked up the hall, passed him, stopped, looked, and eventually walked over. "Uh, Stan? You ok?"

Stan looked at O'Neal with an expression that O'Neal wasn't familiar with. "If you're both shocked and stunned, would you be considered shunned or stocked?"

O'Neal looked at him puzzled.

"Damn it! I need a drink!"

"Alcohol is not allowed on the base," O'Neal reminded him. Stan had heard that somewhere. It did not quell his desire in the least.

"Where do you keep yours?"

O'Neal sighed. "This way." Randy was pretty sure it was going to be a long night.

11
O'NEAL

Stan eventually passed out around four o'clock. Randy didn't get much sleep either. He listened patiently to everything Stan spilled in his drunken stupor. He'd only kept one bottle in his room. Now he'd have to find a way to sneak another one in. He didn't drink much, but having it as an option was nice.

There was supposed to be more combat training that day. Especially for Stan/Remix. Randy cancelled the whole thing. There were other things that needed to be taken care of. Lots of paperwork. A damn lot of paperwork.

He still got a late start on it. He couldn't find a clean HYDRA uniform, eventually settling for one that wasn't that badly stained or smell bad. He'd set up the GNAs for more martial arts classes, sims and testing. It had been two weeks and they still weren't sure what Glacier's upper-limits were. And it had never occurred to them to test his agility as well. But leaping the truck in the sim gave them a clue.

His office was filled with paperwork. He'd gotten three sheets in when there was a knock at his door. Slightly annoyed at the interruption he turned to the door and said, "Come in."

The door didn't open, but Joahn 'popped' in anyway. She was not wearing jeans and a Van Halen tee shirt. Not exactly regulation, he thought, but it looks good on her. "You wanted to see me, sir?" she asked.

He sighed. "Yeah, but I need this to stay between us."

"Ok."

"Stan's passed out in my room. Don't ask why. You really don't want to know."

"Mel talked to him didn't she?"

Randy tried to hide a surprised expression. "Why am I always the last one...?" he muttered. "Um," he looked at Joahn, "yeah. Would you mind popping him back into his room?"

"Not a problem. Anything else?"

"Yeah, who else knows?"

"Just about everyone," she shrugged. "I would have told you but I assumed you knew too."

Randy felt a headache coming on. "Right. Thanks, Jo."

"Like I said, not a problem." She popped out.

Randy turned back to his desk. *Assumed I knew? How the hell would I know? I didn't go to school with them.* He picked up his pen, the paper he was working on, and looked at his computer screen. It said "Press Any Key." He almost chuckled at the old "where's the 'any' key?" joke, when there was another knock at the door.

He put down the pen and paper, closed his eyes and rubbed his right temple. "Come in," he called.

The door did open this time to reveal a smallish man wearing yellow camouflage, which incidentally almost matched his complexion (or was that a reflection of these damn walls), who immediately stepped in, stood at rigid attention, saluted, and proclaimed, "One of the GNAs is missing, sir!"

Randy rubbed his other temple. The headache was getting worse. "Fred," he said with more patience than he felt, "you're not in the military anymore. You work for Hydra. Lighten up a bit." He stopped rubbing his temples and looked at the former soldier. "Who's missing?"

"Remix is not in the practice room or in his quarters, sir!"

Missed the whole thing didn't he? he mused. "Check his room again. I saw him there earlier. He wasn't feeling well," he lied, hoping Jo had actually popped him there already.

"Sir, Yes Sir!" Fred turned on a heel and marched out of the office. *Maybe I should have left a drink for* him.

Randy turned back to his desk, picked up his pen, the paper and looked at his monitor. It still said "Press Any Key". He reached for the keyboard when the phone rang.

Randy looked at his watch. It said Monday. *Of course. Monday.*

He dropped the pen and paper and finally answered the phone on the third ring. It was Edwards. "Hope I'm not disturbing you, O'Neal."

Randy rubbed his temple with his free hand. "No sir. Not at all. What can I do for you?"

"We were looking for the report of the sim. Haven't you finished it yet?" he asked tersely.

Randy looked at his desk. The pen was lying on the paper he had just dropped, which was, of course, the sim report. "Working on it now, sir. Should have it done within the hour."

"Very good, O'Neal. Have it on my desk by C-O-B." Close of Business. Not that they ever really closed here.

"Yes sir." The phone clicked off and Randy hung it up. He rubbed his temples twice before picking up the pen and paper. He did not have time to look at the screen this time before there was another knock at his door.

He dropped the paper and pen. He didn't care that the pen bounced off the desk and landed on the floor or that the paper missed the desk completely and floated nicely to the floor under the desk.

He rubbed his temples, and said "What?" a bit louder than he meant to. It was Dani. She, too, was out of uniform- jeans and a tee shirt. *Why did I put this thing on anyway?* he thought, knowing full well that Edwards would probably have Slash filet him if he didn't.

Dani did not say a word. Simply moved, almost glided, to his desk and placed a small bottle labeled "Migraine Strength" on his desk with a bottle of highly caffeinated cola. She leaned forward and kissed him lightly, motherly really, on the forehead. He got an image, presumably from Dani, of Jo at a liquor store getting him a new bottle of Hennessy.

She gave him a small smile, which he gratefully returned. She turned and glided out the door. She was so... angelic. She mothered everyone. He felt downcast again. He stared at the bottle of medicine simultaneously knowing that he should do more about her situation and knowing that he couldn't do anything about it.

He took two of the pills. Drank half the *Coke*. Fished the paper out from under the desk, picked up the pen, looked at the monitor. "Press Any Key." Then, he dropped everything when the door knocked again.

"I really hate Mondays," he whimpered to himself, burying his head in his hands. He sighed, looked up, and said, as politely as possible, "Come in."

It was Fred again. He came in, saluted and said in a voice entirely too loud for Randy's headache, "Remix is in his quarters sir!" Fred snapped off another salute, turned on his heel and left, again.

Randy just stared at the space where Fred was. *His voice hurts*. Eventually Randy blinked, shook his head and turned back to the monitor. *Screw the paper. I'll do it from memory.* He looked at the monitor, then down to his keyboard. *Right! Where's the 'any' key?*

He closed his eyes and banged his head on the keyboard.

12
DANI

Randall O'Neal was a very nice man. She'd felt his headache two levels away. Of course, she felt most of the things that happened in the complex. Stanley had been hard to deal with last night. Between the sim, Eric and Melanie, and when Geraldine found out what happened, the amount of guilt in the complex was almost overwhelming.

She'd hoped to avoid this kind of a situation. She tried to repress Mel's feelings on the situation. Everyone knew except Stanley. *Hmph, men!* she thought sarcastically. It made her feel better to help Randall.

She had trouble thinking of them in their code names, or anything other than their full names. She didn't much care for nicknames. She tolerated 'Dani', even though her name was really Erica. 'Dani' came from her last name, Danube.

Her husband was the only one who called her Erica. Her daughter-in-law might. If she ever got one. If she could rebuild the relationship with her son. If she ever got to see him again. She tried to remove that thought as quickly as possible. She couldn't think about him. Ever. At least, not if she valued her sanity.

She entered the control room overlooking the training room. It was technically one level above the training room proper. The control room was similar to a press box overlooking a football field, except the training room was bigger.

Melanie/Recoil was on the far side of the room, facing the wall and pointing two handguns at it, one per hand. She was shooting targets on the wall about 500 yards behind her.

Richard/Glacier was dragging a large block across the room. Someone had playfully spray painted "16 Tons" on the side. She suspected Jason, the

Monty Python fan of the group. Although, judging from the size of the block, it may be accurate.

Sandon/Thermal was in the middle of the room alternating pop-up targets, freezing one, igniting the next.

Jason/Hack and Chris/Dot were in the control room, thoroughly engrossed in their respective computers.

Mr. Yook, Edward Martin, Shaun Michaels and Jerome Paynter, the last three hovering over their readout monitors with Mr. Yook hovering over them, were observing the action in the training room. Dani had never had trouble remembering names. She remembered every teacher, every student, every person whom she had ever had contact with.

The door to the room had open silently. Yook had almost noticed she was there, but she created a telepathic illusion of the door still being closed, which it did anyway when she took one step to back out of the room.

She liked being able to go unnoticed. Her telepathy allowed her to wander the base almost completely free, except the basement levels. Her telepathy did not help with electronic key locks. For that, she needed Jason. And he was busy.

She returned to the elevator and went two levels up to the living quarters. There was someone she had to talk to. He would be very helpful later, and since he was not expected to be anywhere, now would be a good time to ask.

She stood before Stanley/Remix's door when it opened. Stanley looked quite hung-over. His costume pants were on but the shirt was mostly off, the left arm was only pulled up to his elbow. He was barefoot. His normally very neat cornrows had given way to a *Don-King-on-a-bad-hair-day* style.

"Why am I even awake?" he asked her drearily, then winced at the volume of his own voice. She smiled up at her friend. Despite what she knew he did when he drank, she still considered him a good friend. Someone safe. Someone who would help her with her problem when it came time. She raised a finger and gently placed it on his forehead. He winced again and waved her inside the dark room.

"Don't take this the wrong way, Dani, but I have this massive han- hang- hung..." She smirked at him. It had taken a few moments, but he finally realized that his hangover was gone. "Uh," he began, more lucidly, "did you?" He gestured to his forehead.

"Yes, Stanley. Your hangover was making *my* head hurt. And I need to talk to you."

"I hate it when you call me Stanley."

"I know. Sorry," she swallowed deeply, "Stan." It really was difficult for her to call him that. "But I need your help and no one can know about it. It does have something to do with your inability to ask the questions you want to ask."

That definitely caught his attention. He motioned for here to sit in the room's chair. He flipped the lights on and tossed the covers back on the bed before sitting on the edge. Dani looked to the windows and smiled. "You've got a beach. How lovely." Stan looked puzzled. "My room has a rainforest. It's always raining there. It's very soothing." The statement did not help Stan's puzzlement.

She turned back to him and smiled. She had such a disarming smile. "It's a hologram, dear. I think everyone's room is different." She chuckled. "Mr. O'Neal has a hard time keeping Jason from reprogramming his. He keeps turning it into flames or spacescapes."

"Let me guess," Stan quipped, "Chris keeps programming naked women."

"He does trouble me."

Now Stan chuckled. "We just need to get him laid. I think he's always been like that."

"Actually," she said, "that's close to what I need to talk to you about."

Stan became puzzled again. "You want to do Chris?" She looked offended. "Sorry, I forgot. Marriage." Dani was known for wanting to remain a virgin until she was married in school. Stan didn't understand that at all, but he knew he was raised differently, and he respected her choice.

Dani looked sad, tears welling in her eyes. Stan moved from the bed to the chair and tried to comfort her. "Dani, geez. I'm sorry. Too much smartass juice last night I guess."

Dani quickly composed herself. "You may want to sit down for this. And please, hear me out completely. You're not going to be happy about it."

"Oh-kay. What's going on?" He attempted to steer the conversation onto its previous course. "You said something about why I can't ask the questions in my head."

She was suddenly unable to look at him, turning her head toward the 'window' then staring at the floor. "You can't ask them because I won't let you." Stan started to rise and protest but she raised a single finger and slowly lowered it so it pointed at the bed. As the finger lowered, so did he. "I asked you to hear me out."

Stan took a deep breath. *In through the nose. Out through the mouth. In through the nose. Out through the mouth.* That was the mantra he had been taught to achieve a state of calmness. It wasn't working very well.

"There are people here," she continued, "who do not what to let us go. They want to keep us locked up and use us for whatever *missions* come up. There is a larger picture but I do not know what it is.

"When they activated me," she held back a sob. "When they activated me, they told me I had to suppress everyone natural tendencies to be independent. To make sure that the whole process felt normal. To make sure that things like what happened last night don't happen. For that, I am sorry. But I'm going to need your help."

Stan was outraged. *She knew about Mel? She knew about what happened with G? She's keeping everyone here... mentally sedated?* He couldn't move. He attributed that to Dani's mind control. He could speak though, and only one word came to mind.

"Why?"

She dried her eyes with the back of her hand before sitting on the edge of the chair and looked him in the eye. "Because I *am* married, Stanley." Tears flowed freely as she held up her left hand. "They took my ring. They took my pictures. They took my life." She tried to compose herself and dried her eyes again.

"And they have my kids." Drying her eyes was futile at that point. Her mental hold on him broke just before he caught her collapsing form as she leaned forward a little too far. He held Dani and stroked her hair. Suddenly, the events of yesterday didn't seem as bad.

"How do we get him back? Where are they keeping him?" He was full of questions, but the only ones that concerned him now had to do with Dani's kids. Stanley's biggest weakness was for children. He wasn't sure anyone had actually noticed that in him. Of course, he didn't notice Mel, either.

Dani looked up at him, her sobbing quieted. "I don't know where he is. I know one of the directors know but I can't read either of them. They're blocked to me." She sat back in the chair and dried her eyes again. "But once I find out, I'll let you remember this."

Her eyes glowed a soft blue, and Stanley fell backwards onto the bed. She stood and smiled at him. "I know you love kids," she whispered. She turned and left quietly. She couldn't let him remember this conversation, yet. She was still setting up her 'resistance group'. Three so far. Soon, she would have to get all of them together. Soon... but not now.

***

Omnipresent. That's what the GNA had done to him. Cursed him with omnipresence. Not in a global sense, but certainly a several mile radius. He was glad the base was isolated. Being aware of more presences would not have been good for his sanity.

Being unable to move wasn't particularly good, though, sanity wise. The 'Sensory Deprivation Chamber', as Edwards had called it, wasn't terribly effective at depriving his senses. It did dull his feeling, his ability to speak and, in any other manner, communicate. But he was still aware of his surroundings.

Several things he found interesting. Stan/Remix's guilt was unexpected. Randy's attempts at seducing Carol Baumann, one of the lab techs, was expected, but always amusing in his failure to succeed. Edwards's inability to see what an opportunity he had with the project was unexpected. He had seemed like an intelligent person. This was disappointing. Ranj's attempts at escape were surprising in their inability to succeed. Dani's plight angered him. But there was nothing to be done about it. The part of him that might have been able to do something was not there anymore. The spirit. The will. It had left. All he could do was observe. It was not good for his sanity.

13
PUBLIC SHADOWS

Three weeks had passed since Remix had had the worst day of his life. During that time, he dedicated himself to the project. Learning everything he could about combat techniques and how to refine his powers. The idea of being able to focus the sonic blasts without screaming at something was foremost in his mind.

The combat techniques were going well. He had learned from Randy that his GNA was developing what was called 'photographic reflexes'. Basically, that meant that when he saw something done, his body would be able to reproduce it. This was true of the entire GNA-enhanced group. Initially he got a sense of accomplishment, thinking he was advancing in his martial arts training at a speed that had never been achieved before. Black belt in Tai Kwan Doe in a week? Surely that had never been done before. Except by the other GNAs who had gotten there before him; an ego-deflating notion that he quickly got over.

His testing with Chris/Dot and Jason/Hack, who was getting less annoying daily, were progressing well. While his most powerful blasts were still when he screamed at a target, he could create blasts by focusing the sonic energy through his hands. It wasn't as powerful a method of blasting, but it was more accurate. He also learned that he was able to detect sounds at frequencies that normal humans could not hear; an ability that could come in useful.

Randy had also been briefing the whole group on tactical errors that were made on the failed sim mission. After the reports were analyzed, it was concluded that groups should not be made up of more than four people. More than that would just get in the way of each other. Glacier was aware that his truck jumping, while successful, would have been more so if he hadn't taken out Kat and Breeze as well as the 'bad guys'. Several more sims had been run to support this conclusion. All of them were successful and the collective confidence was growing. Breeze, Kat, Thermal and Recoil, the 'senior' group, had been on two more successful missions, foiling another attempt at arms theft and a group of drug runners. Randy felt it they were ready for something more public. The previous missions had all ended with the group 'popping' out before anyone got to see them. Edwards, making his first group meeting since Remix had first met him, agreed, it was time to go public.

They agreed that it should not be something as big and potentially dangerous as thwarting a bank robbery or rescuing hostages in the Middle East, but something where the public could view super-powered beings helping society and not be intimidated by the groups' sheer power, but be awed and thankful for their presence and assistance.

CNN and Mother Nature provided an almost ideal event, a Hurricane Caraline in Miami. No one in the group could really prevent the hurricane from hitting, but they could assist in cleanup.

It was decided that two groups would be used. The first group, Breeze and Thermal, would be assigned to attempt to quell the force of the hurricane. Breeze countering with this own winds; Thermal would attempt to disrupt the hurricane by evaporating as much of it as possible. The second group, Kat, Glacier, Remix and Com, would work with local rescue teams.

The six suited up and met at the staging room. Breeze and Thermal were 'popped' first to a location just off coast, where they applied their talents to disrupt Mother Nature's tantrum. Kat, Glacier, Remix and Com were 'popped' into central Miami. The streets were, naturally, deserted. A heavy rain pelted the costume-clad group. The buildings dulled the wind, but it still strong enough to make the palm-trees that lined the streets to touch the ground.

A red flashing light caught their attention. The group followed it to a series of ambulances and busses that lined a building that may at one time have been multi story. The drivers and attendants of the vehicles were attempting to shield themselves from the wind by standing behind their vehicles, none of them able to actually do much in these conditions. Two men leaning against the back of the ambulance at the end of the line were the first to notice the costumed group. They understandably looked at each other in puzzlement. When the group was close enough, the one on the right, possibly the senior official of the group given his graying hair, asked, "So what the hell are you supposed to be?"

"Halloween isn't for a few more months," quipped the younger man, who laughed twice before, realizing that Glacier really was that big *and* within arm reach, stopped and stared.

"We are here to help," said Com, in her remarkably calming voice. "I assume there are people trapped in there," she said pointing at the collapsed building. "What kind of building was it?"

"Our HQ," said the senior man, standing to face the group. "It was also doubling as a shelter. We just can't get to anyone. The walls have collapsed. We can't get through to anyone who may still be alive in there."

"Mind if we try?" rumbled Glacier, who looked at the buildings, rolled his shoulders and rubbed his hands expectantly.

The senior man, whose name badge said 'Bart', looked understandably skeptical, but shrugged and gestured toward the building. "Hmph, go ahead."

"Bartholomew, I would appreciate you and Jeremiah," Com said gesturing to the younger of the pair, "to accompany us. We don't know the layout of the building. And all the hands we can get will help. Where would most of the people have been sheltered?"

"In the basement," he said, "I'll try to show you where. And for Christ's sake, it's Bart!"

"She does that to everyone," muttered Remix. "You'll get used to it."

Glacier moved closer to the ambulance to act as a shield against the wind. The GNAs had no trouble moving despite the wind, but all of them had enhanced strength. Upon reaching the collapsed building, Glacier mentally asked Com a rather pertinent question, *How am I supposed to get under the walls to lift them?*

Com nodded receipt of the message to the giant and turned to Remix and sent him a mental plan. Remix nodded and knelt by the edge of the rubble. All the sound of the storm ceased, which visibly and understandably confused Bart and Jeremy, who looked to the sky as if to confirm the storm was still there. Remix closed his eyes and balled his fists to concentrate the sound there. Slowly he unfurled his fists slowly releasing sonic energy. The sonic waves struck the massive pile of rubble, shattered it piece by piece and sent enough of it flying away to create a passage to the lower levels of the building.

Everyone's ears popped as the sound of the storm came rushing back. Remix slumped a bit, obviously drained from the experience, but he recovered quickly and was on his feet before anyone had a chance to help him.

Com turned to the other members of the group. "Glacier, try to keep the rest from collapsing. Kat do a quick recon and see if there are people left alive down there. Do not move any of the injured…"

"…and come back up and tell you when we can get the rescue crews in," Kat finished. The two quickly disappeared down the hole.

Dot turned to Bart and Jeremy. "Is there an alternate shelter?"

Bart and Jeremy looked at each other, "Uh, dunno," Bart started. "Jeremy, go find out," he pointed at the rest of the ambulance line, "and get everyone over here! These people can't do all of it by themselves!" Bart turned his attention back to the hole and rubble beyond it.

The rubble pile quivered before rising slightly. Kat sprung out of the hole, landing in front of Bart and Com. "There are people down there! Still alive! But I think the main support column just went. Glacier's literally holding most of that stuff up."

Jeremy and the other ambulance crews arrived and looked expectantly at Bart, who, in turn, looked at Com. "It will be safe for a time. Evacuate the people now." Her voice was soothing and hypnotic, but the crew sprang into action. Jeremy leading the workers, Kat and Remix into the damaged building; Bart and Com directed traffic topside. Soon refugees from the storm were being loaded into the ambulances and busses.

Within fifteen minutes, Kat reported that the building was clear of refugees. The busses and all but one ambulance had moved to the new shelter's location. Bart and Jeremy remained at Com's request. "So how are you going to get *him* out?" Jeremy asked, referring to Glacier. "If he moves, the whole thing will collapse and then he'll be buried.

Com answered with a mischievous smirk. Her eyes briefly glowed a light blue, and the remains of the building collapsed into the basement. Bart and Jeremy tried to rush to the rapidly filling hole but were held back by a large, blue-gloved hand. "What the hell are you doing?" cried Bart. "Your friend is still down there! We need to…" he broke off and stopped struggling against the barrier holding him. He looked at the gloved hand holding him back. *Blue?* He followed the hand to the arm and eventually up to the smiling face of the man he was trying to rescue from the basement of the collapsed building. He felt Jeremy on his other side stop struggling and come to the same realization.

"How?" Bart asked Com. The diminutive woman simply smiled. "It's what we do," said Remix.

Jeremy looked as though he had an idea. "If one of you can teleport, why didn't you just teleport all the people out?" Remix, Glacier and Kat tried not to look expectantly at Com. *That was a good question*, Remix thought at her.

"Our teleporter, who is not here, is actually doing just that," Com's hypnotic voice resonated. "But it drains her considerably to do mass transports. It's better to send us to help."

"Oh," Jeremy looked deflated. He thought he'd had a good idea. The words *it was a good idea* ran through his head, in Com's voice. He looked up just enough to catch her wink at him.

"So," Bart looked at the group, "you guys really are superheroes?"

"We're just getting started," smiled Kat. "Let us know how we do."

The next several hours were spent with Bart and Jeremy, traveling through the city, helping those in need.

14
RECUPERATION

The door to the staging room opened letting the worn-out but highly spirited trio of heroes exit. The experience had done wonders for everyone. It always felt good to help others, and with as many as they helped today, they couldn't get higher. Com had returned early at the request of O'Neal. But the rest of the team, with Bart and Jeremy, had functioned admirably as a group.

They would get national exposure for this. Too many people had seen them. There would have to be press conferences. Remix and Glacier liked the idea; Kat, not so much.

Their 'high' was interrupted by the appearance of Breeze behind them. He'd appeared helmet-less and with his uniform in shreds. He didn't even look at his teammates, but brushed passed them at a sprint. The trio, belatedly recognizing that Thermal's absence and Com's early departure was not a good sign, took off after him. They noticed him enter the elevator at the end of the hall. He looked back the trio in pursuit. "I'm not waiting for you," he said as the doors began to close. Kat, being considerably faster and more agile than Remix and, certainly, Glacier, thus closer, sprung between the doors gracefully without touching the reopening mechanism.

Glacier skidded to a stop. Remix didn't. He turned sharply and called to the behemoth behind him, "Down or up?" Noticing the directional indicator on the elevator Glacier moved after Remix toward the staircase. "Up!"

* * *

"What happened?" Kat inquired. Matt did not answer. He simply stared at the elevator panel as if he could will it to go faster. The trip did not take long (it was only two floors) but the trip only added to Kat's tension. Something had gone wrong.

The doors parted and two took off at a sprint. The only thing on this floor, that Kat knew of anyway, was the medical bay. Kat, her ability allowing for greater speed, did get there first, although not by much.

They were solemnly greeted with nods of acknowledgment by most of the others: O'Neal, Jason, Mel, Jo, Gigi, even Edwards. A loud pounding in the hall signaled the approach of Rich, with Stan, most likely, just ahead of him.

Indeed, Stan burst into the room. Rich stopped in the hall and ducked through the doorway. Had he not done that, the doorframe would not have survived the impact. "So what the hell happened?" he rumbled to the room, hoping someone would answer.

Matt looked expectantly at O'Neal, but, surprisingly, it was Edwards who answered. "Sandy Drose has been injured. They seem to have him stabilized at the moment. Erica and Chris are assisting his recovery. As for the details…" he trailed off, looking at Matt.

"He was hit by a car," he said weakly.

Even the stoic Edwards seemed surprised by the statement. "You were supposed to be over the ocean dispelling the storm. How the hell did he get hit by a car?"

Matt stared at the floor. Jo and Gigi led him to one of the seats that lined the walls and sat flanking him. No one else seemed able to sit; tensions in the room running high. "We were off the coast," Matt began softly, "I was trying to create a wind that would counteract the hurricane. And it was working. I just wasn't paying attention. I heard him shout something at me. Probably 'look out!' or something. But I guess I reacted too slowly. I felt him tackle me. I turned to yell at him…" he began to sob, "but he wasn't there anymore. All I saw was a car falling out of the wind."

"He saved my life and I was going to bitch at him for it." Jo and Gigi, each with an arm around him, tried to comfort him. The room was, otherwise, quiet. No one could muster the strength to say anything. Eventually Matt looked up at Edwards. "When are we going to know?"

Edwards couldn't answer. He didn't know how long it would take. All he could do was shrug and look sympathetic. The expression was not easy for him; his demeanor did not often call for sympathy.

A door to an inner room of the medical bay opened revealing Dani and Chris, both of whom wearily entered the room and collapsed into chairs. Neither said anything, drawing the ire of some in the room. "Well?" asked O'Neal.

"He'll be fine," stated Dani, "eventually."

"We reattached his spinal cord," said Chris. "It had been severed." This drew a moan from Matt, whom Chris looked at. "It's ok, man. We got it done. It's just going to take a little time to recover." Matt looked relieved, as did everyone else.

"Can we see him?" asked Kat.

"Not yet," answered a voice from the door. It was Jim Yost. He was wearing surgical scrubs. "We're going to keep him sedated until morning. Actually, he could be up and moving by tomorrow afternoon.

"We forgot something," he said looking at Edwards. "Recuperative Abilities. They're remarkable really. Where we had to cut into him has almost healed. He might have healed without surgery." He turned to Jo. "Of course if you hadn't popped him up here he would have drowned." Jo smiled.

Most of the room was still staring at Yost. "*Doctor* Yost?" Rich asked.

"Yes, Richard. I have two medical degrees in addition to my scientific ones," he said with a fair, and deserved, amount of pride.

"If there's nothing we can do until morning then," Edwards interjected, "I suggest we all get some rest. I will want a full write up of this from everyone involved by noon tomorrow." With that, he left.

"Wow! He's even a bigger asshole than I am," quipped Jason, drawing smiles from around the room.

* * *

The following morning, they all met in the cafeteria, sans O'Neal, Edwards and Yost. They had all slept and cleaned up. To reward themselves they were all dressed casually, mostly jeans and tee shirts. When Stan arrived, he was the last to do so; he heard Rich talking about holding up the remains of the building yesterday.

Stan got his breakfast and joined them at the long table, sitting next to Dani and Jo opposite Rich. Figuring he'd lived the story yesterday, he didn't need to hear it rehashed today. He received a warm smile from the two women, and returned it. "So, Dani, you really took charge down there. Where did a sweet little thing like you learn that?"

Dani rubbed her temples. *He's flirting again. That's a good sign, right?* Jo nodded and Dani smiled at her friend.

* * *

Randy O'Neal was half-heartedly listening the group from his office over the security channel. His attention was primarily on a monitor showing satellite images from the rescue part yesterday. He was trying to ascertain the source of the car that hit Thermal.

Cars being hurled by hurricane's was not an uncommon event, for smaller cars. The satellite image showed identified the flying car as a mid-70s Buick, something entirely too large to have been tossed about by the wind.

He manipulated the computer at his desk to plot the trajectory of the car back to its source. The computer did so with a minimal of fuss. The car came from the area of the beach, about three miles away from Thermal and Breeze's positions.

He adjusted the satellite controls to show the time and location of the cars 'liftoff'. HYDRA's satellite technology was second only to the HUBBLE, only it was pointed at Florida during this event. *Its good to have your own satellite*, Randy mused with a smile.

The smile faded when the image cleared. The car was launched by a large mass, dressed in black. *They're here.*

15
BAD NEWS

Jim Yost hated people. Not individuals, but people as a whole. There were some individuals he did like. O'Neal, Dani, even Remix, to an extent. But he did not like his superiors. They constantly wanted results that were not possible to attain. He could not comprehend how he was expected to get two years worth of results in six weeks. If he said two years, it would take two years. At the moment, his patience was being tested by one of his superiors on the phone. "Yes, I am aware of the time difference. And I've taken that into account. There will be no further problems with the second…"

The door unceremoniously slid open, interrupting his train of thought momentarily. He heard his secretary, Ms. Richardson, attempting to stop someone from entering the office. But judging from the fact that the door was open and O'Neal was entering, he assumed she was unsuccessful. "Something has come up," he said into the phone and placing it back on its receiver.

The good thing was that he had an excuse to hang up on his boss. The bad thing was… "I know you don't like to be interrupted," O'Neal began in an attempt to preempt the lecture. "But you need to see this." He held up a disc briefly before walking to the monitor and player on the wall. Yost was seething, but he also knew how O'Neal thought. He wouldn't do anything like this unless it was vitally important. It wasn't in his character.

Yost took several calming breaths while O'Neal loaded the disc. "What are we looking at?" he said with infinitely more patience than he felt.

"Sir, it's a satellite image from the mission. It contains a vital piece of information concerning the injury to Thermal. The car that hit him was not thrown by the wind." He adjusted the monitor and queued the disc to show a large black mass hurling the car.

Yost's eyes momentarily widened but he quickly assessed the situation. To O'Neal, he assessed it incorrectly. "So?"

"So!?" O'Neal replied incredulously. "Sir, that being is obviously a... an enhanced human! There isn't a machine or construct that can throw a car that size that distance! The shape is human but the size... it's almost as big as Glacier!"

"And?"

"And!? Someone else has figured out how to make super-powered beings. And judging from Thermal's injuries," he struggled briefly with a way to make this sound ominous, "they're not nice, sir!" *That was lame.*

"Not nice, eh?" Yost mocked. "No, they're not. They are part of a parallel program. Not run by us. Not created out of high school *chums*. That would be your government at work, O'Neal."

At each of his statements, O'Neal felt his jaw drop farther. "There's another program? I was under the impression that we had the only EHG." Enhanced Human Group.

"You thought wrong, O'Neal." He sighed and shook his head. "Wake up boy! We're in a competitive business. Why shouldn't there be other enhanced humans? We're all trying to market the same product. Do you think Pepsi got excited when Coke was invented? Or whichever came first." He waved away the whole idea. "The point is, we need to get ours in top fighting shape. We are competing against them. But they made the first strike. I don't intend for our group to get caught with their pants down again!"

"The government has a group?" O'Neal queried.

"Probably, but that guy may or may not be part of it," Yost replied matter-of-factually. "Doctor Forrest went to several companies to pitch his 'super-hero' idea. Eventually the moron patented it. So everyone had access to his information. The problem is that no one seems to have been able to create a stable version." He looked at the monitor. "Maybe someone figured it out. Who knows?

"Anyway, the government doesn't like monopolies. They made sure that everyone who wanted to create these genetic freaks had access to the blueprints, as it were, including themselves."

"There is a government group, Randy," he said as sympathetically as his genetics would allow. "We've never seen them. But I know they exist. There are other corporate groups. This is the first I've actually seen of them, but I knew they existed. Judging from his makeup, it's probably not a corporate group. Hell! It could be a terrorist group! We have no idea.

"Look, I have not committed any of our resources to finding them because I had no *proof* they existed. Now," he said pointing at the monitor, "we do. So, now we start doing some… corporate spying. I want you to get Squeak and Dot. They should make a good espionage unit. See if you can work Gi and Recoil in with them. One's got the scanning ability and one's got the training. Hell, all of them have the training. I just can't see someone like Glacier trying to sneak, well, anywhere."

"Yes sir!" O'Neal turned to get started on his new assignment.

"But, O'Neal," Yost continued, "you are not to tell anyone else in the group." O'Neal appeared confused. "I want them thinking they are the biggest and the best. They may not be but if their attitude changes it will be bad for all of us.

"You are not to discus this with *any*one. Do I make myself clear?" O'Neal hesitated. Not telling his group about a threat that could potentially kill any of them at any time on a mission went against his nature. "Com isn't the only one missing a kid," he finished threateningly.

O'Neal bristled but regained his composure quickly. "Yes sir." O'Neal left with considerably less enthusiasm than when he came in. When he got to the hallway he touched the earpiece / communicator in his right ear. "Squeak, Dot, Gi and Recoil, please meet me in the briefing room."

16
SURPRISES

O'Neal found himself in a darkened room. He'd found himself there before. He knew it wasn't the Staging Area. He was comforted by the soft blue glow from a computer monitor on the table to his left. He knew it would be brighter if Jason were not blocking most of it. He sat up, uncertain of how he physically arrived; he was never really sure of how he got there. He did know that the table he always woke up on was never comfortable. "Dani?" he asked the darkness. "I don't remember us having a meeting scheduled."

"We didn't. I called you here to ask you about the tank. I figured you'd know more than we would," replied Jason's silhouetted form thumbing at Dani's silhouetted form standing next to him.

"Why is it still dark? You usually raise the lights a bit when I..." he broke off when he heard a groan from somewhere else in the room.

"Oh, great! I've been abducted again." O'Neal turned quickly to see Stan sitting up on a table on the other side of him from Jason and Dani. Stan rubbed his eyes and looked around. His eyes adjusted to the darkness and spotted O'Neal. "Hmph. They got you too, eh?"

"Truly funny Stanley."

That voice had to be Dani. The two tabled persons stood and congregated at the monitor. After standing, the room brightened to an almost dawn state. Stan looked about the room in astonishment. It was a large room, almost the size of the practice room, filled to the top with equipment, most of which Stan had never seen before, including a large black tube in the middle of the nearest wall. "Ah, Isaac Asimov's basement, I presume." The rest of the group let out a collective groan.

"He does have a point," O'Neal finally said. "I still don't know where we are."

"That's for your own protection Randall. If you don't know where we are, you can't give away the location can you?"

"I don't even know where we are when we're not in here," complained Stan, his memories of the secret conversation before with Dani slowly coming back "So; I guess this is about finding your kid? What do you need me to do?" O'Neal shot Dani a puzzled look which she quelled with a subtle glance. The word *"Later"* swam through his puzzled thoughts. He felt a mental sigh, *yes I told him.*

Just surprised, he tried to send back. Her grin signaled to him that he was successful.

"Actually this isn't about the kids," Jason answered. "It's about the two refugees."

"Refugees?" Stan inquired.

"Two" O'Neal added.

"I count, don't I?" asked a voice from directly behind Stan's head. He turned quickly to see a slightly distorted face. A quick appraisal revealed the face to not be distorted, just upside down. "Hi Stan! Been a while!"

"RANJ?!?" Stan cried. He started to hug his old friend but realizing he would only squish his head, stopped and looked up to see what Ranj was hanging from. Ranj appeared to be hanging from a pipe that crossed the ceiling. What was remarkable was that the pipe was almost fifty feet above the floor. Ranj's body was stretched.

Stan's hands appeared to be trying to form a question without speaking, several attempts at pointing at Ranj's head, his feet and the extraordinary distance between the appendages. Ranj simply smiled mischievously.

O'Neal patted Stan on the shoulder. "He does this to everyone he meets down here. He thinks it fun."

"It is fun! It's not like there's anyone down here to interact with. They think I'm unstable so they shut me off in one of those… coffins." The last word coming with a shudder that traveled the whole length of his body, making a rubber-band type noise.

Stan turned to look at Dani. "You want to let me in on what's going on?"

Dani smiled. "Short or long form?"

"Uh, short?"

Dani's eyes glowed a light blue and the short form began. It was a telepathic burst. The events of the room over the last several weeks were suddenly available in Stan's head. The discovery of the room via Jason's hacking. The discovery and details of Ranj's escape from a capsule like the black one over there. The occupant of this capsule and the current problem. Stan leaned back on the table.

It was a lot of information to process at once and it gave him a mild headache. But now he understood. Dani wasn't the only telepath in the group. The other one was under heavy sedation to keep his cognitive processes at a minimum while his telepathy was being used by an external source to keep everyone under control. The problem was that the sedatives weren't as effective as they used to be. He was waking up.

"Wow," he mumbled. "So it's not just you screwing with our heads." he mocking accused Dani. "How did he end up like that?"

"He was prematurely activated," responded Jason, whose eyes never left his screen. Stan finally looked at the screen, which was flashing spasmodically. He realized that Jason was scanning the computer for information. The screen was scrolling faster than he could comprehend. *Electrokenetics*, he thought, *Jace probably understands every bit of it.* He wondered if Jason every really stopped. He could only think of one time he had seen Jason here without a computer.

"So what do you want me to do?"

"Listen."

"OK, I'm listening. What do you want me to do?" They all looked incredulously at him. Jason even stopped scanning to turn and stare at him. "Oh," he realized, "like that." He moved to the capsule. *It does look like a coffin.* A cryogenic sensory deprivation tank. That was the term that had come with Dani's 'short form'. He tuned himself in and listened for any movement inside the capsule. He got nothing. Not even a heartbeat. He looked at O'Neal and Dani and shook his head.

"Good," Jason answered immediately. "If he doesn't wake up, that's a good thing."

"Why don't we wake him?" asked Stan. "If were all affected by what's being done to us through him, and we want it stopped, then let's wake him." The argument sounded logical to him. Besides, he had a few things to say to him.

"We can't," Dani said. "Not yet. If he wakes, everyone will know. I can block enough to keep us safe from what's being done. But if he's out, he may not be happy with us. I know he won't be happy with HYDRA."

"I think he'll be fine," said Ranj. He released one of his feet from the pipe, stretching it to the floor before repeating with the other foot so he was standing upright. "He doesn't have much resentment toward anyone except the guys who put him in there." They all looked surprised at the statement, except Stan who looked surprised at the inhuman display of flexibility. "What? We play cards."

O'Neal looked to Dani, "Should we put him back in his tube?"

"Don't panic Randy!" Ranj said patting him on the back, from about ten feet away. "I'm perfectly sane. He just gets out a bit more than you guys think." He looked at Stan, "you've seen him."

Stan looked at the other three in the room before turning back to Ranj. "I what?"

"You've seen him." Ranj looked exasperated. "That first training mission, the one where Rich blew everyone up, right? With me so far? I was watching on the monitor Jace set up for me down here. That's what's keeping me sane," he said as an aside to O'Neal. "Anyway, that shadow from the truck." Stan felt his eyes getting larger. "That was him!"

"The shadow?"

"Yes! We play cards when he comes down here."

"Ranjigan Serikan, are you expecting us to believe that you play cards with shadows?"

"No, Dani, just his," he jerked his thumb in the direction of the capsule.

"Uh, Dani," Stan interrupted, "I have seen this shadow. I don't know if it's him or…"

"It is!"

"But it is real. Maybe it's good at cards."

"Ranjigan, how do you know it's him?"

"He told me."

"Can we get back to the problem?" interjected Jason. "I don't much care about the shadows. I just want to keep him under until we can get the kids back."

Something clicked with Stan. "Kid-uh-ZZZ? As in plural?"

"Yes, Stanley, plural. Ours," she said motioning to herself and Jason.

"Wait a minute," he stuttered. "You mean you and Jace…"

Jason lowered his face into his hands. "Not ours as in with each other. We both have them. With other people. They took mine since Dani can't seem to do much with my head."

"Maybe we should get Bobby. He did a pretty good number on your head back in, what, 3rd grade?"

"No, he did a good number on my face. My head is fine. Anyway, we'll need to bring you back here periodically to check on him. If he starts moving…"

"Ok, so what do I do now?" he asked. The last thing he saw in the room were Dani's glowing eyes. He awoke in his room the next morning. He was aware of what happened, but, unsurprisingly, found himself unable to even talk to himself about it.

17
MORE SURPRISES

Most of their missions had been very similar to the first one, disaster relief. Glacier did get to stop a bank robbery in New York by, naturally, landing on the hood of the getaway vehicle. It gained some reasonable press. *Large Man In Costume Foils Robbery*. Not the best headline, but it was on CNN.

This mission was more typical. The dispatched group, consisting of Glacier, Remix, Breeze and Com, were assigned to help repair some damage caused by a tornado that had ripped through a small Tennessee town.

Waverly was a very small town. Remix had heard of it before from a friend in college who had what he called the misfortune of living there. "It's called Wave-early, 'cause if ya don't, you're gonna miss it." *Not an unfair assessment*, he thought with a tension-lightening chuckle.

There was probably more to it before the tornado, though. The main shopping center, a grocery store and attached strip mall, had been relocated to the nearby river. The town center building appeared to be the only untouched structure in the town. It seemed a good a place as any to house the refugee shelter.

Glacier spent most of the time picking up toppled buildings, sometimes a wall at a time, when they held together, to rescue people trapped underneath. Remix used his sound waves to disintegrate rubble blocking passageways. He tried not to find himself in a situation where he'd need to clear rubble from a collapsed building. None of the buildings here were terribly big, save the seven-story government center; most appeared to be two-story, at most. He was afraid that any thing he could clear from the buildings would liquefy the people he was trying to rescue. Breeze had gone after the storm system in hopes of preventing further tornadoes.

Com was helping local medical staff and the recently arrived Red Cross disaster team with injuries, supplies and relocation of the now homeless. She used here telepathy as a wide spread tranquilizer; not putting people to sleep, but making them more at ease.

The shelter was already filled to capacity so tents were erected outside the building. "For such a small town there certainly are a lot of people here," Com mentioned to one of the locals she was bandaging.

"It's a sleeper town," the woman replied. "People come here to get away from the big city stuff. It's quiet. Well, it was until this happened. My shop is gone. My house is probably gone too." She began to sob. Com attempted to soothe the woman's mind. "Why are you in a costume?" the woman finally asked.

"I'm with them," she motioned to Glacier and Remix, who were still visible from the Town Center. "I guess you could say my abilities are not in the same category as theirs." The woman looked at Glacier, who, at that moment, was holding the roof of a building over his head.

"So, he's really strong. And he makes stuff disappear," she gestured to Remix.

"Actually," Com began to interrupt. *Would she understand audio-liquefaction?* "Well, that's close enough. I guess."

"What do you do?"

Com hesitated. Some people in her group were apprehensive about the concept of a telepath. Almost against her better judgment she found herself saying, "I can read people's minds."

The woman paled and pulled her not-quite bandaged arm away, horrified. Com noticed the paramedic on her left and Red Cross worker on her right, along with their respective patients, have similar reactions. Com hung her head, shaking it slightly. *This is going to happen a lot.* The Red Cross worker's patient began shouting. "Police! We need help over he-yer. She's stealing our souls! He-yulp!"

Com looked incredulously at the hysterical man. "I'm what?" she half-muttered, half-giggled. She almost immediately realized this was probably not the best reaction. Several people had gathered and were staring at her accusingly. *Rich! Stan! I could use your help!* she mentally broadcast. She wanted to back away from the crowd but she soon realized that there was nowhere for her to go without running into or over one of the townspeople. She felt Glacier and Remix approaching and felt a momentary tension release until two things caught her attention.

The first was that the eyes of all the people closing in on her were green. The second was a loud crunching sound. The town center was not as stable as it had appeared. The foundation was now noticeably weakened. Several bricks on the outer wall of the first floor shattered and the building began to topple, toward Com.

Com's first reaction was to send a telepathic 'scream' of danger. Most people realized the danger and began to scatter. Several of the people closing on her, continued to do so despite the obvious danger. The closer they drew, the more she noticed their eyes; the green was not their color, but their glow.

She tried to send a telepathic mayday to Joahn to 'pop' them somewhere out of the path of the collapsing building when she realize she was no longer in front of the building. In addition to the mild disorientation, there was an accompanying motion sickness. She realized that she was now several blocks away from where she was. Her would be attackers began to materialize around her again. She noticed their eyes were no longer glowing.

She looked back to the town center, hoping that Glacier had somehow gotten to the building and was able to hold it up while it was evacuated. While she couldn't see him, she could see an orange glow surrounding the building, preventing it from toppling.

None of her team had that kind of ability, at least, none that she knew of. She found herself, and several of the workers being drawn back to the building, partially out of a sense of duty, but, for her, also a sense of awe. As she got closer, she noticed an ebon-skinned woman in a red costume standing before the collapsing side of the building. The woman's arms were outstretched; her hands glowing the same color as the field around the building. Her face was hidden by a skullcap/mask as her teammate's faces were. Rather, she wore a simple mask over her eyes.

Glacier and Remix stood on the other side of the mysterious woman, apparently struck with the same awe as Com. None of the three stood by for long. Glacier and Remix moved toward the building to help with the evacuation. Com used her telepathy to coordinate the rescue among the GNAs and the workers. It took a fraction of the time to empty than it had to fill it. Com realized that the female newcomer was not the only one to join their rescue party. She caught sight of a blur moving between the building and where she had been relocated. Something was moving people from the danger zone to a safe location at an astonishing speed.

Com moved toward the woman with the glowing hands. "Is there something we can do to assist you? Or do you have a way to control the collapse of the building?"

"I was hoping you'd ask," she replied. "I can hold it here. But probably not forever. I'm very open to suggestions." The dark skinned woman smiled, although she was obviously straining to maintain her hold on the building.

"Remix! Glacier! We have a new plan!" she called. She told Glacier to act as a brace at the building at the weakened foundation. Remix stood between the woman and the building gathering his strength, his sound vacuum gathering all the sound in the area. This startled the woman holding the building momentarily loosening her grip on the falling structure. Com quickly explained Remix's powers, and the plan, telepathically. The woman nodded an assent and strengthened her hold on the building. Glacier was in position holding up the building as best he could, allowing the woman to focus her grip on the upper floors.

A man appeared by the woman startling Com. Presumably this was the speedster who helped with the evacuation. Com mentally briefed him as well and asked if the building was clear. He nodded. Com sent a mental 'go' signal to Remix. He looked to the top floors and screamed. No sound was heard, but the top floors began to evaporate. Soon, the top three floors had been removed.

This was enough for the glowing woman and Glacier to stabilize the building on the remains of its foundation. They couldn't have saved the whole building, and what was left would need repair, but it would not collapse. Remix, however, did collapse. The speedster caught him before he could reach the ground. Before disappearing, he motioned to Com in the opposite direction from the refugees. Com understood him as wanting to talk privately with the other enhanced humans. The glowing woman apparently also understood and began to float away in the direction the speedster indicated.

Com had hoped she and Glacier would be able to join them. She was uncomfortable with an unknown wandering off with an injured member of her group. Unfortunately, from the crowd of refugees burst a small army of cameramen and people with microphones. Com looked panic stricken. She'd never cared for public speaking. Fortunately, Glacier loved it. She looked to the giant and mentally suggested that he try to downplay the whole thing. The last thing she heard was someone asking about New York before she found herself facing Remix, who was leaning against a tree.

She took a moment to reorient herself. She was standing on a hill overlooking the town. She gave a sideways glance at the speedster, dressed in an appalling orange suit with matching orange mask. He shrugged. "I hope de big guy's ok wit de press. I canna carry someone dat big. So, Remix here say you called Com." He shook his head and looked at the other woman. "I tol' you we needed some good names, but every-won say, 'Jeremy, you nuts. Why we need codenames? We not in a comic book.'"

An orange glow appeared over his mouth, followed quickly by a disapproving look. "You can shut up now," she began before looking at Com. "My name's Janelle," she said extending her non-glowing hand in greetings. Com took her hand and introduced herself, naming Glacier as well.

"Hmph," grumbled Jeremy. "He look like that wrestler dat disappeared."

"And she looks like someone I went to college with," Remix playfully interjected before removing his skullcap.

"STANLEY?!" she cried. He simply smiled, stood, and started to hug her. Rather than return the embrace, she slapped him, hard. "You said you'd call me! 'I've got an early class' you said. And I waited on your ass! But did you call? Noooo."

Jeremy began to laugh. Com tried not to. "You aren't having the best luck with women are you Stanley?"

Stan, for his part, looked mortified. "I guess not," he mumbled. "I suppose saying 'I meant to' wouldn't do any good, would it?" She replied simply with an incredulous look.

"Hmph, men."

"I always call you de next day, cherie!" Jeremy piped in. She turned her look to Jeremy.

"*You* are not going there!" She turned to Com. "So, anyway, who are you guys affiliated with? I thought we were the only super-group."

"So did I," answered Com. "This is the first time we've come across anyone else with powers." She raised an eyebrow at Janelle. "G-N-A?"

Janelle looked surprised. "Yeah, they said we were injected with it when we were kids. They just turned it on recently. A couple of months ago. How about you guys?"

"Same for us," answered Remix. "How many in your group?"

"Fourteen," said Jeremy. Com and Remix knew there were the twelve 'public' faces in their group, but knew of other two in the capsule room. *Did they have the same problems?*

"Same here," replied Remix. "Think that's a coincidence?"

"Probably not," she began. She quickly put a hand to her ear. "Not yet. We just found... I know but..." She looked at Stan and vanished.

The two exchanged a look. "We need to talk to Randy," said Remix.

"No, Stanley. We need to talk to Yost."

* * *

A pair of binoculars was focused on the behemoth talking to the press when he vanished. "He's gone. We should have had them." The voice was calm and decidedly feminine. The voice belonged to a woman in a skintight black suit, similar to the other GNAs. Her eyes were an emerald green.

Her two comrades flanked her on a different hill overlooking the ruined town. On her left was her own giant, dressed all in black, including a complete facemask that completely hid his face. The other, also in black with a full facemask, was smaller but radiated an indescribable power. "We will have them soon enough," said the smaller. "We know where they are and what they can do. It is the other two we should be concerned about. We did not anticipate their participation in this exercise."

"No matter." She turned to the pair and grasped their hands. "We will deal with the others as well."

18
QUESTIONS

The briefing room was fuller than it normally would be. O'Neal was sitting at the head of the table. Sitting around the table, from O'Neal's left, were Thermal, Com, Breeze, Hack, Slash, Pop, Kat, Glacier and Remix. None of them looked particularly happy. Remix had told Glacier about the meeting on the hill and briefed Breeze on the whole incident.

Thermal, Kat and Slash had just returned from a mission of their own. Remix did not know the details of that mission but judging from the air that hung heavily on the room, theirs was not the only group to encounter other super-beings.

Judging from O'Neal's expression, he had known other groups existed, and everyone had picked up on that. "I want to let you know, first of all, that this meeting did not take place." O'Neal looked uncomfortable. He did not like keeping secrets, and this job was forcing him to do just that, repeatedly. "I am not allowed to tell you that one of Jason's abilities is to be able to block the security system. There are... people in this organization that would not appreciate us meeting like this to discuss the others."

Several *thank you*s were mumbled from around the table before he continued. "I know you have had encounters with other GNAs. We've only recently been able to confirm their existence ourselves. I'll tell you what we know so far."

"Hang on Randy," interjected Sandy, "shouldn't we wait for Chris and Mel?"

"They're not here," he answered matter-of-factually. "I'll get to that shortly." He took a deep breath before continuing. "I first became aware of them a few weeks ago. That car that hit you, Sandy, was not thrown by the wind." He let the statement sink in. It didn't take long before the whole group was in an uproar. O'Neal looked at a seething Remix and tapped his ear. Remix, hesitantly, activated his vacuum silencing the room. They continued to yell despite the soundlessness of their own voices. Even in the complete silence, it took a few moments for everyone to calm down.

Remix relaxed the vacuum. Only one voice was still going. Thermal was apparently still stringing a long list of expletives at O'Neal. He stopped when he realized that he could be heard again, mumbling an apology.

"That's OK," O'Neal said apologetically himself. "I didn't want to keep it from you but there was nothing we could do anyway, so why get you upset about it? I'm just glad none of you started breaking the furniture." His humor diffused their anger a bit.

"What we know so far, and we don't know their affiliations, is there's a speedster named Jeremy and a... matter manipulator named Janelle. Those two worked together and met Glacier, Remix and Com in Tennessee.

"We also know about an unnamed pair from the other mission in Texas. A hydrokinetic and an avian." His announcement was met with numerous looks of confusion. "A guy who can control water and a guy with wings," he clarified. "There was a news story on a girl of pure energy and we also have reports of a super-fast swordsman, a telekinetic, a hypnokenetic and another strong guy. This last group appears to be... well, I hate to use the term evil."

"But if the other big guy is the one who hit me with the car," quipped Thermal, "go right ahead."

"We don't know they're evil," Kat said. "Maybe they're a bit misguided."

"He threw a car at me!" Thermal cried.

"Actually, I think he threw it at me," Breeze chimed in, drawing a glare from Thermal.

"He's got a point," O'Neal stated. "And it was the big guy who threw the car."

"My point is," said Kat, "that we don't know what *they* were told. Maybe they were told that you two," indicating Thermal and Breeze, "were the cause of the hurricane and he was trying to stop you from doing further damage."

Thermal, Breeze and O'Neal sat a little farther back in their chairs and contemplated her point. "Maybe she's right," grumbled Glacier. "We don't know. We shouldn't jump to conclusions." His comments drew nods of consent from around the room, except from Thermal, who simply sat almost dazed.

"What's the matter, Sandy?" asked Pop, with a big smile. "*Kat* got your tongue?"

"Ooh, I like that idea," said Glacier with a big goofy grin. Kat swiped her hands at her comrades on either side, leaving matching claw marks on their cheeks for the comments.

Sandy turned toward the three at the other end of the table and leveled a finger at Kat, "That," he said emphatically, "was evil." This drew laughter from the room, except Pop, Glacier and Kat, the latter simply donned a very evil, feline grin.

"Um, kids," O'Neal said in his best parental voice, "if we could get back to the subject. We have no idea of where these groups are based. We have no idea what the extent of their powers. We don't even know if they are actually one group, or several."

"So what are we going to do about them?" asked Slash. "Should we be teaming up to work on bigger things? Are they... what, our arch-nemesis... sz? Nemesi?"

"Arch-what?"

"Bad guys."

"Evil villains to be thwarted at every turn," Glacier's rant ended quickly when Kat placed a clawed hand on his upper thigh. "I'll stop," he said sheepishly. He knew the GNA's healing properties would take care of the scratches on his face, but he didn't want to test their ability on some of his more sensitive parts.

O'Neal stood, placing his hands on the table, "Look, we have too many questions right now. I know that already. I wanted to let you know that I'm going to try to keep you all up-to-date on this situation. Recoil, Dot Gi and Squeak are already looking for answers. We may not hear from them for a while."

"They're beginning to suspect something," said Jason, drawing confused stares.

"Ok," continued O'Neal. "I want all of you to be thinking about what to do when you encounter more GNAs. Do not discuss this outside Jason's presence. He can block security, but only for so long. We'll meet back here periodically. I want all of you to train hard. These newbies may not be friendly. I'll tell you more when we have the time. Dismissed."

The group filed out and went their mostly separate ways. Com, Pop and Slash went to the cafeteria. Thermal and Breeze went to the training room. Hack did not leave the room apparently content to be electrokenetically wired into... whatever he was wired into at the time. Kat and Glacier seemed to wander off together flirtatiously. This left Remix and O'Neal standing in the hall, basically wondering which way they could go and look inconspicuous. "Wouldn't have pegged them as a couple," stated Remix, watching Kat and Glacier meander down the hall.

"Are they?" O'Neal wondered. "She did take part of his face off in there."

"I hear he likes it rough."

"You were at that camp thing too?" O'Neal asked, eying Remix curiously.

"The wha...?" Several things ran through his head eventually coming back to the conversation with Sandy and Rich in the costume department. "Uh, no! Do you know about it? 'Cause I don't."

"Come on," O'Neal said, "I'll buy you a drink and tell you all about it."

Remix followed for about three steps before commenting on his sudden realization. "The drink I'm good with. I *don't* want to know about the camp thing."

* * *

In the capsule chamber, Ranj sat on cross-legged on Jason's potentially dangerous capsule with a hand of cards. Solitaire was a very boring game to him. At least it had become so. His only regular companion had left in search of more information.

As usual, this left Ranj alone. It was something he was used to. He loved being around people, but people, he felt, didn't want to be around him. Being alone so much had given him a special non-GNA related gift, an excellent sense of hearing. He'd had it all his life so he really couldn't attribute it to any modification by some loony doctor. Any little sound he had always been able to hear; which is why his parents never caught him doing anything he wasn't supposed to. So he was a bit startled when he heard the activator for the door. His reaction was exactly as he had been told it should be. "*Grab one of the pipes in the ceiling and pull yourself up there,*" Dani had said.

Every so often, technicians would come into the room and adjust some devices that Ranj did not recognize. He'd never been particularly technologically inclined. He could use a remote and surf the net. That's about all he cared about.

This time the technicians, whom Ranj did not recognize, did something different. They opened the 'Jason's' capsule. Immediately the room's temperature dropped about 20 degrees. He realized he could see his breath and hoped no one else could. His black jumpsuit, a less armored but more stretchable version of the costumes everyone else had, would keep him camouflaged in the ceiling area, but a white puff might give him away.

Fortunately, no one looked up. Unfortunately, he could not tell what they were doing. All he knew was that it took about two hours to do it.

19
CONFRONTATION

The group learned about another room in the HYDRA complex that had just 'gone on-line': the Scanning Room. There were six people, called Monitors, who worked in the scanning room. These people had been modified with cybernetic implants. The implants allowed them to be directly connected to a vast global observation system that monitored every police, fire and emergency communication. The HYDRA scanning room was primarily interested in domestic issues, but one of the Monitors was set global for anything big like a tsunami or meteor strike.

The Monitors were reporting any situation that the group could effectively deal with directly to O'Neal. This was, of course, a filtered list. Any member of the group, possibly including Squeak, could handle a liquor store hold-up. These were deemed tragic but the GNAs could not cover *every* crime in the country. It simply wasn't practical.

However, since the Scanning Room had gone on-line, their missions had become exponentially more frequent, and not just during daylight hours. This lead to some expected grumbling amongst the group; most of them actually liked the idea of sleeping through the night.

Many of them had been assigned solo missions since only one person had the particular needed talent. Thermal, for example, had been assigned to repair a bursting dam. Freeze the water and melt the stone back into a more 'dam-like' structure. Slash would not have been a good option for that particular mission. Breeze had been assigned to numerous weather related events, mainly tornadoes. Kat would not have been a good choice to handle that situation. O'Neal worked very logically in assigning missions. He also seemed to be working 24-hours a day. So was Pop, since she was the one actually sending the GNA on their way.

There had come a certain amount of press with these events. Several members of the team had become, in the most literal sense, super-heroes. Thermal, Breeze and Glacier were almost 'media-darlings'; the former because they could fly, the latter because of his size and ability to 'play to the camera'. Remix shied away from the cameras and reporters. He wasn't much of one for self-publicity. Although, Glacier had made sure everyone knew all their group's names. At least the one's who had appeared publicly. Hack, Dot, Recoil, Pop and Squeak hadn't gotten public notice and O'Neal thought it would be good to keep them as a secret reserve. After all, two hackers, a markswoman, a teleporter and a hyper-intelligent mouse might not go over too well with the public. That and Dot, Recoil and Squeak had not returned from their hunt for more enhanced human groups.

* * *

Glacier appeared in the middle of the Campanile Drive in San Diego. He knew his mission was one that could endanger bystanders, or so he was warned, *ad nauseum*. A small masked group had just robbed Tony Gwynn Stadium, home of the San Diego Surf Dawgs. Most of the people in the stadium were unaware the stadium had been robbed. After all, they were only in the third inning of the first game of a double-header against the Reno Silver Sox.

The suspects, whom Glacier thought was an odd term since he could clearly *see* them leaving the stadium with bags of money, automatic weapons and ski masks, were piling into a red Hummer. Two police cars were smoldering nearby, riddled with bullet holes. No one actually appeared to be injured, but the cars were toast.

The Hummer sped out of the parking lot and headed, conveniently, for Glacier. Glacier smiled and pounded a fist into his other hand. He loved doing this. Stopping a robbery by smashing a car's hood into the ground, the publicity that accompanied it. He loved the spotlight and this was as close as he could get to being back in it after he stopped being a wrestler and started being a super-hero. *Not a bad upgrade*, he mused.

As the Hummer barreled toward him, he caught the expression on the drivers face. When Glacier had done this before, usually the driver had a panicked expression. This driver, who was mask-less, wore an expression of confidence, as though nothing could stop him. *Probably on drugs*, Glacier thought.

Then a car hit him. The Hummer he had expected. The Buick in the back, on the other hand, he hadn't counted on so he wasn't braced for the impact. It threw him out of the way of the Hummer, which casually sped away. At least, as casually as a car can speed away being chased by two police cars.

Glacier's first thought was to check the car that hit him. He may not have been injured by the impact, which totaled the car, but the driver might. Had there been a driver. Out of the corner of his eye he saw a something large and black speeding toward him. This time he braced for the impact of another car. Unfortunately bracing for a car is not the same as bracing for a fist.

Even in all his time as a professional wrestler and super-hero had Glacier felt an impact like this. Not only did he feel it, it sent him flying through the outer wall of the stadium eventually to land in leftfield. He heard a mass panic from the crowd in the stadium. Lots of screaming. The sound of a stampede to the exits. Even the players panicked and ran. Of course, that would be expected of almost everyone if someone his size had just flown through a wall at them.

Glacier attempted to stand. The impact of his landing had made a mess of leftfield. The leftfielder, ironically, still stood at his position staring at the large man who had just landed next to him. "Glacier?" he mumbled.

"Rickey?" Glacier mumbled in recognition. The conversation did not get any farther as the large black mass bounded into the stadium and in one step covered the distance between the fence and the super-hero and connected with a double fisted swing, sending Glacier flying from the stadium. In another leap, the black mass of muscle leaped after him.

Two. Three. Four. Glacier counted silently in his head. He wasn't sure if he was counting how many blocks he had flown or how many teeth he felt were loose. When he got to six, he landed, hard. In a sense it was lucky he'd landed in an intersection. If he'd landed in a house, people would have definitely gotten hurt. As it was, the intersection had no traffic. Nor would it have traffic for a while since the impact of his landing turned it into a crater. Glacier staggered to his feet and looked back at the stadium. It was not visible from where he was but he had a feeling that the man in black was following him.

Not surprisingly, Glacier spotted him in the sky, about to land on him, pancake-style. But this was more of a situation that he was used to. Being blindsided had thrown him off, but his ACW years taught him a trick or two about people about to land on him. Glacier easily sidestepped the incoming behemoth. He caught enough of an expression to know that the man's abilities were similar to his own. Super-strength. No ability to fly. *And no crash helmet*, he noticed. *Poor bastard.*

As the man in black fell past him, Glacier swung both fists down into the man's back with all his strength. He realized too late that using all his strength *might* be too much. The crater increased in size almost exponentially. Glacier did get 'sucked in' a bit more, but he was nowhere near as damaged as the man in black.

A crowd had formed at the edge of the crater. It wasn't often two beings of immense size fell from the sky and did this kind of damage. Most didn't even see what had made it, but the impact shattered windows for blocks around. The crowd cheered when they saw Glacier carrying another person his size out of the crater on his shoulder.

He heard several kids say something about a super-villain and how it was about time one popped up. Glacier just rolled his eyes. *That's all we need*, he thought, *super-villains*. He wanted to whip the other man off his shoulder, slam him to the ground and question him. He was reasonably sure this was the same guy who threw the car into Thermal. But that wouldn't look good for the cameras, which were arriving. He also knew he didn't have answers that would appease the media.

He held his hand to his ear, activating his comlink. "Uh, guys, now would be a good time to get me out of here." All he received was static. The comlink was apparently broken. *Oh shit!*

The first of at least fifteen cameramen and reporters shoved a microphone into his face, "Glacier! Who is this guy? And what happened to the guys who robbed the stadium?"

"Uh, I have no idea. To either of those."

"How do you know that other guy wasn't trying to stop the robbers too?" cried a second.

"Probably 'cause he hit me with a car," Glacier deadpanned.

"Who's going to pay for all this damage?" asked a third.

Glaciers eyes got bigger. "Uh, well, I think, um…" Suddenly an idea came to him. He began slightly bouncing the shoulder with the man on it. "Back off! I think he's waking up!" His cry sent the reporters, and most of the spectators scurrying. *DANI!!!* he thought furiously, *GET ME THE HELL OUT OF HERE!* Mercifully, he vanished.

As the crowd dissipated, a figure in black smiled.

20
EXPOSURE

"I want to talk to him!"

O'Neal looked up at the behemoth. "That would not be a good idea, Rich. He just tried to kill you."

"Yeah, and I want to know why!" Glacier for his part had remained relatively calm. Dani had been in the staging area when he returned and made sure the monster was asleep. Technicians had entered the room and took him from Glacier and strapped him to a table before scurrying out again. He was now in O'Neal's office trying to remain calm and not smash things. His skullcap was impaled in the wall opposite the door, and O'Neal did not look happy about that. Glacier had apologized, but was still not happy.

"We want to know why too, Rich. That's why we have Dani scanning him, trying to get any kind of information from him. We're also thinking about turning Slash loose on him."

"I need to be there in case he get free! If he swats Dani she'll splatter on the nearest wall. No one is capable of handling him other than me."

O'Neal sighed. As far as Glacier knew he was right. O'Neal knew this would have to come out sooner or later. He rose from his desk to told Glacier to follow him. O'Neal led him through the maze of corridors and up two levels to the med bay, or so Glacier thought. On the other side of the med bay was another door. Glacier had not noticed it before, but whether that was because it wasn't there before or not, he didn't know, and O'Neal didn't tell him.

O'Neal entered a code into a keypad next to the door, which politely opened and admitted them into what looked like a typical office, except for the large window on the far wall. Beyond the window were several technicians 'tweaking' a large torture rack of a device containing the man in black. The hands and feet of the rack completely covered the man's appendages to the joint. His waist was surrounded by what looked like a solid metal band that covered his upper thigh to his pectoral. His head was held in place by a similar looking device.

Glacier looked almost impressed, but skeptically asked, "Are you sure that's gonna hold him?"

O'Neal sighed and looked at the floor. "It was designed to hold you."

Glacier felt his ire rising again, "You want to try that one again Randy? What the hell do you mean 'designed to hold me'?"

O'Neal sighed again and looked Glacier in the eye. "When you guys were activated, we didn't know if you'd be stable. We had to come up with a method of detaining all of you in case you weren't. If you'd been activated and gone nuts," he gestured to the rack, "we'd have had to put you in that."

Glacier let out a long sigh. It did make sense to him. But he still didn't like it. "So," he began, looking at the man in the rack, "do we know anything yet?" He gave a small startled jump when he realized that Dani was standing directly before the window. O'Neal touched a switch on the wall next to a speaker.

"Well?"

"I haven't found out much," Dani answered. "The whole situation was a set-up. It was designed to get Glacier out in the open and 'take him out'." Her statement included the bunny-rabbit finger quotes. "We don't know where the robbers went, or, I should say, he doesn't. But I think the police can handle that. I have been able to get his name."

O'Neal and Glacier exchanged glances before turning to the diminutive woman on the other side of the glass. "Well?" they asked simultaneously.

Dani cleared her throat and looked up at her giant apologetically. "Um, I'm sorry Richard, but he calls himself... um... Mammoth."

"I guess he doesn't have a legal department," O'Neal quipped in what he knew was a vain attempt to lighten Glacier's mood. And, as expected, it didn't work. Glacier seethed. Had he been a cartoon character, this is when his face would turn bright red and the steam would shoot out of his ears. O'Neal thought the man looked somewhat frightening normally, just on size, but now he was petrified because if something that big looked this pissed, most people would panic and run, which is what he felt like doing.

"I'M GONNA TEAR HIS FUCKING HEAD OFF!!"

* * *

Remix was in his room resting. His assignment for the day had been relatively benign. He was experimenting with Breeze on the effects of sound waves on weather patterns with surprising results. He had disrupted a tornado without screaming at it, just focusing the sound through his hands.

He felt rather good about saving that trailer park. He had removed his skullcap and unzipped part of his shirt when he heard a deep rumbling noise that he knew could have only come from one place.

Well, he thought, *Rich sounds a bit pissed.* He reached out with his mind to find Dani and see if any help was needed.

***

Two floors below Remix, Ranj examining the capsule's case, trying to figure out what had been done when he heard the same scream of anger. He'd only heard that sound once before and he knew then that getting out of the way was preferably to being within two blocks of Rich. He hoped four floors would be enough.

***

Dani had also heard Rich make this sound once before. This time, she stood directly between Glacier and Mammoth. Glacier had moved quickly enough to break through the window and surrounding wall. He did this with remarkably little effort. Dani had also moved quickly to stand between her giant and the monster sealed up behind her.

Glacier froze, first because of Com's telepathic interference in his neural system, second because Thermal encased his legs in ice. O'Neal slowly approached the big man. "I think the two of them could handle him."

"Yea," came an unfamiliar Brooklyn accent, "if dey can handle yooz. Dey can shirly handle me." Mammoth's mocking tone grated on everyone's nerves, but especially Glacier's. "Hey, aint' you dat wrestler? Dat's where I got da name from, y'know."

Glacier seemed to deflate. He almost looked as if he could cry. Not only had this guy stolen his name, but he knew he had stolen it. And O'Neal, Com and Thermal wouldn't let him get close to removing his head, either. Though they did look sympathetic. Thermal did encase the lower half of Mammoth's mouth in ice. Glacier felt a slight vindication and smiled weakly at Thermal when a voice came from a speaker on the wall. "O'Neal and Com to Staging Area!"

He tapped the comlink in his ear. "What is it? I'm kind of in the middle of something?"

* * *

Thermal was left in the room with Mammoth when the rest of the group, including a hastily thawed Glacier, was popped down the two levels between the interrogation room and the staging area.

The staging area had two occupants. O'Neal knew there was only one person out on an assignment that may return, Slash. And Slash was, indeed, one of the occupants of the room, the other was a skinny, ancient-looking man dressed in a black jumpsuit, impaled on Slash's right hand.

Despite the obvious injury to the man's torso, he was obviously still alive. A telepathic burst from Com did not render him unconscious. A smack on the head from Glacier did, though. The impact also dislocated Slash's shoulder.

"Omega Protocol!" O'Neal called out. Almost instantly, technicians arrived in the room and strapped the old man to a table and rushed him out. Slash retracted his claws, popped his shoulder back into place, and looked puzzled at O'Neal.

"Omega what?"

"We had to have something in place if we captured any other super-powered beings," O'Neal explained. "We would hopefully render them unconscious and take them off to be studied."

"Good," Slash grinned. "I'll help with the dissection."

O'Neal hung his head. "Not that kind of study." He returned Slash's gaze. "So what can he do?"

"I'm not too sure. There were several people around me who looked like they had died of old age. But there was something wrong about it. I mean some of the people were really short and had toys. I'd rather not think about that at the moment if you don't mind. But the short form is, I think he ages things."

"And he looks like his powers affect him too," Dani added.

"How are you going to contain this one?" inquired Glacier.

O'Neal didn't answer. But Com knew what he had in mind. Another Capsule.

21
OMEGA

The Omega Protocol was not only an order to restrain incoming and possibly hostile GNAs. It was a signal to Doctor Jim Yost that things may be going wrong. And, indeed, things were not the way they were supposed to be. Unidentified GNAs had been springing up globally for several weeks.

Yost was able to maintain control of his group with Dani's help and the use of the main capsule's occupant. It was sheer dumb luck that he discovered a way to use the occupant's powers without the occupant being conscious. GNA was compatible with the computers he used to study DNA. It was the main reason he'd been put in charge of this group. If there was a group that he couldn't control, and they'd made their way here, well, there were too many things that could go wrong.

Having Mammoth brought back unconscious didn't send up any red flags. If anything it gave Yost the opportunity to study a GNA who was not in his group. Check for similarities and see if refinement is possible. But having not only a live GNA, but also a dangerous and psychotic one pop up on the base was unacceptable. If the main capsule were to be damaged, it could mean the end of the program. His program. He couldn't let that happen.

And his visitors would be arriving any time now.

Yost kept his office immaculate just in case his superiors decided to show up. And the Omega Protocol meant they would. Always in threes. Always that damnable militant bastard sniping at him. Always that absolute bitch harping about how the program was unholy. Always the mute who simply stared into space. He hated them all. And judging from the image on his wall monitor, they were here.

* * *

They exited the elevator on the top floor. They walked down the hall in uniform steps, pyramid formation. They passed the secretary with no acknowledgement of her existence. They entered his office and stared at the small aging man seated behind the desk.

"Infiltration is unacceptable," said the woman at the point. "Your program has been compromised. You must have not been keeping up with your prayers, James. The good Lord is not pleased with you."

"Marcia," Yost began, rising from his desk, "what would have had me do? We couldn't leave Mammoth just lying around in San Diego, could we? And the other one... what would you have me do?" *What would Jesus do? God I hate that woman! Is that a pun somehow?*

"Your job is to make sure the groups do not intermingle," objected the militant bastard, also known as Kent Edwards. "You made the group too public. You've already had contact with fifteen other GNAs. AND you've sent out a locator group to find more. You've already got two of them that do not belong in your group in your complex." He sighed.

"I understand you want to study Mammoth. That's fine and dandy. What if he escapes, Jim? Have you thought about that? You know this location is not exactly safe for a rematch between him and Glacier."

"The Lord did not intend such things."

Yost stood his ground, feeling more intimidated by the stoic third member of their group than the unreasonable ones. "I still have not heard an alternative. Mammoth could not have been left unobserved. The other one had murdered numerous people and came attached to one of my group. Slash might be dead if he weren't popped back here."

"Then that is what the Lord had intended."

Yost was appalled. "I will not sacrifice any member of my group just to keep your sense of *what should be where* satisfied. I don't give a damn what your Lord intended!"

Marcia Nichols visibly paled. Edwards cast his eyes toward the floor. The third member's eyes began to glow intensely red. And for the first time in the six years Yost had know him, he spoke. His voice an eerie reverberation. "You should not blaspheme."

Great, now they'll break out in a rousing version of kumbiah. "Blaspheme? What the hell? When did this become a Jehovah's Witness program? My job is to take care of my group. Group interaction is inevitable. There is no way for you to prevent it. Your *Lord*," he filled the word with as much spite as he could muster, "is a fool if he thinks they'd never..."

"MY PLAN WILL NOT BE INTERRUPTED!"

Yost's eyes widened. That was a voice he had never heard before. It had no origin in the room. It came over no speaker. No phone. The voice was in his head. It had no sound; only the words. He had been contacted telepathically before, but this was more intense than any previous contact.

"Wh- wh- who is that?" Yost asked anyone who would answer. The trio remained unmoving and silent.

The last communication Yost received said, "I AM THE LORD!"

* * *

The trio left the former director slumped over his desk. They returned to the elevator as stoically and methodically as they had arrived. The room remained quiet, save for the breathing of its unseen occupants.

The first occupant did not actually need to breathe. The shadow simply left the cabinet it was attached to and slipped under the door.

The second occupant was in an air duct over the desk. He'd witnessed the whole debacle, but was not privy to the telepathic communication. He simply observed Yost fall over after his outburst. He'd assumed telepathy. It would have been useful earlier in his mission to have a telepath along. He'd discovered three so far.

But now he had a problem.

His mission was to discover who was in charge of GNA groups, and he had certainly found out. Apparently the Lord was in charge, and it wasn't the religious Lord. There was a powerful telepath in charge. And that was probably not a good thing, at least judging from the bloody mess that was now seeping out of Yost's ears and nose.

He'd discovered the capsule chamber. He knew the occupant of the main capsule. He knew about Ranj, even let Ranj know he was there. Ranj could be trusted.

His problem was that the person who came up with the idea to send him on this mission was now slumped over his desk. The problem had become infinitely more complex, which was an ironic way to put it.

22
SURRENDER?

Ranj watched from his hidden area in the pipes as another capsule was wheeled into the room. This one was no different from the first, except, most likely, the occupant. But even that was something that Ranj wasn't ready to fully rule out yet. With so many strange things happening since his 'initiation' it might somehow be possible for the same person to be in both capsules.

The second capsule was placed next to the first and wired into the same type of monitoring system. This might have been advantageous if Ranj knew how the first one had worked. Jason would know how, but he wasn't here. Again, all Ranj could do was watch and wait for someone to come and help him decipher the meaning of these events.

* * *

The getaway car was smashed. The engine completely removed from the car itself. It still moved, albeit slowly and sparking heavily from where the undercarriage dragged along the ground. After all, cars weren't supposed to drive only on rear wheels.

The cars occupants were bewildered and panicking. The car had a front end just a few moments ago. Then everything went quiet. Their little heist was pulled off perfectly. They didn't have to use the guns. And that was a good thing. They wanted the money but not the potential murder charge if they got caught.

And now it looked a lot like they'd get caught. Barry, the car's passenger jumped from the car when it had slowed enough. Not out the door, out the front. There wasn't anything in the way, so why not? He carried his not-at-all-legal-but-fully-automatic rifle in one hand and tried to drag a bag of, presumably money, behind him.

"Let me get this straight," a voice said from behind him. "I just liquefied the front end of your car and you think I'm just going to let you walk away?"

Barry spun around to see a man in a black spandex-like suit with a red skullcap sitting cross-legged on the roof of the car. The man's smile was irritating but the fact that he appeared to be vibrating the air around him was unsettling. He pointed the rifle at him and pulled the trigger. He felt the gun fire repeatedly, but it made no noise. Actually, he heard no sound at all. None of the other street traffic. None of the pedestrians talking. No birds. Nothing. None of his bullets seemed to reach their target. They all hit the vibrating air around the costumed man and vanished.

When his clip was empty he dropped his gun and stared in bewilderment. The driver shaken from his state of shock at having a gun dropped on his legs began to scream. The scream didn't last long as the costumed man placed a hand on the roof of the car and silenced the noise. The rest of the world resumed its normal volume, but Ben, who looked like he was still screaming, was mute. "You done?" the costumed man asked.

Barry could only nod. The costumed man slid off the front of the car as two police vans and an ambulance pulled up. Barry dropped to his knees and put his hands behind his head. Two officers ran from their vehicles to take him into custody. As he was being led to one of the police vans he heard the name of the man who had outwitted him.

"You're Remix, right?" one of the officers asked. "Hmph, never met a super hero before."

Remix sighed. "I don't consider myself a super hero. I'm just..." he shrugged, "a concerned citizen trying to help."

The officer shook his head. "Uh, yeah. Where exactly is the front end of the car?"

Remix pursed his lips, then grimaced. "Actually I was just going for the tires. Sorry." He looked back at the officer who was looking down at the driver, still sitting in the car screaming silently.

"I guess you, uh, defeated them, eh?" Remix followed the officer's stare and noticed that the driver's feet would have been in the front part of the car, if the front part of the car was still there. The driver's feet were gone as well. Remix's sound vacuum faltered for a moment and both were startled at the screaming man's attempt at his own sonic scream.

Remix quickly regained control and the man fell silent again.

He didn't know what to say. It certainly wasn't his intent to… de-feet this man. Stop him. Yes. But not this. He felt sick. The office could tell. "You may be black and red all over, son, but you look green."

"I didn't mean to… do this." He shook his head and looked apologetically at the officer, then the driver. Something new struck him as wrong. He had better control than this. There is no reason the whole front end should have blown off. This man should still have his feet. *This man should have taken a breath by now.*

Almost as if on cue, the driver closed his mouth and smiled a perfectly evil smile at Remix. The driver's face exploded striking Remix in the chest and sending him flying back into one of the vans.

Barry, seizing the opportunity, broke away and ran back toward the remains of the car. His body turned almost liquid halfway and turned into a wave of flesh before joining with the driver. The mass of flesh eventually became a whole, humanoid figure holding a wicked looking cannon-like weapon.

"Hmph. I guess that would mean I just mastered the Remix," gurgled the composite being, his voice sounding as though he were underwater. Most people were have at least looked startled at the event. The officer, however, hadn't moved from his spot. Instead, the back of his shirt ripped open revealing a pair of leathery, reptile-like wings.

"I think he fell for that one, Barry," smirked the faux-officer.

"That was fun. I think I'll do it again." Barry smiled and pointed the weapon at Remix's head. Remix was in no condition to dodge the shot, nor could he concentrate enough to focus his powers. And while the suit may be able to take the impact, the lower part of his face was uncovered. Another trigger was pulled creating a massive explosion from the police van.

Remix, however, found himself in the staging area. "It's ok, Stan," Pop's voice said over the speaker. "I just sent a back-up team to get them." Remix slumped to the ground.

* * *

"That was so cool!" cried Barry.

"Don't get too carried away," warned the avian. "We know they usually only send one for a job like this, but we don't know how they… *whulmph!*" His sentence was cut off as a large blue and white figure landed on his back.

Glacier looked up and slightly over Barry's head. "I told you popping up over him like that would work."

Barry heard a sigh from behind (and over?) him. He turned to see a half-blue, half-red figure hovering behind him. "Don't make a habit of jumping people like that, though. There's just no sport in it," replied Thermal, who then coated Barry in ice.

"Besides," he continued, "doesn't this seem too easy to you?"

"Yeah. It does. I mean…" the four vanished from the street and reappeared in the staging room, "even when I went up against Mammoth, I only hit him once. And that was it."

"Yeah," muttered Remix, still on the floor, "way too easy."

Thermal looked down at his friend, "Ok, apart from you getting hit like that. I mean, we've captured four of the five super villains we know about. If that's all there is… should we… what, savor the last one?"

"Maybe we're just better trained," rumbled the giant. "I mean, come on, O'Neal and Yost have been pushing us pretty hard. We don't go anywhere. We just train and do missions."

"He does have a point," said Remix, finally coming to a seated / propped position. "Maybe these guys just don't train as much as we do."

Thermal had to concede the point. All they did was train for situations like this. But there was still something that did not feel right about it.

INTERLUDE
CHANGE OF PLANS

Three hazy holograms 'sat' in the briefing room. The holoprojector was replaying the events of Remix's adventure with the shape shifter and the avian. "They are progressing well," said the hologram at the head of the table.

"But they are still a bit raw. Should never have been caught off guard like that," said the one on his right.

"It's too late for that now," said the third. "Everything is in place for the groups to come together. Operation Cliché is ready. Is there a particular target either of you have in mind?"

"That depends on how cliché you want this to be," said the second. "New York is the obvious target. The casualty rate would be astronomical but the publicity would be almost equal."

"California," said the first. "There are numerous media outlets there. I can even see one of the movie studios pulling their equipment in to film it."

"That may be for the best," said the third. "New York has the potential for too many things to go wrong. Hollywood? Or maybe Oakland?"

"Venice?"

"Too much water."

"Venice, *California*."

The third noticeably dropped his head in shame. "Sorry."

"Atlanta," said the first with a note of finality. "Hasn't been done before and is big enough to cover the media."

"Hmm, Atlanta it is."

The three holograms winked from existence. The holoprojector ceased functioning. And a shadow from under the table slid under the door.

23
CLICHE

The quartet stood in the staging area. Remix, Glacier, Thermal and Breeze. The four heaviest hitters of the group. Able to cause the most damage in the least amount of time. The group had been chosen by O'Neal for the biggest, and most surreal, adventure yet.

"Are they serious about this?" Remix asked O'Neal.

O'Neal, in the control room, shrugged. "Edwards just sent in a message saying that Atlanta is scheduled to be attacked by something big. I'm just following orders here."

"This is still weird," rumbled Glacier. "Why are we being spaced like this?"

O'Neal shrugged again. "Edwards said it would be a good idea to have you appear in different parts of town. Wherever this thing pops up, if it pops up, one of you should be close by to start working on it. The others will be popped in shortly."

"And the reason we're leaving now instead of when it pops up is…?" asked Breeze.

"Because Edwards told me to send you now."

"I never bought that reason from my parents," grumbled Thermal. "'Mom, why do I have to go to bed now?' 'Because I told you to.' That always seemed lame."

"Weren't you the one who said this was getting too easy?" countered Glacier. "We may get something big now."

"Yeah," he sighed. "Whatever."

* * *

Jason and Ranj looked over the new capsule. There was nothing extraordinary about the exterior; at least compared to the other capsule. Jason had deduced the 'aging man' had been put inside.

The shape shifter and the avian were also being kept here. The 'shifter still encased in ice and kept in a cold storage unit and the avian in, essentially, a large birdcage. Mammoth had been moved down here, as well. Dani was telepathically keeping him asleep while Jason worked.

"This is not the same type of unit as his," Jason whispered, gesturing to the other unit. "This one is doing something I don't understand. Something with a temporal signature."

Ranj looked puzzled. "That means it's doing something with time," Jason explained.

"No, I got that part," Ranj said. "I just don't understand why you don't get it."

"Huh?"

"They guy inside is the one who aged everything right? Wouldn't it make sense for his coffin to prevent his powers from working?"

"Ranj, that is…" *absurd? ludicrous?* He thought a moment and chuckled to himself, "absolutely brilliant. That does make sense." Out of the corner of his eye he caught a shadow. This would not have been something alarming, except the shadow was growing and looming closer to Ranj.

He tried to grab his friend and move him out of the way, but Ranj's body mostly stayed put. The part Jason grabbed to move him, did move, the rest of him did not. Ranj looked puzzled but did turn his head, completely around. This made Jason somewhat nauseous, but if it had the same effect on the shadow…

"Hey!" Ranj said, realizing his voice may be too loud, he repeated softer. "Hey, shadowman! Whazzup?" He turned back to Jason. "Told ya he was real."

The shadow enveloped Ranj completely. Jason wondered if Ranj could breathe in there. Just before Jason's panic set in, the shadow separated and Ranj had a look of enlightenment.

"I know what's going on now," he said with a clarity and finality that his friends had never heard him use before. "We don't have much time. Open the primary capsule. There are things we need to do."

* * *

Remix found himself in a section of Atlanta that he'd never been in before. Of course, he'd never been to any other part of Atlanta before, but it was still a bit intimidating to find yourself in a place you've never been before.

But there was something seriously wrong with this picture. He was surrounded by large glass office buildings. He was in the middle of what should be a busy street at any time of day, but it was completely deserted. There were cars parked along the sidewalk, but none actually moving up or down the road itself. No pedestrians. No animals. Nothing.

He looked around, feeling very nervous. Cities like this simply didn't have the population disappear overnight. Even if there were some sort of disaster and a government order to evacuate, there'd still be someone here. Then an even more disturbing thought hit him.

There was no sound.

Here he was, about to face some big, unspeakable foe, and there was no sound for him to absorb and focus. He touched his ear to activate the comlink. "O'Neal, where the hell is everyone?" He tried to sound calm, although his skullcap was absorbing a large amount of nervous sweat.

No answer. "O'Neal? This better be some damn training exercise! This is just wrong! Where is everybody? Glacier? Breeze? Thermal? Somebody come in!"

"-e-ix?" came a heavily static-laden reply. "wha- -e—ck?—re we?"

"Glacier? Try again. I can barely hear you!" He moved to an intersection to get a better signal. There were still no signs of life down the newly visible streets. Several parked cars and… a glowing black sphere in the middle of the road about two blocks away?

There was a flash and one of the parked cars behind him exploded, throwing him farther down the street. His suit absorbed most of the blast but a piece of shrapnel gouged his left arm. He landed with a thud on the other. He quickly assessed his injuries and realizing that nothing serious was wrong, looked toward the sphere, the only thing that seemed out of place.

The sphere was gone but a small figure stood in its place. It was wearing a costume that was almost the inverted version of his own. Where his was black and red, this one was white and green. The figure was quickly replaced with a growing, glowing black sphere, and it had soon covered most of the block.

"Not good! Not good!" he muttered as he scampered away from his prone position and dove between two parked cars. He tentatively peered over the hood toward the black sphere in time to watch it quickly shrink to the size of a ball in the hands of the white-clad figure. The ball then burst with a bright white light and the road where he had just been lying exploded. This time his cover had been adequate.

That would explain the flash before the explosion. He moved closer to get a better look at his adversary, trying to use the cars for cover. She, and upon closer inspection, this was definitely a she, appeared to be satisfied that her last blast had vaporized her foe.

Damn, she wears that suit nice. Shame she not on our... Tink-whir-whir-whir. He glanced at where he felt his toe had contacted with something. *Beer bottle. Cute girl. Spin the bottle. Yep, I'm back in high school.* "You're not that good y'know!" she called. *Cute voice.* He slowly raised his head over the hood of the car. "You should always check your path. You never know what might give you away."

In her hands appeared two small black glowing spheres. Her eyes glowed with a purple intensity. *Purple eyes?* He tried to gather as much sound as he could from the bottle and the exploded but still burning car, now two blocks away. The two spheres in her hands were expanding, creating a dark void around her. Her costume now seemed gray instead of white, as if she were being covered with a shadow.

Remix realized it actually was a shadow about the same time Glacier's feet hit the ground behind her. Glacier's impact shattered the pavement and made a small crater, which threw her back into his enormous arms. He hoisted her in the air with one hand wrapped around her waist. He started to smash her into the ground. He hesitated as he found her weight had more than doubled. He looked at the girl over his head and realized that she wasn't the only person attached to that arm. There was also a small man with an obnoxiously orange costume. "Please don' smash her big guy. She's really is on yo' side."

Remix released some of the sound energy he had built up and looked inquisitively at the newcomer. "Jeremy?"

The orange-clad speedster put a finger to his lips and hissed. "Dat's suppose' to be a secret. I'm 'Rush' now!" he proclaimed dropping from Glacier's arm and posed, hands on hips, below the behemoth's appendage.

"You know him?" The question was asked in a bizarre stereo with the giant's rumble and his feminine prisoner's equally feminine voice to their respective teammates, who responded in an almost equal tone "Yeah we met about..." they paused and looked at each other, before resuming, "we need to stop this."

Remix rubbed his temples. Jeremy -*strike that*. Rush chuckled. Glacier put down the woman in white and looked apologetically at her. "Sorry about that," he rumbled. "It just looked like, well…"

"'s ok. I'm Nightlite." She extended a hand to the big man. "Good to meet you."

"Likewise. I'm Glacier. This is Remix," he swept a hand toward his teammate, who shook hers in greeting.

"Glad we're actually on the same side." He hesitantly turned toward Rush. "We are on the same side, right?"

"Far as I know."

"Good, I'll just chalk it up to a mix-up and let it go." He turned back to Nightlite. "What what the black… sphere… thing?"

She smirked and seemed to blush a bit under her white skullcap. "Well, I absorb light, focus it and turn it into… energy blasts." She sighed. "The problem is that when I absorb the light it creates a complete absence of light around me and I can't see a damn thing, so," she shrugged, "I miss a lot."

"That sounds like what I… do," Remix commented. "I just do it with sound." He looked to the giant. "That's too weird to be a coincidence isn't it? I mean we do the same thing in principal, kinda."

"Not as weird as this city. I mean, where the hell is everyone?"

"I've searched most of it so far," said Rush, "and apart from my group and yours, I didn't find anyone." He shrugged. "I mean I heard Boise can get a bit boring but this is overdoing it I think."

Glacier and Remix exchanged worried glances. "Boise?" Glacier asked carefully.

"Uh, yeah."

"Idaho?" Remix asked.

"That is what I've heard about you," came a womanly voice from above, followed by the descending forms of Janelle, Breeze, Thermal and… someone new, presumably the fourth member of their group.

"You're still bitter about that aren't you?" Remix asked. The only response he got was an acidic expression. "Uh, yeah, well…" He turned to the person he hadn't met and extended a hand to the purple-clad flyer. "Remix." All he got in return was an icy stare.

"That's my brother mix-boy," sniped Janelle. "He's Vigor and I'm Vim."

"Oh that's cute," mumbled Glacier.

"Great, so you're both holding a grudge." Vigor didn't respond verbally but Remix was glad that his Vigor's powers didn't include 'death vision.' "Meanwhile," he turned to the speedster, "did you say Boise?"

"What are we doing in Boise?" asked Thermal.

"Idaho?" asked Breeze.

"No, he's da' 'ho," quipped Vim.

"Ok, we can stop that now," said Remix in a tone that suggested he was actually trying to be serious. His third attempt to ascertain their location was almost cut off by another rant from Vim. Instead, he cut off her rant by absorbing any sound she made. This, of course, infuriated her, and after a few moments of attempting to scream through it, subsided and allowed Remix to continue his question. "Who told you this was Idaho?" he asked Rush.

"We were told that something big was going to hit Boise," answered Nightlite. "I figured it was you. I mean, we don't really come across many costumed people. Well, at least we don't." She looked to the rest of the group for confirmation, which Vigor and Rush gave with a nod. "So if its not you, then... wait a minute. Where did you think you were?"

"We were told the same thing, except substitute Atlanta," responded Breeze. "Hey, I've never been there... or Boise, for that matter. Unless there were people I probably couldn't tell them apart just by looking at buildings. Where the hell are all the people anyway?"

"Breeze, is your comlink working?" Remix asked.

"Nope." He looked at the others who all shook their heads, from both groups. "Hmph. I guess somebody screwed up."

Rush looked frustrated. "I am so going to kick Edwards ass when we get back."

Remix, Glacier, Breeze and Thermal all exchanged glances of surprise, but before any of them could ask, a loud explosion sounded from a few blocks over. Rush, understandably, was the first to react. His sudden disappearance was accepted as his burst of speed toward the only sound not made by the group. The flyers were the next, taking to the air and heading the direction of the explosion. Glacier followed, leaping over the buildings.

This left Remix and Nightlite staring blankly at their respective group members. "They do this to you a lot?" she asked.

Remix groaned. "Yep. You?"

"All the time." They looked at each other and sighed, chuckled, and grudgingly jogged after their friends.

* * *

Remix and Nightlite joined the group in a most unexpected location. Two blocks from where the two groups had met was… nothing. Not a no-buildings nothing. Not a field useable for a park. There was a void. No visible ground, no visible far side to the void.

Just a large white space of nothingness. It wasn't an overly bright nothingness. Almost a pale brightness, like staring into a soft-white light bulb.

It was very disconcerting to the group. Most of the group stood, or floated, at the edge of the nothingness. Remix looked to the others. All of them appeared dumbstruck. Except all of them weren't there. Someone was missing, someone big. He looked up at Breeze, who was still floating with an almost natural ease. "Where's Glacier?"

Breeze, shaken from his idiot-stare, looked at Remix and swallowed into a grimace. "Um. He overshot. He's in there somewhere," he replied, indicating the void. "We pulled up once we saw it but—"

"There was no way we could have stopped something his size that quickly," Rush interrupted.

"And no one thought to go after him?" Remix was incensed. He turned from the group and ran into the void, followed by Nightlite. The pair disappeared three steps in.

Rush fidgeted, bouncing from foot to foot. "Damn!" He ran after them, followed by Thermal and Breeze.

Vim and Vigor remained outside the void long enough to be engulfed by a larger black void.

* * *

Running full speed after someone in a white void where you're not really sure if you can see two-feet in front of you is generally not a wise decision. Even less so if you can run several hundred miles-per-hour.

Rush found this out the hard way by running into what felt like a brick wall. His garishly orange suit protected him from most of the impact, but still knocked him backwards onto the previously invisible ground. Actually the ground was still mostly imperceptible except for several black cracks leading up to a pair of really large, white boots, which were next to a considerably smaller white pair, a red pair, gray pair, and a mismatched red/blue pair.

"Ha!" he proclaimed, picking himself up. "I knew I'd find you eventually."

"Eventually?" rumbled the giant. "You ran past me twice. I just landed and stayed put. I figured you guys'd find me eventually."

"We just followed the cracks," Thermal stated. "You did make quite an impact, y'know."

"Probably the only time doing crack is good for you," quipped Remix to a chorus of moans from most of the group. He did notice Nightlite stifle a laugh and smile at him. Glacier apparently noticed her reaction as well, giving Remix a trio of hand subtle hand signals. A swipe of the index finger, followed by poke and a small thumbs-up, their old sign for *don't screw it up*.

"And I'm glad you did follow the crack," came a familiar voice. "It saves me the trouble of trying to round all of you up in here." The group turned from Remix to find a very nice wooden desk with a rather ornate carving on the front of the HYDRA corporate symbol. Behind the desk sat Randall O'Neal.

The group exchanged startled glances with each other. The entire group looked to the man at the desk. "Randy?" they all asked simultaneously, followed by an equally stereophonic "You know him?"

Randy cocked an eyebrow, "You guys seem to be doing that a lot recently. I guess it's a good thing that the initiation is over."

The void changed from white to black. The last thing Remix heard was O'Neal's mumbled "Boise?"

PART II
PAST

24
REBOOT

He hated his job. He *really* hated his job. Seven years of college with two degrees in communications and the best he could get was a secretarial position, with a crap company, in another country.

It's not like he didn't try to get other jobs. By his count he'd sent out about 1,400 resumes. Only heard back from 12. Only one brought him in for an interview. The church he grew up in; the church where he spent seven miserable years as an altar boy.

Eric Duffy figured if anyone were going to finally hire him, it'd be them. After all, he'd found out that he was the only one of the final four applicants who was already part of the religion. He was overqualified but didn't mind working in the area where he grew up. His parents would be close by and could watch the kids occasionally so he could go out with his wife. It could work out.

Unfortunately, they didn't hire him.

Ultimately his wife, Anna, a woman he pined after and flirted with voraciously in college and loved more than life, got a wonderful job offer in another country. They paid for the house. There were English-speaking schools for the girls, Monte and Allison. And he eventually got a position as a secretary.

He did get paid, just not that much. His work was more appreciated by the people in the office next door (same building), whose computers he fixed rather regularly. His boss didn't seem to be very interested in having him in the office, much less doing anything useful.

There were meetings with other agencies in the area. He wasn't allowed to sit in on them. The part of that that annoyed him the most was when he heard that someone had commented on the company website he had created.

That's all he knew. Someone commented. Was it good? Bad? Were there suggestions? No one ever let him know.

He hated his job.

On this particular day, his boss was out of the office. He did like it when she wasn't there. It wasn't that the boss was a she, he'd worked with women before and didn't have a problem with that. It wasn't that she mistreated him either, really. It was mainly that she didn't treat him at all. He was invisible to her.

He wasn't particularly interested in accolades, but being acknowledged as being there would be nice. There were even times he heard her say to someone on the phone that there was no one to watch the office. That was probably the most annoying part of his job.

He would be just fine if she left permanently. He'd been running the office for the past year and a half anyway. She had the title of manager, but he had no idea what she did apart from sit at a desk and bitch about people who came in.

He *really* hated his job. Thankfully, something else came along. Just not at all what he expected.

He was sitting at his desk / cubicle. It was a L-shaped desk with a wall on one side that held two cabinets full of paperwork that wasn't really necessary since all the information was in the computer. The monitor fit on his desk, but the CPU and printer were underneath. Most of the desktop was covered in more useless paperwork and scribbled notes.

He kept the office door open so he could hear signs of life next door. People came to the office next door. Very few came to his office. On this day, he heard something that he would not have expected. A familiar voice.

The office next door processed paperwork for people coming into the country. He knew that eventually someone would come in that he knew. He didn't know very many people here and did not speak the local language. Not that he really wanted to learn it. Typical American stubbornness.

But that voice next door was like a waft of fresh air. Someone he once knew and cared deeply for. Geraldine Davis. Gigi. They had dated in high school years before. To say they had not separated on the best of terms was putting it lightly. Catching your best friend in bed with your girlfriend… not the way to break up.

He supposed that it would have surprised most of his old classmates to know that they had reconciled their differences and become quite good friends. But even that friendship was years ago. He had not seen her since he got married ten... no, eleven years ago.

But her voice was here. It was a sound he'd never forget. He stared into his computer monitor contemplating what he should do. Should he go over and say 'hi'? Why not? He'd heard she was married now with kids of her own. Would she want to resume their friendship? Would she even recognize him?

He had changed a bit since high school. His hair was still longish and thick. Always had been really. He'd put on a few pounds. Who doesn't? He'd even bulked up a little. Which isn't really saying much as he always considered himself scrawny. That and he finally figured out that he could, indeed, grow facial hair, now in a moustache-goatee combo.

Her voice was growing closer. Apparently he didn't have to get up after all. She was going to walk right by his office.

He knew then how he'd handle the meeting. Just casually say "Hi Gigi" as she walked by. In his head it would take about two steps before she realized that someone had said "hi" to her and another three before she realized that person had called her by name.

He loved doing that to people and didn't get to often enough. Some people said that made him something of an asshole. He didn't really care about the opinions of those some people, though. She'd stop and realize who he was and there would be a relatively happy reunion of sorts. He'd help them get moved in and show them around and stuff. He liked being helpful. And it would be nice to have friends to reminisce with?

Of course, all of this only happened in his head.

What he saw and heard would change his life. First he heard the voices. They were raised. She wasn't happy about something. The first thing he saw was a stroller wheel, followed, of course, by the stroller. In the stroller were two small children, maybe one year old. *Twins? She had Twins?* He couldn't determine gender from his position, roughly 90 degrees to their left.

Their words were now a bit more audible. Her husband, presumably, was complaining about her spending money and how they needed to start a savings plan. The last thing he heard was her sarcastic reply:

"So, darling, how do we initiate *that*?"

* * *

She didn't want to be in this country. She hadn't been out of the US in years. She took classes on the language back in high school. Her boyfriend at the time had ribbed her about it. "Are you planning on going there?" he'd ask.

"No," she'd reply. "I just like to learn new languages." Of course she found it somewhat ironic that she'd met Eric in a foreign language class. It was a requirement, but she knew he hated learning new languages. God, she hadn't thought of him in years! What would he think of her now? She was married and had twins. She'd heard he was married as well with two kids. Both girls. That would serve him right. *They'd torture him for years*, she thought smugly. She shook her head slightly to clear it of these absurd thoughts.

The lady at the front desk was nice enough. She got a "welcome packet" full of things to do in the area and other organizations that should be visited to make sure their paperwork was in order. And there was plenty of paperwork, especially for the kids.

Pregnancy wasn't something she figured she was cut out for. She was rather short and skinny. How she carried twins was still a mystery to her. But she did love her little ones, Persia and Tiger. One of each. And they were the light of her life.

Michael, her husband, had gotten upset about her spending money on new car seats. Mike was a very practical man, but he did not realize the things that would have to change since they had kids. Having two at once may seem practical, but it really wasn't.

"Here you go Ms. Wood," the lady behind the desk said, handing her a small stack of paper clipped documents. She was being nice and helpful. Gigi was a bit worried when she had seen the woman's large, blonde hair and equally large breasts. Several "blonde" jokes ran through her head but were quickly quashed by the woman's apparent competence in her job. "You'll need to go to the customs office to get *that* paperwork straightened out. Then," she smiled, "you're done."

"Thank you, Nikki," Gigi replied.

"It may be shorter if you cut down this hallway," Nikki said indicating the hallway to her right. "It goes straight out of the building and the customs office will be right in front of you."

Gigi and Mike looked down the hall briefly before again thanking the helpful woman and starting on their way. They got about two steps before he started up again. "We need to keep the money in a fund. We've got two kids to put through college and they'll be going at the same time. Do you know how much that will cost?"

It was nice to know that he was thinking about the children, but the conversation was getting rather tedious. "So, darling, how do we initiate *that?*" At the end of her annoyed question there was a thump from a doorway to their left. Through the doorway was a man slumped over a desk, and from the entranceway they could tell there was a small, but growing pool of blood under his face.

The event shocked Gigi for two reasons. One: she wasn't good with blood and, two:

Is that Eric?

25
INTANGIBLE

The light was terribly bright and shining directly into his face. He hated mornings anyway. Never one for bright lights. He really didn't like this morning since he awoke and wasn't sure where he was. There were only two places he slept regularly: his house and, when no one was paying attention, the office. This was neither place.

There was a sound on his left. A faint beeping? He turned his head and saw a vision-blurred medical device. *I'm in a hospital?* he wondered. He tried to sit up, and succeeded quite easily.

He furrowed his brow. If he was in a hospital, shouldn't he be connected to the beeping machine? He raised his arm and found no connections. But he was wearing a long-sleeved black shirt. He considered this to be another oddity since he really did not like long-sleeved shirts.

He looked about the room. It was rather sparse. His bed, the beeping thing, a chair and a full-wall mirror opposite the bed. There was a door to his left. He contemplated seeing what was outside but decided to do a physical inventory first.

He flung his legs over the side of the bed and tried to stand. He didn't remember having any kind of accident, but if he was in a hospital… Maybe his legs were broken. No. He stood fine. His legs were covered in pants made from a black material that he couldn't readily recognize. They weren't tight. Actually, they felt remarkably comfortable.

His feet were also covered in (possibly) the same material as his pants. They looked like tabi boots; the kind ninjas wore in the movies. He'd looked the name up on the Internet once in a fit of boredom. *Let's hear it for Google!* he thought wryly. *I know what my shoes are called.* He couldn't recall ever owning a pair of them before but he'd liked the idea. *Ok, someone bought me some new shoes.*

He glanced at himself in the mirror. He looked thinner. His hair was longer and pulled back into a ponytail. Actually, he thought he looked rather good. That, in and of itself, was odd since he was fully aware of his almost complete lack of self-esteem. But there was something else odd in the mirror.

Someone was still in the bed. And it was him.

* * *

An indeterminate length of time later, Eric woke up on the floor. He slowly raised his head and looked up to the bed. The occupant certainly looked like him. Only the person he was looking at was different somehow. He stood and looked closer at the body.

This one was hooked up to the beeping machine. His torso was bare save for the two chest hairs his wife had always teased him about. But it really was him. Actually he felt it was more him than he was. This was the him he was used to seeing in the mirror every morning. Not the him with the tabi boots. He sat in the chair. This whole train of thought was making him dizzy.

The door opened and a man came in. Eric estimated the newcomer to be in his fifties with a close-cropped buzz cut. He was wearing gray military fatigues with the rank insignia of a major. His sewn-in nametag read "Edwards". The man took a clipboard to the bed, read a few things off the beeping machine and wrote them down. "Well, it's about time," he muttered. Then he left.

"That's ok," Eric muttered. "I'm not really here anyway." He ran his hand through his hair and sighed. Maybe he wasn't really here he thought. Maybe this was an out of body experience. But why would he bother being dressed?

He stared into the mirror, looking at himself and, well, himself reclined. A few moments later the door opened again. Edwards entered followed by two men in orange jumpsuits rolling what looked like a large, black, aerodynamic casket.

"Make sure all of the connections are secure," Edwards was saying to the two men. "We're going to need to access his GNA to make sure that the others are controllable."

GNA? What's G-N-A? Eric thought. He usually prided himself on being up-to-date on scientific things; it kept him busy at work. But GNA was a new term. And seeing as how the three men didn't notice he was there, he was pretty sure asking wouldn't help.

Or would it?

"Um, excuse me," he began, his voice sounding hollow in his ears. "What's GNA?"

As he had expected, no one answered him. No one even looked in his direction.

He rose from the chair, his annoyance becoming anger. He reached for the technician, who was closest to him. His hand passed through the other man's shoulder.

Eric's eyes widened as he slumped back into the chair. His surprise quickly gave way to curiosity. He couldn't touch the other man but he was tangible enough to sit in the chair and not fall through the floor. *Maybe...* he thought as he rose again and went to the mirrored wall.

He put his right hand up to the mirror. He felt the mirror, but he felt nothing when he had tried to touch the technician, who was still working on taking Eric's prone body and putting it in the... container. He couldn't bring himself to think of it as a casket. How could he be dead and still be watching this?

He resigned himself to worry about the tangibility issue later. For now, he was concerned about what was being done to his body. The two orange men had moved his body into the container and were connecting his arms and head to electrical leads.

The leads were connected to a monitor and keyboard built into the head of the container. The monitor sprang to life as the first lead was connected. It displayed technical jargon that Eric did not understand. When the last lead was connected, the far-side technician tapped a code into the keyboard and a black plastic-like sheath began to cover Eric's body.

Once in place, the sheath made Eric's body look like a mold for a manikin. There was a hissing noise followed by a 'fwump'. Eric had heard similar noises before, but they were usually associated with airlocks on sci-fi shows. *My body's sealed in a vacuum?*

"The connection is complete, sir!" the keyboard technician stated. "It appears that his GNA is completely accessible by the system. The computer says his GNA will be able to subdue the others."

"Good," Edwards replied coldly. There was something about this guy that Eric didn't like. It wasn't just that the man had put his body in a vacuum tube and hooked him up to some machine to help 'subdue' others, whatever the hell that meant. It was a lack of ... emotion. Like he was some sort of cold automaton. And maybe he wasn't human. Eric guessed there was enough sci-fi type things going on in this room to make Rod Serling's head spin, so why not an android?

"Take him to chamber 42," Edwards ordered. The two orange-clad men snapped off the obligatory 'Yes Sir's, closed the lid to the casket (*May as well call it that since you can't breathe in a vacuum, right?*) and wheeled it through the door followed by Edwards... and Eric.

The hallway outside the room was an obnoxiously pastel yellow. The men with his body had turned right and were heading toward what looked like elevator doors at the end of the hall. They passed several doors on the way with strange labels, like: 'Staging Area' and 'Control'. All of the doors were closed and Eric did not want to take the time to explore now. He wanted to know where his body was going. 'Chamber 42' didn't mean much to him.

The doors at the end of the hall parted to reveal the expected elevator car. Edwards did not get in the elevator, but instead turned down the hallway to the left. Eric did enter the car. The casket took up most of the room with the two orange men on one side with the buttons.

Eric was standing in the doorway when the doors closed. He did not realize this until they had, according to the lights on the wall, moved down several floors. He took a step forward to move completely into the car. He reached around to make sure his whole body was there. He surmised that he should check just in case he literally left part of himself behind. As near as he could tell he was all there.

What Eric didn't notice was when he stepped forward; he bumped the casket, which juggled slightly. The two technicians gave each other quick, worried glances before chalking it up to a hiccup in the elevator.

When the doors opened, Eric, out of habit, quickly backed out of the elevator and got out of the way. When he turned he realized he was not in a hallway, but in a large... well, science lab are the words that readily came to mind. The room was easily the size of two football fields.

The wall to the right was lined with computers. Not just the standard CPU and monitor, but servers and larger systems covering the entire wall to the ceiling, which may be twenty-five feet up. The far wall was too far away to make any distinctions as to what may be over there. But the left wall was a honeycomb of cavities, most of which were filled with more of the black, aerodynamic caskets. There was enough room for several hundred of them. It was impossible to tell if the caskets were occupied.

The technicians moved Eric's casket to one of the vacant honeycombs and inserted it. The previously black wall surrounding the hole came to life with numerous readouts and blinking colored panels.

"Is the chamber completely active?" came a voice from over Eric's shoulder. He started a bit at the sound as he had not heard anyone come up behind him… much less Edwards. *How did he get down here? The elevator wasn't that quick?*

"Yes sir!" came the reply. "All readings are in the green." Eric thought that was a strange thing to say since the panels he could see were all showing reds or blues.

"Good," Edwards answered. "We need to prepare more of the chambers. They'll be filling up soon. This is progressing faster than we had anticipated. If Wood hadn't found this poor bastard we could have activated him on our own terms and taken it slow. But that's not going to happen, now. Get the other teams ready. We're expecting to have twenty more by the end of the week."

The techs snapped off salutes and gave the requisite 'Yes Sir!'s and went back to the elevator. Eric studied the readouts outside his honeycomb. The reflective surface of the panels showed Edwards remained standing behind him.

Eric put his hand on one of the panels. He found that with minor concentration he could move his hand through the panel. He tried the same concept with his foot and the floor and found he could pass through the objects with only minor concentration.

He turned to face Edwards. "What the hell have you done to me?" he asked, his anger quelled knowing he would not receive an answer. Edwards blinked and his eyes changed from a piercing blue to a glowing green.

"It's not what *we* did to you. It's what was done to you a long time ago."

26
NUMBER FOUR

"Discussing this further here may disturb the others in the chamber," Edwards continued. "Would you please follow me?" With that he turned and headed toward the elevator.

Eric looked puzzled. He turned to see if someone was standing behind him. Could Edwards really be talking to him? Was he just ignoring him until now? Hesitantly, Eric followed the strange man (machine?) to the elevator.

Partially to see if Edwards was talking to him, and partially to see if he could do it, Eric walked through the door into the waiting car. The doors parted shortly thereafter and permitted the permanently tangible Edwards to enter. When the doors closed, he pushed one of the floor buttons, turned to face Eric and spoke. "You should be careful when doing things like that, Mr. Duffy. If the car had not been here you may have fallen."

"You can see and hear me?" Eric was rather calm about the situation. After all, his body was in a vacuum-sealed coffin while he was also in the elevator with someone who may be a robot. How much weirder could the day get?

"Yes, Mr. Duffy. Hearing you has not been a problem. Seeing you on the other hand is requiring an adjustment to my optics."

"So," Eric started hesitantly, "you *are* an android?"

"Yes," he replied. "One of six designed specifically for this program. All of us look similar. Mostly the programming is the same but there are some quirks. I would like to apologize for the behavior of the model you met upstairs. I've been told he has a tendency to be rude."

"Uh huh. So when will Rod Serling will be making his appearance?"

"I can assure you, Mr. Duffy that this is not an episode of the *Twilight Zone*. Nor is it a *Candid Camera* or," Edwards tilted his head as if looking for a term, "*Punk'd?*"

"Never watched that one but I know the concept," Eric confirmed. "And it's Eric. Mr. Duffy is my dad."

"Very well, Eric." This Edwards model was, at least, more polite than the other one. The elevator 'dinged' and the doors opened. "Follow me, please. I will tell you that I should not talk to you in the hallway. Please refrain from asking more questions until we reach the briefing room."

Eric nodded but quickly realized the futility of that gesture as the only person who could see him had already started down the hall. Eric moved ahead of Edwards and started sticking his head through doors to see what was inside. Most of the rooms appeared to be living quarters of some sort. Some were finished and some were not, but they all appeared like one-bedroom apartments.

Eric did not realize that he had gotten so far ahead until he heard Edwards clear his throat before entering a room on the other side of the hall. Eric trotted over to the door that Edwards had already gone through and closed. *Did the android just clear his throat?* He chalked it up to pretty good programming and walked through the door, literally.

Eric found himself in room with a large wooden meeting table. At the head sat a slightly older, less well-built, more balding version of Edwards. To his right sat another Edwards, with the one he had followed sitting to that models right. *Thing one and thing two,* Eric thought, reminded of the song from the *Cat in the Hat* cartoon.

Opposite the Edwards and to the left of... *the older model?* was Geraldine Davis. "I'm sorry to have to inform you of this Mrs. Wood," the man at the head of the table was saying. *Wood? I guess she did get married.* "but Mr. Duffy has died."

"THE HELL I HAVE! I'M RIGHT HERE DAMN IT!!!" he cried. The Edwards he had followed was the only one to react. And that reaction was only to turn his head toward Eric and fix him with a quick glare that said, quite plainly, "shut up."

Geraldine sniffled, dried her eyes with a tissue and sighed. "Why? Why did he die when I was there? I mean, that was a coincidence, right?"

"Actually, Ms. Wood," began the other Edwards, "it was not coincidence. You killed him." The other Edwards and the man at the head of the table looked appalled at the pronouncement from the android. And Geraldine, poor, sweet Gigi, combined expressions of horror, sorrow and anger all at once. Tears streamed down her face.

"What?!" she cried. "I didn't even see him until after he collapsed on his desk!"

"Nevertheless, it was mostly your responsibility, whether or not you were aware of the situation," the Edwards model, which Eric decided should be called the Evil Android, stated. "Dr. Yost and I have decided that you will not be brought up on charges concerning his death, provided you agree to work with this project."

Gigi looked to the man at the head of the table, presumably Yost. "How could I be responsible for this? I hadn't seen him in years. I didn't even know he was there!" Eric sympathized with her plight. How *could* she be responsible?

"Mrs. Wood," Yost began in an attempt at a soothing voice, "Gigi. There are parts of this story you don't know yet. Please let me try to explain."

The 'evil android' suddenly rose from the table and began to leave. He muttered something about coddling and how the project should move forward faster. He paused in front of Eric, who was still standing near the doorway. Eric noticed that his eyes were the same glowing green as the other android. As another experiment on his new 'condition' he took a swing at the android. His fist passed harmlessly through the androids head. The android's only reaction was to snort derisively and leave, walking through Eric's body to reach the door. Eric seemed stunned by another being, even if it was just an android, passing through him.

"Mrs. Wood," Yost began again," first I would like to apologize for the conduct of my... ahem, colleague."

"He doesn't have a particularly good attitude, does he?" she quipped. "Good twin, bad twin?" she asked the remaining Edwards, who simply shrugged in reply.

"Unfortunately," Yost stated in an apologetic tone, "in a very strict sense, he was right. But in the most common sense, so are you." He held up his hands to stave off the obvious questions that were inevitable. "Let me explain.

"Several years ago," he continued, "there was a project called GNA. Genetic Nanotechnological Advancement. The purpose of the project was to see if there was a way to advance the evolution of the human race. There was a team of doctors who developed a nano-technology device that could be inserted into the nucleus of human cells and create, essentially, a third strand of DNA."

He pressed a button on the tabletop and a holographic projector sprung to life in the middle of the table, startling both Gigi and Eric. "Sorry," Yost said sheepishly. "Should have warned you about that." The hologram showed a standard DNA strand, save for a third string dissecting the helix.

"It was hypothesized that the third strand could activate some latent abilities already present in the human genetic structure. The initial experiments were, well, not terribly successful."

"Meaning?" Gigi and Eric both asked. Eric immediately looked abashed as he realized that not only could he probably not be heard, but also that Gigi was a smart woman and could probably do better at getting answers that he'd be able to if he were there.

"Do you remember that rash of Bigfoot sightings back in the 70s and 80s?" Gigi nodded. "That's how wrong they went. Fortunately we got everything back on track and, well, you and several people you know got caught up in it." Gigi looked puzzled. Eric suspected that he did as well, despite not being able to be seen. Habit he supposed.

"When you were a child, you, like just about everyone at that age, got sick, at some point, and were taken to a doctor. Now, when this specifically happened, I don't know, but, you were given an injection that infused you with a GNA sequence. One of the more important ones, really."

Gigi looked horrified. "What the hell have you done to me? What is this going to do to my kids?"

Yost held up his hands, partly to calm her and partly in case she found something to throw at him. "We don't know yet. We're examining your children now actually. Everything so far appears to be fine. As for you, you are the linchpin to the whole batch of GNAs. We've determined that if you are within hearing distance of any inactive GNAs, and say a specific word, they will activate. Now, we're not entirely sure which word it is, but it's probably some synonym of activate."

The remaining Edwards finally spoke. "Do you remember what you were talking about when you found Eric?"

Geraldine furrowed her brow in concentration. "Mike and I were talking about money." Pause. "He said something about starting a college fund for the kids." Another pause. "Would *initiate* count? I said it sarcastically, but..."

Edwards nodded. "That was probably it. When Eric heard it, which he could have done with you in close proximity to him, he activated. We weren't expecting to have anyone ever activate from your... batch. But this would be number four."

"Four?" Gigi and Eric asked.

"Yes," Yost replied somberly. "The first was, well, you. It was in your... programming to be the one to activate everyone else.

"The second was Joahn Carey. She was activated in a manner we weren't expecting. There is a failsafe that activates an ability if the person's life is in danger. In the case of her accident, her power manifested at the point of impact." Yost sighed. "Unfortunately none of us were expecting what happened." He grimaced.

Gigi excitedly looked back and forth between Edwards and Yost. "Jo's alive?" she asked, echoing Eric's question.

"Well, no." Yost inhaled deeply and uneasily. "Her ability was teleportation. As near as we can tell she teleported at the moment of impact during an automobile accident. But her momentum kept her moving when she reappeared. She... well, she appeared on the roof of a nearby building and the momentum... threw her off and she landed on her own car."

Edwards took up the story. "Witnesses say that they noticed no one in the car but thought it was very unusual for a suicide to occur at the same moment."

Gigi stared at Edwards and blinked repeatedly. She's accepted Joahn's death some time ago. She didn't like it, but she'd accepted it. Now, to find out that Joahn was saved only to die again seconds later was... one of the strangest feelings she'd ever had. Judging from how he read her expression, Eric shared the feeling.

"Ohhh kay," Gigi finally mumbled before looking at Yost. "Who was the other one?"

"Sergeant Melanie Greene, US Marine Corps," Yost answered. "She was in a skirmish in the Middle East when her ability to target and manipulate any projectile to hit the target kicked in."

Useful for a Marine, Eric thought. He'd known she was interested in the military, almost as interested as she was in Stanley. Of course, the big goof never noticed. Maybe if he had, he and Gigi... best not to go down that road.

So if they're going to blackmail Gigi into working for this project, how is she going to explain it to her husband? For that matter, how would he explain this to his wife? He had no idea how long he'd been here. What had she been told? Was she fed the same BS story Gig was?

"Yes, Ms. Greene is part of our project." Yost's comment broke him from his trance-like and depressive musings. "She's set up to work primarily as a solo operative. I'll be re-introducing the two of you later."

"So," Gigi sighed, "what else can I do besides kick-starting the power thing?"

"You can also turn them off," Edwards responded. "Once you've started all the GNAs, we will place them in a testing unit to determine if they are stable. If they are, we'll recruit them to be part of the program permanently. If not, we have a method of removing their memories of the testing, have you turn them off and return them to their lives."

"That's it?"

"That's it."

"So basically," she started with a bit more ire in her voice, "you're blackmailing me into working for you so you can create a superhuman army out of my old friends and holding my family hostage until I finish? Did I sum this up properly?"

Yost looked nervously at Edwards, who replied, "I don't know that I would have phrased it that way, but you are essentially correct. We prefer to think of it as being proactive given the situation."

"Oh, really?" she quipped.

"Please think of this situation. Say you're at your school reunion. All of the GNAs are there and you mention, for whatever reason, the word 'initiate'. Do you really want to trigger everyone at once where they all have the possibility of being killed by their activation? Or would it be better to make sure they all can be cared for on an individual basis?"

Gigi's brow furrowed and she glared at Edwards. Eric knew this was her angry face. It wasn't terribly intimidating on someone of her stature unless you knew how hot her temper could get. She finally sighed, realizing that she wasn't winning a staring contest with a person she had no way of knowing was really an android. Her head drooped and she sighed again. "Ok," she whispered. "I'll do it."

27
HERE KITTY KITTY

Katerina Parker's apartment was a mess. It usually was. It had the potential of being a lovely loft apartment in downtown Paris. If it had been Paris, France, she might have kept things up better. But, she figured, Paris, Tennessee? Why bother?

She often wondered how she ended up here. Of course, she knew the answer: Troy. The idiot boyfriend from college who grew up in the area and wanted her to move in with him. Not really being that interested in living with him, but needing a roommate to help with the bills, so she said yes.

What a mistake that turned out to be! Two weeks together she caught him in bed with another woman and two guys! She wasn't really hurt, seeing as she didn't really care for him that much anyway, but there was still a feeling of being let down. If she had been cuter she might have understood. As it was, it just shot her self-esteem all to hell.

Here she was, a pretty, svelte-but-well-endowed woman, and she was being tossed aside for someone who looked like an inbred whore with too much make-up. Well, this was Tennessee. Maybe she was inbred. But it was time for Tammy Faye and her posse to get up out of here!

So, since the apartment was in her name, she got to kick him out. Now she had the place to herself. She'd gotten a decent job at a local law office, so the pay was good and she could live comfortably. Unfortunately, she wasn't paid enough to afford to more somewhere she could get a life.

Were there places in town to meet guys? Sure, if you liked the country music bar scene. Occasionally she'd venture to Nashville, which, oddly enough, had a pretty decent rock scene. But most of the guys there were not her type. On-line dating? Not in this lifetime.

So she was stuck in a not-as-bad-as-it-could-be-but-not-as-good-as-she'd-like situation.

At least she still had her painting. Her hobby / passion took up most of the room in the apartment. Canvasses, paints, brushes and easels littered her the whole place. Several half-finished pieces hung on the walls, more leaned against them. This was her newest problem: finding inspiration in a town that has none.

In this midst of a furious stroking of the canvas with the most hideous shade of purplish black she could make, the door buzzer echoed through the room, breaking her angst-ridden concentration on her latest masterpiece: Unfinished Bastard.

She threw the brush across the room and kicked the easel, knocking the still wet painting onto her face smearing it in what surely must look like garish bruises. She stopped and took several calming, deep breaths. She walked to the small speaker by the door and pressed the button. "THIS BETTER BE FUCKING GOOD!" *Calming breaths my ass*, she thought bitterly. *I should probably work on that.*

"Kat?" replied the speaker in a soft and familiar voice. *Kat* wasn't a name she'd used since high school. She'd insisted everyone call her that. She couldn't really remember why anymore. She pushed the door button allowing the front door to the stair open. What's the worst that could happen? Someone would come up and kill her. *Crime is terribly rampant here in hickville.* Her bitterness usually manifested itself in sarcasm.

Shortly there came a knock at the door. Katerina opened it, forgetting her face was still covered in painted bruises. A small woman wearing a blue hooded cape stood at the door. *Little Blue Riding Hood?* "My god, Kat!" exclaimed the small woman. "What the hell happened?"

"Gigi?" Kat queried. What was Gigi doing here and what was she… the paint. It was still on her face and must look horrible. After a momentary pause, she grabbed her smaller friend in a warm embrace.

"Gigi! It is soo good to see you." Katerina literally pulled her friend inside and kicked the door shut. "Sorry about the paint and, well, the mess. I don't get much company."

Gigi looked a bit startled by the response. She always somehow imagined Kat to become a dominatrix or something. But finding her here, in Tennessee, wearing paint covered jeans and a tee shirt wasn't what she expected. "I'm really hoping that's paint on your face too."

"Hmm," Kat absently wiped her face with a cloth. "I guess so. Ooh. That probably looked like I got my face kicked in or something, didn't it?"

"Yes, actually," Gigi chuckled. "I can't think of any man who'd be able to do that to you... and live."

The two shared a laugh. Katerina unearthed her couch from the many canvasses and the two sat and caught up on their lives. Kat thought it was really good to have someone from the "old school" to talk to. It did make her feel better.

"Kat," Gigi started hesitantly, "I may have a job offer for you."

Kat's eyes widened. Could it really be? Not only to find an old friend, ok, have an old friend find you, but to have her offer her a job? This could be wonderful. And without thinking about it at all she blurted, "Hire me! Get me the hell out of here!"

"You don't even want to know what it is?"

"Do I look like I care? I hate it here and can't get out. Yes. Take me. I don't care if I'm selling my body in Vegas... not that I can see *you* hooking me up with something like that, but I don't care. Take me!" she cried, overdramatically flinging her arms outstretched.

Gigi smirked. "I don't know how this is going to work completely. This is the first time I've done it," she seemed to choke on the word, "purposefully."

Kat, arms still outstretched, looked inquisitively at her friend who looked her in the eye and said one word.

* * *

Hut! Hei! Clank! Clang! Flip! Stab! Hei! Flip! Flip! Swat! Flip! *God I love my work*!

Steven Callahan was one of the happier people on the planet. He loved his job, which was rare. He was still single, which, while not rare, was something he reveled in. Whenever he needed someone for physicality, he could usually count on one of the waitresses. Cut! Flip! Stab!

Being a teppan-yaki chef at a hibachi / Japanese Steak house had its advantages. He'd always loved to play with knives. And once he found he could make a living at it... there was nothing else in the world he'd rather do. Stab! Flip! Swat!

He made more money here in the last year than he had in his career as a knife juggler for state fairs. The thought of that old job almost made him shudder. Almost. He'd disciplined himself enough to know that one does not shudder when cooking. Flip! Pour! Avoid flame!

This group he was cooking for was here for a birthday party, or so he was told. Most of them looked like a typical, if not large, family. Mom, Dad, three boys, two girls. Slice! Flip! Flip!

It was the eighth person at the table that didn't fit in; a petite woman with a blue hooded cloak, the hood around her shoulders. He'd seen her before, but was not placing her. She was seated at his extreme right, almost behind him. If he could turn, he might get a better look and recognize her. Flip! Cut! Stab!

But he couldn't really take his eyes off the food. That would be dangerous. Flip! Stab! Flip onto birthday boy's plate. Shrimp dead center. "Careful, it's still hot!" he warned in his own amusingly flippant way.

Another ten minutes of choreographed cooking led to everyone at the table enjoying the show and the meal. *Damn I'm good*, he thought a bit smugly. As he turned to leave and he finally recognized the woman in blue. The face was a bit older, the hair was shorter, and the smile gave it away. "Gigi!" he exclaimed and rounded the table to give his old friend a hug.

Everyone wants to hug me, she mused. "Hi Steve," she replied. "You're looking good." And he was. He'd lost a lot of weight since school. It probably also helped that his hands weren't as cut up as she remembered. Actually she didn't remember ever seeing the cuts, but the pink bandages clashed with his yellowish-skin tone.

"So what are you doing here?" he smiled. "I haven't seen you since, what, high school?"

"Yeah," she replied as she popped a shrimp in her mouth. "This is delicious. I know who we're going to use as a cook."

"Oh really," he asked. "'We' who? Cook for 'what'? And it's 'chef', thank you very much," he added a tie straightening gesture at 'chef', which looked silly to Gigi as he wasn't wearing a tie.

"I have a job offer for you, Steve. I think it's something you may like even more than this."

Steve looked skeptical. "I don't know, Gigi." He swept his arm in a gesture to the restaurant. "I really love this place." He felt a menu swat him in the back of the head. He turned to see one of the waitresses behind him. "Sumi!" he scolded. "What'd'ja do that for?"

"You said I was the special one, Steven," she replied sounding hurt. "And here you are with her!" She stabbed an accusatory finger at Gigi. She 'fwapped' him with the menu again and stormed into the back room. He turned back to Gigi and noticed that not only was Gigi smirking at him from behind her hand, trying to contain a laugh, but also the birthday-partying family was looking at him uncomfortably.

"Uh, Gi," he began lamely. "I'm going to go to the back for a minute. Uh, finish your dinner." He leaned closer. "It's on me," he whispered before leaning back. "I'll, um, be back in a few minutes."

* * *

Gigi sat in a chair staring at a bed with two snuggling bodies in it. Both were covered and unconscious at the moment, but it still made her uneasy. She sat with one elbow on her knee, propping her head in her hand. She sighed.

The male figure, the one on her left, stirred slightly and got out of bed. He moved carefully enough not to disturb his companion. Steve wandered through a door near his side of the bed, still naked, presumably to a bathroom. When he returned, he noticed Gigi sitting in the chair near the bed. He jumped slightly and covered himself.

He half-stormed, half-scurried to his old friend in the chair. "Gigi," he whispered intensely, "what the hell are you doing here?"

She stifled a laugh. "I told you. I came to talk to you. You, my dear friend, left me," she said waving an accusatory finger at him. "Just so you know, I had intended on paying for my own meal."

He hung his head. "I'm sorry, Gee," he muttered feeling appropriately abashed. He turned his head back toward the bed. "Um, but this might not be the best time to talk about this. I mean… Sumi was pretty hot at both of us. I think I'm back on good terms with her," he shrugged, "but my tongue is still a bit numb."

She rubbed her temples in a vain attempt to thwart a headache. "That's more than I wanted to know. Thanks Steve." He shrugged, and then realized he was still naked and quickly covered himself again while looking around the room for something to put on.

He found his pants near the bedroom door. He scurried over to put them on when Sumi stirred and looked dazedly at him. "Come back to bed, baby. I think you missed a spot. Right here."

Gigi couldn't tell which part Sumi was specifically pointing to as she was holding up a blanked to show Steve, but she could guess. Steve looked at Sumi and glanced at the chair where Gigi… was.

He dropped his pants in surprise. They, of course, fell to the floor, as he hadn't gotten that far in putting them back on. Gigi was gone. Sumi, however, did not know that Gigi had been there and took the gesture as something completely different, and quickly reached out and grabbed him. "Ok baby," she said in a silky voice. "We'll give your tongue a break. You can use this now." She pulled him back into bed by what may look like a handle, but genetically isn't.

* * *

The following morning was mostly a blur. Sumi had finally left. Her appetite was insatiable, and it had nothing to do with his food. He put on a bathrobe staggered into the kitchen. Breakfast? The thought of food turned his stomach. He was still tired. Maybe he'd call in sick today. Another night of Sumi may actually kill him.

And what the hell was up with Gigi? Did he hallucinate the whole thing? No, Sumi and the birthday party had seen her at the restaurant. Ok, partially hallucinate? Was she really in his room last night? How could she have been? He wasn't in the phone book? But then she had mentioned something about a job offer. How did she know where he was?

"She is gone, isn't she?"

He jumped and spun at the unexpected voice, which was a mistake as he slipped on the tile floor and landed on his posterior, the robe falling open, revealing himself to her again. He attempted to cover himself and stand at the same time but mostly succeeded in flailing around on the floor. Eventually, he regained his composure, and his verticalness. "Don't do that!" he cried.

Gigi sat on cross-legged on his couch; her head drooped into one hand, shaking in back and forth. "Well, that was embarrassing, wasn't it?" she quipped. "Are you ready, yet? Or do you have another woman coming over?"

Steve felt abashed and offended. "What are you, my magical pimp? How did you get in here anyway?"

She smirked at him. "It was magic," she deadpanned.

He sighed and walked to the chair next to the couch and flopped into it. Part of him flopped out of his robe, but he didn't seem to care anymore. Gigi blushed, which made him feel a bit better. *Ha! So there!* he thought. "So, tell me about this job. Apparently it's really important to you. You'd think you were trying to initiate me into some fraternity or something."

She smiled at the irony that he didn't understand… until she spoke again.

28
FAMILY

Eric sat in an Edwards' office. He wasn't sure which Edwards actually owned the office. He just hoped it wasn't 'Evil Eddies', as he'd come to call the personality deficient android. He had only met the two Edwards. They apparently had different first names. The one he knew was Micah. The one he didn't like was Kent. This was unfortunate since he actually knew a few 'Kent's and liked them.

Despite the naming, he could not tell them apart physically. So when one opened the door and entered, he tensed. The Edwards that entered lowered his head to look at Eric and almost rolled his glowing eyes. Micah.

Micah had explained that his body and his mind and / or soul had become detached from each other. The way he perceived himself now, was his 'astral self'. His body was being well taken care of in the hibernation capsule.

He felt terribly lonely, though. It's not as though there weren't people to talk to. He talked to almost everyone in the complex incessantly. Unfortunately no one could see or hear him, except the Edwards.

He wanted to talk to Kat and Mel. They were old friends who he hadn't seen in years. Kat did look different with claws, even if they could be 'retracted' to look like really long fingernails. Mel looked different with short-cropped hair, but she was still a very beautiful woman. Stan was an idiot for not seeing that.

He really would have liked to communicate with Gigi. Just to let her know that he wasn't really dead. His body may register as brain dead, but that was because his brain was out wandering around all on its own.

Most of all he wanted to talk to Anna. To hold her again. And Monte and Allison. He couldn't very well show up and say "Hi, its me!" Actually, he could, but they wouldn't be able to see or hear him. He missed his family.

He really empathized with Gigi. She had newborn twins! How could she not be suffering like he was? He remembered how excited he was when Monte was born. She was the most beautiful thing he'd ever seen. She had such big eyes. He used to tease her that she'd have to grow into them. Not that a newborn would understand his teasing...

He had been given assurances that his family was ok. He didn't know what they'd been told about him. He'd been told they were given a substantial "surprise inheritance from a long-lost uncle", so they were financially set. Not that he felt his job gave them *that* much money.

He had to see them again. To know that everything was ok. To know that everything *would be* ok. And he knew that there wasn't anything the Edwards could do to stop him from leaving. So, he left.

* * *

This was not going to be as easy as he'd hoped. Once outside, he had no idea where he was. The exterior of the complex was huge and looked vaguely like a college campus. He knew the complex to be even larger since it was mostly underground.

The problem he now faced was... where the hell did they put the campus? There was nothing visible for miles in any direction. He'd hoped, unreasonably he assumed, that since he was intangible he could fly. After several attempts at it, he realized he couldn't.

Since there was virtually no traffic on or off the complex grounds, he decided to go to the cafeteria area. Not that he was hungry, he'd realized a while ago that that was probably a good thing since he couldn't pick up any food anyway, but to see if any supply trucks were there, coming, or, preferably, leaving.

Finally he had some luck. He'd waited in the loading area for about an hour before a delivery truck arrived. He waited another half-an-hour before it was unloaded before climbing into the back of the truck. How hard could it be to stow-away on a truck when you were invisible and intangible?

After riding in the truck for what seemed like hours, the truck finally stopped. Eric pushed his head through a wall to see if they'd reached civilization. There were a few buildings around, but nothing that stood out as an actual city. But outside the truck he heard something that would probably make his job much easier... the sounds of a small airport.

Leaving the truck, he entered what he thought were the airport's grounds.

As it turned out, it was a military airbase. *Just as good*, he thought. *They still have planes.* He boarded a cargo jet. Eventually, he'd find civilization, and a way home.

* * *

Two weeks. It had taken two weeks for him to get home. He'd learned several things in that time. The most useful had been how to transfer from one moving vehicle to another. This was handy since there wasn't an airport near his house. Hitching rides in cars going in the right direction was easy. If they turned from the way he wanted to go, simply slip out of the car and into the one behind it.

Two weeks since he'd been in the complex in, well, whatever town that had been. He still didn't technically know the name, but he could find his way back. He'd always considered himself to have a good sense of direction. Having been someone once, he could usually find his way back, which in this case was a wonderful thing. He couldn't really stop for directions, could he?

But he was here. Finally standing in front of the house he lived in. Home. His wife and kids... he paused. His wife and kids probably thought he was dead. And there was nothing he could do to prove them wrong.

But he wasn't here to do that. He was here to make sure they were ok.

As near as he could tell, it was Saturday. Judging from the sun, about three in the afternoon. The van wasn't parked at the side of the house. They should be home, but, of course, they could be shopping.

He walked up to the side of the house and pushed his face through the wall of what should be the living room. And it still was, technically, but it was someone else's living room. Where there were pictures of Monte and Allison, there were pictures of, well, someone else. All the furniture was different. He removed his head from the side of the house. He wasn't sure if he was capable of crying in his current state, but he definitely felt like it.

"I could have told you they weren't there."

Eric was understandably startled by the voice and fell over. He looked up to see a man in a military-type suit looking back at him. "Don't f*king do that!" One thing he'd learned with kids is how to censor himself, kind of.

"I apologize," whispered the man. A woman passing on the street at that moment gave the man a strange 'who are you talking to?' look. Eric snickered. "If you had wanted to see your family in person, all you had to do was ask."

"Who the hell are you?" Eric asked in a very bewildered tone. He had seen the man before at the complex but the man had never given any indication that he could see Eric. The name badge over the left breast of his jacket said O'Neal, something Eric had never bothered to notice before.

"Sorry, I'm Major Randall O'Neal," he whispered out of the corner of his mouth. "I'm the head cyberneticist for the Campus. Call me Randy." Eric noticed the man's eyes glowed a slight purple. "Let me guess, you're wondering how I can see and hear you?"

"Well… yeah."

"I developed some new contacts and adjusted a couple of my cybernetic implants to hear you."

"You're a cyborg?"

O'Neal smirked, "Yes, but I've tried to keep that mostly invisible. I figure I can tell you since, well, the only other people you can tell right now are the Edwards, and they already know.

"Speaking of the Edwards, Micah was upset that you left and asked me to find you. I figured you would have come here," he said. "Hey, we lost track of you two weeks ago. Kent has even given you up for lost. As long as he has your body, I honestly don't think he cares about this part of you." Eric rolled his eyes in agreement. "However, Micah was programmed to respect life in all its forms. I'm not sure Kent was. Would you like me to take you to your family?"

Eric's eyes widened. "Y- Ye- Yes!" he stammered. "Hell yes!"

Eric blinked and suddenly felt disoriented as he found himself on a sidewalk outside a house he'd never seen before. He looked to Randy, who looked completely unfazed by his new surroundings. "Matter teleporter," he stated as an explanation. "How do you think we got to you so quickly? The campus" *not complex*, Eric noted, "isn't even in the same country."

"So you knew I'd been activated since you're, what? Keeping tabs on us?" Eric querried.

"Of course," Randy replied seemingly confused by the question. "Can you imagine how disastrous it could be if one of you activated without us there to make sure nothing went wrong with the process?"

"Good point," Eric conceded. "Wait, how did the transporter…"

"Get a lock on you?" O'Neal finished with a smirk. "The computer that runs it can see you. We've been able to keep track of you with the systems at the campus. But when you left, I changed one of our satellite monitors to keep an eye on your old house and popped over when you got there. Sorry we couldn't get to you sooner."

"Um, that's... ok. So where are we?" he asked taking in his new surroundings. It appeared they were in a suburb type environment next to a two-story brick house. It was now clearly night time, as opposed to the daylight that had been there only moments ago. A familiar car was parked in the driveway. The yard was not overly large, but well kept with green grass, a pair of dogwood trees and a small flowerbed. *She must have hired a gardener*, he mused. *She'd never been good with plants.*

"I'm going to take a walk around the block," O'Neal suddenly announced in a whispered tone. "It would look odd to the neighbors if I stand here talking to myself. Take as much time as you want. I'll keep an eye out for you." Eric nodded an assent as O'Neal began his trek down the sidewalk.

Eric cautiously walked toward the house. He felt terribly self-conscious. He knew, logically, that no one could see him. No one would ever know he was there unless somehow they knew O'Neal and connected it. He thought that was highly improbable.

He walked, literally, through the front door and into an entrance hall. The pictures from his old living room were now in a hallway, including the wedding picture. He sighed. He knew that at this rate he'd never get to hold his wife again.

A door off the hallway opened into a living room. He noticed most of the furniture was the same. A new-looking plasma TV hung on the wall opposite the couch. He assumed that the financial situation had to be better since they hadn't been able to afford one before.

He returned to the hall and found a staircase leading upstairs. As he ascended, he found new pictures hanging on the wall. They looked like new school pictures of the kids. Monte had gotten a haircut. She looked so much more mature. Allison looked grown up, too. Her curly golden hair still draped over her shoulders, though.

As he reached the top, he heard a familiar sound that he'd felt like he'd never hear again. He followed the noise to a rather large bedroom. In the middle of the new bed in the middle of the room was Anna.

He really loved his wife, but she had the ability to recreate the most unusual sounds in her sleep. He'd heard everything from freight trains to digital microwave ovens. Tonight she was in 'cell phone mode'. He knew that she always seemed to sleep best when she made dialing noises. He smiled and moved to the side of the bed. He leaned over and (tried to) kiss his wife's forehead. "I'll try to come home soon," he whispered.

He went to Monte's room next. His oldest daughter looked so grown up.

He'd always been proud of her but always felt like he had never actually done a good job of expressing it. She, too, was sleeping soundly; her arm tucked around her stuffed white tiger. Pictures of dolphins lined the walls.

A picture on her dresser disturbed him slightly. It was of Monte and a boy at what looked like a school dance. He hadn't been ready for her to start dating. Still wasn't, really.

He leaned over her and kissed her on the forehead, too. "If he hurts you," he whispered, "I'll find a way to hurt him." He smiled down at her, still feeling that fatherly protection thing.

Allison's room was decorated much in the same way it had been before. *Winnie-the-Pooh* and *Dora the Explorer* had always been her favorites. Allison was sleeping in her own room now. They hadn't been able to get her to do that before. More proof she was growing up. Thankfully there was no sign of a boyfriend for the little girl. She'd always liked boys, but six-years-old was way too young.

He leaned over to kiss her when she opened her eyes and stared back at him. She raised a tiny hand and stroked his cheek, and he actually felt it. "I miss you daddy," she mumbled before closing her eyes and going back to sleep.

When he found the old house with new occupants, he'd felt like crying. Now he did.

* * *

Eric found O'Neal almost two blocks from the house. He called out to him, and O'Neal replied, oddly. He dropped his head, snapped the fingers of his right hand before turning and walking back to Eric.

When the two were within whispering range, Eric asked, "Forget something?"

"Good," came the major's whispered reply. "I was hoping that's what it looked like. I have to keep up appearances. Anyone watching may think it's odd for a stranger to be walking down the street as it is, but to randomly turn and walk the other direction? They may call the police."

Eric stared at him in wonderment. That did make sense, he supposed. "Are you feeling alright, Eric?" O'Neal asked. "Your eyes appear swollen."

Eric sniffed and reflexively wiped at his eyes. "Yeah, I'm just swell," he deadpanned. "Randy, I need my body back."

29
LITTLE PROBLEM SOLVERS

Doctor Christopher Rock stood before in front of 300 students in the main lecture hall. This was the part of his job that he hated most. He didn't mind teaching in a one-on-one situation, or even in a classroom, but lecturing on this scale he'd always seen as pointless.

Nano-technology was new enough that there needed to be more that a handful of people in the field who knew what they were doing before going to do mass lecturing like this. If someone here had a question, where would they go afterward? He didn't teach here. No one at this school knew the field well enough to answer anything. And the students! It's not that they weren't among the brightest people he'd ever met, but if he fielded one more question about the *I-pod* variant…!

He had just finished explaining how the base adjustment of the amide in a fullerene changes the Van der Waals force during the positional synthesis of diamondoid DNA when a school bell rang. The students all rose, almost as one, and began filing out. He hung his head, shaking it slightly.

"They never stay for the whole thing," he muttered with a sigh. He began to disassemble his display, which mainly consisted of letting the screen up and disconnecting his projector from the laptop. He'd spent so much time getting the displays to work to his satisfaction, which was higher than most people would expect. No one had even come up to thank him for coming to visit this god-forsaken school.

He wasn't even sure which school this was. He'd heard of it, certainly. Otherwise he'd never have come here. But as for a specific location, he still wasn't sure. He'd gotten the plane ticket sent to him. Once off the big plane, he was put on a little plane and flown directly to the campus. From there, he wasn't too sure. He'd fallen asleep on the small plane and didn't even remember getting off of it until they'd landed.

He was reasonably sure he hadn't been kidnapped. After all, this looked like a college campus. There were students. He'd given most of a lecture. His cell phone worked. He'd called Martha as soon as he felt conscious enough to have a coherent conversation. But he had a nagging feeling that something was... well, maybe not wrong, but certainly not right.

Maybe it was that the stage of the auditorium was rounded at too sharp an angle. Maybe it was that the screen for the projector was being too cooperative, unlike the one at his school. He finally realized it was the rather smallish, blue-hooded woman who seemed to suddenly appear on the stage with him.

"You're lecture was great Chris," said the small woman in a vaguely familiar voice. "Of course, I only understood the English parts." Beneath the hood he saw a recognizable face smiling back at him.

"Gigi?" he asked with a smile, moving over to his old schoolmate. "What the hell are you doing here?" he further inquired while embracing her.

"I came to see you actually," she replied matter-of-factually. "I have something of a job offer for you."

He broke their friendly hug to look at her questioningly. He chuckled slightly. "Honey, I've got a job. A great job, really. I'm teaching at a prestigious university. I get to make my own hours. I'm on the cutting edge of my field. I even get to pick my own students.

"Besides," he continued, "I finally met the most perfect woman in the world." He paused and twisted his face slightly. "I mean, perfect for me. We all know that there is no more perfect woman in the world than you."

"Flirt," she countered.

"I mean it Gee. I'm doing great. I'm getting married in two months! You wanna come? We've got this big church. Great catering. Great band. You don't even have to bring a gift or anything, just show-" She held up a hand in hopes of cutting off her excited friend's rant. "Sorry, Gee. I'm just... ecstatic about this whole thing," he beamed.

She returned his gleeful look with her own remorseful one. "I hate to do this to you Chris. You seem to have it all together. I always knew you'd do it, of course." He looked proud of himself. *He doesn't deserve this*, she thought. *He's got a good life.* But she composed herself, remembering the warning about uncontrolled activation. "Unfortunately, this is something that can't be refused." She sighed. "And it's something that I have to..." she took a deep breath, *"initiate."*

GNA: INITIATE

* * *

The lights spun over the stage, cascading a brilliant array of colors over the audience. The crowd was getting excited. The music was so energetic it caused everyone to hypnotically rock their heads, or bounce slightly, to the beat.

Or is it too much bass?

Sandon Drose was so anxious about this show, almost to the point of being paranoid. He'd waited so long for a moment like this. He just wanted everything to go perfect, and he was so worried it wouldn't.

"You need to relax, Sandy." Sandy jumped at the sudden pressure of someone rubbing his shoulders. "My your tense. Just relax. Everything is going fine." Steffon's large hands kneading his neck and shoulders released some of the tension. But he'd spent too much time making sure everything would be perfect for his first show and he didn't want to relax. He turned and waved off the massage.

"I can't relax now!" he cried. Steffon looked hurt. "I'm sorry," he apologized. "That came out a bit more harsh than I'd intended. But you need to get ready. You aren't even dressed yet and the show starts in ten minutes!"

Steffon looked abashed, but nodded, turned and walked toward the dressing area. Sandy sighed and watched the tall, bronzed (and naked) man walk off. *Oh the ass on that man!*

He snapped himself out of his fantasy and turned went to check on the rest of his troupe. It wasn't every day that he unveiled his new fall line. His models were all so excited to be wearing his clothes. His clothes! He loved the sound of that. Clothes he designed. Clothes he worked so hard to manufacture. Clothes that, he'd been told, that were so hot they were cool! And he was finally getting a fashion show of his own to show off his work. Not only were all the major fashion magazines and television program represented outside, but CNN had sent a crew as well. If he could pull off this show, he'd be one of the more famous fashion designers on the planet. He just knew it.

Everything *had* to be perfect!

Everyone was dressed, except Steffon, of course. But his bronze god would be the last on the stage anyway. He inspected his company, making sure every last detail was to his liking... and it was. Everyone looked marvelous.

The first model, Michele, was at the top of the ramp, ready to walk on to the runway, when everything fell apart. Not her clothes, of course. They stayed just a fabulous as when they were first designed.

No, it was when he felt something metallic snap around his wrist and heard a stern voice say, "Sandon Thomas Drose. You are under arrest." Sandy looked down at the handcuff he suddenly found on his arm. His eyes followed the chain of the cuffs to arm of a policeman and up to the policeman's unrelenting gaze.

"Wh-what?" he stammered, shock prevalent on his face. "I'm... who? Arrest? Why?"

"Mister Drose," the officer continued, "you are under arrest for the statutory rape and kidnapping of one," he handed the cuffs to another officer who placed the other one of Sandy other wrist while the first officer consulted a notebook. "One Steffon Jamison."

"What!?" Sandy cried. Several of the other models, who had naturally gathered to find out what was going on, were equally shocked. "Kidnapping? He came to me!! And you're telling me he's under aged!" he yelled jerking his head in the direction of the large, now partially dressed, man.

Sandy looked at Steffon and noticed that an older couple was now holding him. The family resemblance told him that Steffon's parents had come. They were crying and saying something about how they'd been looking for 'their baby' for so long.

Sandy looked incredulously at the office. "Look at him! Does he look under aged to you? He's six-foot-seven! He's built like a Greek God! He'—"

"Fifteen-years-old," the officer finished. "And *you* have the right to remain silent. Anything you say can and will..."

Sandy, still in a state of complete shock, looked at Steffon, who returned his gaze. Steffon looked sad and embarrassed. He mouthed an "I'm sorry" and shook his head apologetically.

Sandy simply hung his head. He felt tears welling in his eyes. He looked to the closest model, Janice, and asked her to continue the show without him. But in his heart, he knew he was ruined.

As he was lead from the building to the waiting police car, he noticed the CNN crew had left the building as well. They were filming him. He'd wanted to be a famous designer, just not like this.

His current state allowed him to only focus on the cameras and the officers escorting him there. What he didn't notice was the diminutive woman watching from across the street. If he had seen her, he probably would have told her that the blue cloak she was wearing was not exactly the best fashion decision she could have made.

30
KHAMERON

The campus cafeteria was full. Eric had learned that the above-ground portion of the base was actually a college campus. He'd spent much of his time there upon his return. There was little for him to do, as a non-corporeal being.

He'd come to the cafeteria and watch the students play cards, a popular pastime, and listen to their stories. There was one group of kids that reminded him of his college group. They discussed sci-fi topics mainly. From comic books to television shows to what movies were coming out several years from now. Typical geek stuff. He could relate.

He was extremely interested in one of their conversations about astral projection. One of them, Mitchell Thomas, a psychology major, had theorized that if astral projection was possible, which none of them believed it was, then why would it not be possible for the projection to enter a different body and inhabit it for a while. They all had discussed it and decided that "astral possession" had its merits and would be incorporated into the role-playing game they were designing.

He'd been working with O'Neal on methods of becoming visible, but that wouldn't really do much good if he couldn't actually physically interact. So far, he'd been able to appear as a shadow and spook some of the technicians, but that was relatively useless as a 'super power' as everyone else seemed to have. They never even heard him say "Boo!"

But astral possession, could it be possible for him to possess someone? He'd occupied the same space as someone but it was just a fleeting walkthrough, like a ghost. He'd never actually attempted to make someone else do anything.

If it worked, he'd have to possess one of these kids and let them know. Or, better yet, possess someone like that jerk who was captaining the football team. Have him come over and sit with the 'geek squad', in a dress.

He smiled at that thought, not that anyone would see it. He let himself float through the floor. "I need to find someone to experiment on," he muttered to no one in particular.

* * *

Two levels down, in a section of the campus that none of the students suspected existed, was a massive room with a honeycomb of black capsules along one wall. The room was an almost constant hub of activity.

Eric hovered over the room. (Hovering was a relatively new trick he'd picked up. It wasn't as much fun as full-fledged flying, but it came in handy, especially when he tried to fly in place. He'd ended up flying in circles and got really dizzy. So hovering was a good thing.) He was looking for someone that was going to be 'off-duty' soon so he could follow them back to their quarters and see about possessing them.

He didn't want to pick just anyone. O'Neal was out. He didn't want to alienate the only human who could interact with him. And the Edwards weren't human at all, so that probably wouldn't work. He'd have to find someone that wasn't just, well, ugly. If he couldn't face himself in the mirror... And he couldn't possess a woman. He liked the idea, and there were certainly many women here he wouldn't mind looking in the mirror and seeing... more of. But he decided that would be unethical. He'd have to find someone... like that guy.

Khameron Mitchem, the new guy. Khameron was still trying to fit in. He was a relatively good-looking guy, intelligent, and completely nervous about his new environment. He'd make a good subject. He seemed to be good at what he was doing, which was reprogramming computers. He was new enough that he didn't have a critical job yet, so if something went wrong.

Yes, Khameron would be the test subject. Eric hovered around him for the rest of the shift.

* * *

Khameron Mitchem felt a chill. He glanced around his workstation in the honeycomb room, as it was apparently called. There was no where for a breeze to come from, so how did he get a chill?

He turned back to his computer. The programming he was doing was intense. The calibrations of the honeycombs consisted of a combination of medical terminology, computer languages, and a bit of science fiction.

He knew there were six of the capsules in use now, with another several expected to be in use soon. He knew there were people inside the capsules, but he hadn't been able to figure out what they were doing in there, or if they came out.

He finished his programming quickly. This room made him nervous. He'd preferred to work on troubleshooting, but this job paid so well, he couldn't pass it up. Room and board was included, which was big for him since his parents were still upset with him for... well, everything. Looking back on his life, he realized that he probably should have behaved better for them. He sighed.

"Good work, kid." The voice and the unexpected clap on the back startled him. "A bit jumpy aren't we?" asked his supervisor, Mister Edwards. This man was a mystery to Khameron. Sometimes he was really cool, other times he was a complete bastard.

"Why don't you knock off for the day?" his boss continued. "You've done some really great work here, Khameron. Do you mind if I call you Khameron?" Khameron responded with a shake of the head. "Good, it's good to have you aboard Khameron. I think you're going to fit in quite nicely here."

"Thank you sir," Khameron replied as he rose from his workstation. He had to repress a shudder as he rose. He noticed Edwards eyes darted just over his shoulder, where the chill was. Out of the corner of his eye he thought he saw a shadow, which, of course, disappeared as he turned to look at it. "I think I will go back up to my room, if that's ok, sir."

"Certainly," replied Edwards, now refocused on him, clapped him on the shoulder. "We'll see you tomorrow."

Khameron smiled and walked to the elevator at the other end of the room. *This place is starting to give me the creeps*, he thought. *Weird boss. Chills. Shadows. What's next?*

* * *

His room was not unlike any other dormitory room on the campus, mainly because it really was a dormitory room on the campus. But Khameron didn't mind. It was one of the 'senior suites', as he used to call them when he was in college. Basically it had its own bathroom.

He leaned with both hands on the dresser and stared into the mirror. He sighed. It had been a long day, but a productive one. At least, productive as far as he could tell. He wasn't even really sure of what he was doing. He knew that he got his part of it right. The programs took and ran the way they were supposed to, but he wasn't sure what the overall goal of the facility was.

Oh well, he sighed again. A two-year contract, right out of college making six-figures plus the room-and-board, if you didn't mind the cafeteria, wasn't that bad. Now if he could just find out where the night life was in this area, things would be even better.

He picked up the remote from the dresser and pointed it in the mirror. The television on the opposite wall came to life. There was a news story about some high school student being in a car wreck caused by a lightning strike somewhere in Tennessee.

He shrugged off his work shirt, and opened the top drawer of to get another shirt, preferably a more comfortable one. He felt the chill again. He thought that he might be coming down with a cold or something. *That would really suck*, he thought. *First month on the job and I'm getting sick.*

He glanced back up at the mirror as he pulled the shirt over his head and saw the same shadow that had been in his peripheral vision all day. Only this time, it didn't disappear when he turned to look at it.

Khameron felt oddly calm. Odd in that when one looks at a three-dimensional shadow in the middle of a room, one would usually suspect panic would be the first emotion. But there was no panic. Something was telling him that the shadow meant him no harm. Or, at least, wouldn't harm him intentionally.

The shadow moved toward him, touching him. It moved into him, or through, like a ghost. He felt his head tilt back. He felt his arms grow numb but saw them move upwards. The numbness in his arms spread throughout his body. When the feeling reached his head, he heard a voice.

"Sleep my friend. I'll give it back soon."

* * *

Khameron's mind was completely suppressed. It had finally worked. He turned to look in the mirror and saw... Khameron. No visible differences between now and pre-possession. After two weeks of trying, Eric had finally acquired a body.

After the first week, he had assumed that maybe it was something wrong with Khameron. But attempts with two others led him to the same conclusion: he was just doing it wrong. It turned out to be such a simple process. Simply think about being the person. The merger worked wonderfully, except for one thing.

"Terrific," Eric muttered, somewhat disoriented to hear his thoughts with Khameron's voice. "I finally get a body and the first thing I'm going to do with it is take a piss." He sighed and did something he hadn't done in some time, use a bathroom.

* * *

The buildings and passages of the campus looked different somehow. Probably because I'm using real eyes now, he thought. KhamEric, as he thought of his current combination, was redressed in his work clothes and headed back down to the underground complex.

He had access to the main section, but he knew that he somehow needed to access the restricted areas to find O'Neal or one of the Edwards. He didn't want to unpossess Khameron without medical supervision. Just in case something happened to him.

Soon he reached the sliding doors with the red and white striped border. There was a guard outside the door. There usually was. Even with the numeric keypad combination lock and the retinal scanner, they felt the need to have a guard posted. Eric had thought this a bit paranoid, but this time, it would be helpful.

* * *

Fred Brown enjoyed his job. It was really boring, but he enjoyed it. He was a guard at an underground complex. His job basically entailed standing in front of a door, holding a gun, wearing a military-style jumpsuit. A short, but muscular man in military fatigues and a big automatic rifle was typically intimidating. This would make his job easier, if there was really something to do.

He was told there would be a limited number of people using the door now, but the traffic would increase later. He had also figured out that this was not the only door to, well, whatever was on the other side. It couldn't be. How else could that Edwards guy go in several times without coming out again?

Basically, with only two people regularly using the door, and no one else trying to get in, this was a boring job. His favorite pastime had become playing with reflections. His dark skin reflected some of the overhead light off his shaved head and back down the hall. He would bob his head and see what kind of shapes he could make.

One day, he had just succeeded in creating a reflection of a silhouette of a duck and was contemplating how to capture the image, when someone he had never seen before appeared in the hallway.

He stood at attention, losing the duck reflection, held the rifle across his chest and said, "Excuse me, sir! But you need to go back. This area is restricted." That's what he had been trained to say, but this was the first time he'd actually had to say it. He thought his deep throaty voice made it sound really intimidating. What he didn't expect was the response.

"Hi Fred," the man said enthusiastically. "How's Allison and the kids?"

Fred's jaw dropped momentarily and he looked skeptically at the newcomer. "I… don't know you do I? How the hell do you know my wife and kids?" He pointed the rifle at the strange man at the last question.

"Sorry," the man replied holding up his empty hands. "Look, Fred, I need to speak with O'Neal. I don't have the clearance to get past the door, but I know he's on the other side and I need to speak with him. It's quite urgent."

"I'm sorry, sir!" Fred replied to the newcomer. "But no one gets beyond this door. Not even me. Now go back to where you came from." He mock-prodded the air with the rifle.

"Look, Fred," the newcomer continued, "I need to speak with O'Neal or one of the Edwards."

"*One* of the Edwards?"

"They didn't tell you how many there were, did they?"

"What?"

The newcomer rubbed his forehead with a finger in apparent frustration. "Ok, new approach. Can I speak with your supervisor? I'm not going anywhere, and just so you know," he turned out his pockets, "I'm unarmed."

Fred looked skeptical and started to reach for the comlink on his wrist when the door opened. Fred remained standing before the door, not even turning to see who it was, and said "You need to go back inside sir! We seem to have a situation."

A comforting hand fell on Fred's shoulder. "It's ok Fred. He works here." Edwards patted Fred's shoulder and Fred stepped to the side allowing his supervisor to pass. "What can I do for you Mitchem?" Edwards asked.

The newcomer took a deep breath and replied, "If I told you that Eric wanted to speak with O'Neal..."

Edward's eyes widened and seemed to glow slightly. "Then I'd probably want to tell you to come inside," he replied, gesturing the newcomer through the door before turning to Fred. "You're doing a good job, Brown! Keep it up."

"Thank you, sir!" Fred replied, feeling somewhat confused. He finally the opportunity to do his job, prevent an unauthorized someone from entering, and he gets overruled. He sighed and dropped his head slightly. Out of the corner of his eye, he noticed the duck pattern again.

He thought about trying to bring a camera to see if he could get the duck on film and had almost discarded the idea when someone else came down the hall. It was Edwards. Fred tilted his head in confusion. How did he get out here when he just went in there?

"Good evening Fred! How's Allison and the kids?" Edwards started before giving him a second look. "Are you feeling ok? You look kind of... pale."

Fred resigned the next day.

* * *

O'Neal sat in his office at his desk. It was a rather nice desk, largish, metallic silver, pushed up against the wall so he wouldn't have to look at anything else. Just the way he liked it. He was working on a cybernetic armband when his door suddenly opened.

Through a mirror over his desk he saw two of the Edwards come in with someone he vaguely recognized. The new guy, Mitchem. What did he do to get in this much trouble? No one but he had seen more than one of the Edwards at a time. They'd have to get rid of Mitchem now, which was a shame since he was doing a really good job.

"We have a situation, sir." said one of the Edwards. O'Neal wasn't particularly fond of talking to more than one Edwards at a time. Despite building them, he really couldn't tell them apart by looking at them. O'Neal sighed, put down the micro-welder and turned to face the trio.

"Well," he said expectantly.

"Sir," the same Edwards continued (*probably Terry*, O'Neal thought, *he was the most military sounding*) "this man claims that Eric wants to talk to you."

O'Neal's eyebrows shot up in surprise. He turned to Khameron, "Oh really? Eric who?"

Mitchem's reaction yesterday would have been one of embarrassment. O'Neal knew Mitchem was uncomfortable here. He'd heard something about chills and how he thought Mitchem might be coming down with something. But the reaction to the question was completely different. Mitchem stifled a laugh, but not the accompanying smile, or was that a smirk? "Guess who found out he can possess people?"

O'Neal's eyebrows shot up again. "What?"

"Randy, I am not Khameron Mitchem. I'm Eric Duffy. Like the new body? I think it fits nicely." He raised both arms and rotated like a model. O'Neal covered his mouth with a hand to stifle a laugh before deciding that it was a fruitless gesture and just laughed out loud.

Both Edwards looked at Mitchem, then at O'Neal, and back to Mitchem. Their stereo-like movements bookending Mitchem's pirouette made for a vastly amusing image. Something like a music box, O'Neal mused. Which made him laugh harder.

After two rotations, Mitchem looked at O'Neal and smiled, smirked, smothered another laugh, and asked "Can you hear me now?" This, of course, prompted more laughter. Even the Edwards to Mitchem's right, Micah, the only one who ever laughed, joined in.

After a few moments frivolity, O'Neal asked, "so why did you bring Khameron down here? Just to show off your new trick?"

"Actually, I'm worried about him," KhamEric, a sensible name for the merged being, responded, turning a serious expression. "This is the first time I've done something like this. I'm not sure what would happen to him if I just popped out." He adopted a concerned expression. "I'm not sure I can just pop out."

O'Neal's expression became one of concern. "Hmm. I guess you'd like to do this in the med-bay." Not a question, a statement.

"Well," KhamEric replied, "actually yeah. If that's ok. I mean, I don't want anything to happen to him, y'know? He's a good kid."

O'Neal contemplated the situation for a moment before responding. "Edwards," he began, addressing both of them, "take, well, take *them* up to the non-restriced med-bay. If Mitchem wakes up, I don't want him in this area. Not yet anyway. Eric, do you think Mitchem would make a good addition to the inner circle of the project? I'm guessing you've been studying him for a while so you probably know him better than we do."

"Actually," KhamEric answered, "I think I'm getting some of his thoughts mixed with mine, so, yeah, I guess I do know him pretty well. And yes, I think he'd make a good addition to the team."

"Very well. I still want to do this in the unrestricted area. If he comes out of it in good shape, we'll see what we can do about getting him access."

The Edwards on his left too KhamEric by the arm and the trio left for the med-bay. O'Neal turned back to his desk, picked up the armband and the micro-welder, paused, put them back down and followed the trio up to the med-bay. He should be there for this, just in case.

* * *

The med-bay was the eminent domain of Doctor Jim Yost, a not-overly tall, thin man with short, mostly-graying hair. It was rumored that he actually lived in the med-bay to the point of even having food brought to him. O'Neal didn't really believe the rumors, but he didn't entirely disbelieve them either.

O'Neal, the two Edwards and KhamEric had explained the situation to the doctor who took the whole situation with a complete lack of emotion. "Well, the first thing we need to do is have one of you two leave," he said firmly to the Edwards twins. Both initially looked surprised by the pronouncement. Surprise was followed by understanding, a joint rising from their seats, a moments hesitation, and, something surprising to the others in the room, a quick game of rock-paper-scissors, won by the Edwards on the left. The one on the right looked dejected, hung his head and left muttering something about a thrown rock should be able to break through paper.

"There are times," began the Doctor, "that I think you did a really good job on them." He rubbed his right eyebrow with his left hand. "Then there are times they do things like this," he chuckled as he rose. "I want to examine you first," he said to KhamEric, leading the dual-being to an examining table in the main section of the med-bay.

The med-bay, in Eric's opinion, was very *Star Trek*-ish. Beige walls with more computers and monitors than actual stethoscopes and reflex hammers. As he lay on the table, which was a sensation he hadn't actually felt in a while, a large, glossy, white panel slid from under the table creating an arc over him. After being intangible for so long, the covering made him feel a bit claustrophobic.

Doctor Yost tapped on the panel in several places. The panel, in turn, made several beeping noises that seemed to satisfy him. KhamEric simply lay waiting on the table. Unable to see the topside of the arc, he assumed that the beeping noises were satisfactory scans due to the unchanged expression in the doctor. "So Doc," he quipped, "are we going to live?"

The doctor stopped his scans, stared directly ahead for a moment before turning to KhamEric and almost making a snide comeback. Instead he stopped and looked KhamEric in the directly in the eyes and muttered, "Interesting."

KhamEric raised an eyebrow. "What's interesting?" he asked in a low, confused / worried tone. The doctor didn't respond verbally but pulled a small, pen-like instrument from his pocket. He pointed the device at KhamEric and seemed to push a button on the top. KhamEric couldn't tell that it had done anything.

"What did you find?" O'Neal asked from a position somewhere in the room KhamEric couldn't see.

"His eyes are, well, they're wrong," the doctor stated. "Khameron's eye color is normally a brownish-gold. Now they're a silvery-blue." He made three more taps on the panel, each responding with a beep, before turning to O'Neal and stating, "Apart from the eye-color. He's exactly the same as; I guess you could call it, *pre-possession*." He turned back to KhamEric. "Are you ready to, hmph, split?"

KhamEric smirked. "I guess so. Just in case I don't get to tell you later, since you probably won't see me, thanks Doc."

Doctor Yost smiled and shook his head slightly before closing his eyes. When he reopened them a moment later, his eyes glowed. "Who do you think designed the lenses to let them see you?" He patted KhamEric on the shoulder. "I'll see you again," he said turning back to the panel.

"Ok, I'm ready whenever you are."

KhamEric sighed, closed his eyes and took a deep breath. A shadow passed from Khameron's body and hovered over the table before completely vanishing from normal sight.

Khameron opened his eyes, which were now brownish-gold again. He expression was somewhat panicked. His eyes darted around the room before finally settling on Doctor Yost, a man Khameron had never seen before. "Where am I?" he demanded. "And why do I have this big, uh, whatever this is, over my chest?"

"It's going to be ok, Mr. Mitchem," Doctor Yost said reassuringly. "My name is Doctor Yost. You're in the campus medical bay. There was a gas leak in the dorm last night. We caught it before it spread too far, but you seem to have taken the brunt of it." He lifted a clipboard from the top of the arc and flipped a few pages. "It appears you were knocked out but there don't seem to be any side effects. How do you feel?"

"Um," Khameron stammered. "Uh, thanks, Doc. Sorry for, um, being rude and, uh, stuff. Um. I feel fine, actually." His expression turned thoughtful. "Actually, better than I've felt in a while."

"That would probably be the antibiotic we gave you," Yost said comfortingly. "It was a precaution, of course, but it is, I suppose you could say *laced* with several vitamins and other, well, good things." Yost's eyes betrayed a momentary panic. "*Legal* good things," he amended with a grin. "We would like to keep you overnight, just in case. Besides, they need to finish patching up your room. They kind of made a mess of one of the walls getting to it. That okay with you?"

"Yeah, fine with me," he replied. Yost turned and nodded at O'Neal, who was not visible from Khameron's perspective. O'Neal silently slipped out of the room. He knew Yost would find out more about Khameron Mitchem and see if he would be qualified for the program.

They'd need at least one more soon. The capsule state would only last for another two days, at the most.

PART III
AWAKENINGS

31
DIFFERENT STAGE

Darkness.

That's all he could see when he finally got his eyes open. He wasn't sure how long they'd been closed; he was still a bit groggy from the... whatever it was. What was it? Big white space. Randy? A desk? Then *poof.* Darkness.

He heard several other voices making the noises one usually hears when waking up at a party the next morning. He found himself making the same noises when he tried to sit up.

He put his hand to his head. He shook his head hoping to clear away the cobwebs. It didn't work. Just in case he shook his own hand against his head. That didn't work either. He shrugged and tried to look around.

To his left was a circle of light. He was sitting one the edge of it. The room was not completely dark after all, but looking in the directions he had been; it was plenty dark.

He recognized the occupants of the room... mostly. There was Rich, and Sandy, Ranj, Steve, Chris, Kat, Matt, Mel, some scrawny guy and a cute blonde chick. But something was not entirely right about the whole thing.

The staging area!

That's where he finally realized he was... again. Why was he here again with the lights off? Of course, he felt more comfortable with it like this since the light seemed to increase the 'hangover' he felt.

He looked at his hand, still resting on his forehead. No glove. Ah, that's what else is odd: no uniforms. Everyone was mostly dressed in... well, normal clothes, mostly blue jeans and tee shirts. The notable exceptions were Chris was wearing a suit, Rich was wearing his wrestling outfit, and the blonde chick was wearing a very nice white, low-cut sundress.

Stan moved his hand away from his head and almost out of reflex tilted his head to get a better look at the cleavage on the lovely woman next to him. Unfortunately, for him, she was a bit more lucid than he was and returned his lustful gaze with a very frigid expression. She crossed her hands across her chest and asked "*Do you mind?*" Stan blinked and muttered an apology.

"Anyone else feel like dey jus woke up from a relly bad dream wit' a hangovah?" asked the scrawny guy, who's expression immediately soured as he realized that he probably spoke too loud.

"That would be everyone, I think," muttered Ranj. "And don't talk so loud." Ranj's hand make a 'smack you on the head gesture' toward Jeremy and seemed honestly surprised that his hand stretched far enough to actually do it.

"I guess that wasn't a dream."

"Well, that would actually depend on your point of view," came a familiar, but different, voice that didn't belong to anyone visible in the room.

"Randy?" Sandy asked groggily, trying to get to his feet. He didn't entirely succeed but compensated by creating an 'ice cane' that seemed to appear from his right hand and stretch to the floor. He quickly increased the length of the cane and found himself the first one on his feet.

O'Neal stepped from the darkness into the circle of light. Behind him, the large double door split, sliding into the wall on both sides and revealing a 'path of light' from the doorway to the circle.

Even as the path backlit O'Neal, most of the group noticed several differences in his appearance. It wasn't just the uniform, which looked like a typical military uniform. He looked older. Not a whole lot, but there was about a ten-year difference from when they saw him ten minutes ago at the desk in the white void.

"Randy?" Sandy asked again.

"Uh, dude, you look… older," Matt piped in.

"Now I'm a bit confused," added the scrawny guy.

"Ah," Stan mumbled, "Jeremy. Ok. Got it now."

"Its Rush!" he replied, pointing an accusatory finger at Stan. "But you know that. What I didn't know was that you knew him," he said nodding to O'Neal.

O'Neal put up his hands in a calming expression. "We'll sort that out in a minute," he semi-explained. "First we should all get you to the med-bay to get checked out first. Then we'll meet in the briefing room and I will explain everything."

"This ought to be good," Rich rumbled as he stood.

A group of similarly dressed (to O'Neal) people flooded the room, each helping one of the group to their feet, and ultimately, the med-bay.

They noticed several things upon exiting the staging area. The first being, the hallway they were led into. The walls were colored differently. It wasn't the same obnoxious yellow as before. It was more of a gun-metal gray.

The Hydra Corporation billboard was gone. Another difference.

Sandy, the first led out of the staging area glanced behind him at the others, to make sure they were ok, but then set off a chain reaction of confused glances. Sandy's glance originated when he realized that the staging area was not a circle of light with darkness surrounding it, but a round, well lit room. Sandy's glance had Matt glancing behind him, making an odd expression, and so on.

"Something is wrong," Rich mumbled.

O'Neal patted the large man on the shoulder, which did require a bit of a stretch. "No, my friend. It's just more real this time."

32
GROUP COUNSELING

The med-bay hadn't changed. The doctor had. Jim Yost, the former head of the now, apparently, non-existent Hydra Corporation, was simply the facility's head doctor. Most of the examinations went well, except for Chris's.

Chris almost went into hysterics at seeing Yost. Eventually he was calmed enough to submit to the examination. But Chris's eyes never moved from the doctor during the entire time he was in the room. Yost and O'Neal had asked several times what was making him so uncomfortable, but Chris never even opened his mouth. He simply stared, wide-eyed, at the doctor.

Two hours later, they were taken to the briefing room. The room's color had changed, again, gun-metal gray, but the rest had remained the same... almost. O'Neal sat at the 'right-hand' seat rather than the head of the table, as he had been at the more recent meetings.

Sitting at the head of the table was a woman no one seemed familiar with. The woman, a rather tall, well-proportioned redhead in a military-style dress uniform, sensed their unease, smiled at the group and stood. "I know, I know. You have no idea who I am," she said, acquiring a group of muttered agreement. "My name is Colonel Roberta Schmid. I am in charge of the GNA Project. I trust none of you need an explanation as to what that project is?" she asked the group and received a series of headshakes and murmured 'no's.

Melanie, looking terribly uncomfortable, stood from her chair, the one next to O'Neal's, threw a salute and said in a quite militant voice, "No Ma'am! I believe we all understand about the GNA project!"

The Colonel looked initially surprised by what could be viewed as an outburst since most of the group viewed it as one. Her surprise was replaced by amusement and that quickly by turning her head to O'Neal. "Yours, I assume?"

O'Neal looked up at the Colonel from his chair and gave a curt nod with a smile of pride. "I suppose I should tell you that Ms. O'Neal's former military training is not expected of everyone here. She is formerly military, true. But you are all civilians. We didn't draft you."

The Colonel's statement, one she thought was clear enough, elicited nothing but confused looks from most of the group. Naturally, Stan was the first to ask. "Dude, I knew you looked older, but, um...?"

"Oh my gawd," exclaimed Jeremy. "I knew day was married! I taught *you* woulda known!" The group exchanged quick glances of curiosity resulting in a 'group stare' at Melanie.

"I guess I told the other group," she mumbled.

The replies ranged from "what other group?" to a surprised "you two are married?" But the big question came from Stan. "If you two are married, what about that thing in the hallway?"

Randy O'Neal looked curiously at his wife. "What thing in the hall?"

"We'll talk about that later," she replied sheepishly. "I believe the Colonel has some more important things to discuss now." She looked expectantly at Colonel; her expression clearly wanted someone to get her out of the situation.

"Ahem, yes. I do have some... um..." the Colonel began switching her gaze briefly to Stan. "Thing in the?. Anyway," she continued, returning her focus to the group. "You are all part of the group that was deemed a success as far as this program is concerned. I'll start at the beginning, which I believe some of you know.

"Doctor Emil Fox was a genetic researcher who developed GNA. He could not get permission from either his original corporation, the Hydra Corporation, nor the government to experiment on humans. His lab tests were impressive but there were serious concerns over his testing of humans.

"Eventually he disappeared," she continued, "only to surface later as Doctor Anthony Forrest. I believe most of you remember him?"

"Ah don'" Jeremy drawled.

"Yes, but we've checked your medical records and you did see him once when you were very young," the Colonel answered. "We suspect that was when you were given the injection of the nanotech. The rest of you," she addressed the group, "had numerous visits to see him. That's when he introduced you to his Genetic Nanotechnological Advancement program, or GNA. Actually, everyone in your school seems to have been advanced in some way."

"Everyone?" most of the group asked.

"Yes. Everyone was activated briefly. We sorted through the abilities everyone had and picked you as the ones to remain active as your abilities have the most promise."

"So some of the powers didn't work out that good?" Rich asked. "I gotta know. What kind of things didn't go over too good?" Most of the group was familiar with Rich's odd humor but expressed a similar curiosity.

"I don't think we'll go into all of them," Randy O'Neal replied, "but… May I tell them a few that I was amused with?" he asked the Colonel, who stifled a laugh and nodded. "Ok, how about… Ronnie Jones. He had the ability to… how to phrase this? Uh, he had the ability to hold his breath for long periods of time."

"Um," Kat interjected, "wasn't Ronnie the guy who almost drown at that party at the lake because he didn't know how to swim?"

"And that's why we decided that he would probably not make a good member of the group," Randy responded jovially. "Then there was Julia Barnett, your prom queen I believe, right?"

"Stuck up bitch," Kat mumbled.

"Well," Randy continued, "her ability was to, well, have her face generate makeup." The group reacted with an expected skepticism. "I know, not terribly useful. That's why she's not here. But my favorite glitch, as we started calling the one's that didn't work, has got to be your team's quarterback Matt Young."

"Snotty bastard," Ranj mumbled, with a round of mumbled ascent from the rest of the group, save Jeremy who mainly looked lost through this part of the conversation.

"Funny you should say it like that," Randy laughed. "Apparently his ability was to sneeze acid. So basically once we put his hands back together…"

"Put his what?" asked Chris.

"Hands," replied Melanie.

"He covered his nose," laughed the Colonel.

"Anyway," Randy continued. "we put him back together and sent him home."

"I think that's enough," said the Colonel, composing herself. "They don't need to know everyone since they're not going to be used anyway. Now," she addressed the group, "I know this leads to a lot of questions. Let me try to answer them before you ask. No, no one will remember their abilities. We have a method of removing memories. We simply turned them off and put them back into their lives. Now, I actually have a question for you. And you'll understand why I'm asking it when you answer. How long have you been here?"

"About six weeks," answered Stan.

"Six weeks?" asked Rich. "More like three months."

"You're both half right," quipped Sandy, "six months."

The Colonel held up her hands, signaling for no more answers from the understandably confused group. "You've all been here no more than one week," she said. They took it better than she had anticipated as they were all stunned into silence, which was better then the panicked arguing match she'd expected. "You've all been immersed in a virtual world. That's where we tested your abilities, your group work-"

"So, I've never actually done this before?" Sandy asked, making a small ball of flame appear in his hand.

"No," she replied. "That would be a first. The GNA is basically a small computer. Your interfacing with that computer could be simulated in our virtual world. And since the brain can process things considerably faster than reality takes place, time passed quickly and you were able to learn your abilities faster.

"None of you can recall much of your non-training time over the past few months, can you?" Apart from Stan's glance at Melanie, she received nothing but puzzled shakes of the head. "That's because it wasn't really programmed into the system. There were some routines that Major O'Neal programmed into the system that were carried out, which produced some odd effects." She turned to Chris. "Just so you know, there is no *Lord*."

Randy's eyes grew large as his stare bounced from Chris to the Colonel and back. "He activated the *Lord* routine? I threw that in as a joke. I wasn't expecting someone to actually set it off. Geez, no wonder you looked so screwed up when you saw Doctor Yost!"

Chris looked very perturbed at being, what he suspected was, teased. Instead of lashing out at O'Neal, as Stan or Rich might have done, he calmly looked to Colonel Schmid. "So, none of the last three months has really happened? I'm sorry guys, but I am not really interested in doing this. I'm supposed to get married next month and I have a really good life. I want to go home."

"Actually," the Colonel answered, "you will be able to go home soon *and* remain a part of this group. And we would really like to have you in this group. Electrokenesis is not an ability to take lightly, and your participation would be greatly appreciated."

"We don't *have* to stay here?" Chris questioned.

"Of course not. We had the simulation set up that way because, even with the new organic processor we acquired, we would never have been able to run the program if you all went home. We had to keep you pretty much confined to a single area. You can stay here if you wish, but I do understand your wanting to go home. Martha is a beautiful woman."

Rich and Stan turned slowly to face Chris. "Martha?" they asked.

"Hey," Chris exclaimed pointing a finger at the pair. "Don't mess with my woman!"

Rich and Stan's snickering was interrupted by Colonel Schmid. "That was my mother's name too."

The pair immediately turned to her and replied, in stereo, perfectly deadpan, "And a lovely name it is too Colonel!" They then took on appropriately abashed expressions.

"Sorry about that Colonel," said Kat.

"They did that in school a lot, too," quipped Matt.

"Drove the teachers nuts," added the heretofore unnamed blonde. The group turned to her with inquiring expressions. "No one ever remembers me," she muttered.

She scanned each of their eyes looking for recognition, and not getting any. "Candace Brown," she said hoping that someone would recognize her. "Debate team? Chess club? Damn, none of you have a clue who I am do you?"

"Ah do dahrlin'," quipped Jeremy, who decided to drop the flirtation due to the icy stare he received.

Appropriately, somehow, Stan's eyes eventually sparked some recognition. "Wait a minute! Weren't you... um... a bit, well, bigger?"

"So you remember the name of the *fat chick* you picked on, eh?," she replied. "Yes, I *was bigger!*"

"I do remember you, Candace," Mel said. "Yes, Stan, she was bigger. Personally I'm quite proud of her. She's lost 275-pounds since school. No surgery, nothing. Just correct dieting and exercise."

"Damn," muttered Rich. "That is impressive! For one, I'm sorry I didn't recognize you. I mean, you have changed a bit since school. *275 pounds*? Hell you just lost two Ranjs!"

"Hey!" Ranj interjected. "That's... well, that's close, actually."

"If we can get back to the subject please," the Colonel interrupted. Once the room's attention had been refocused on her, she continued, "Of course you'll probably want to keep your identities a secret as it could draw unnecessary attention to your private life. You are about to become the first *real* 'super-powered' group. We're not sure how the public is going to react to that. We're going to want to do some *real life* studies first."

"And how exactly are we going to do that?" Sandy asked.

"Real missions."

33
REALLY OUT THERE

"Why can't we use our old costumes?" Sandy complained, not for the first time. The new uniforms resembled the old ones, but were more body armor than spandex-ish.

"Because the other ones weren't real," O'Neal responded. "They only existed in the VR program."

"But why do I need one?" asked Rich. "I thought I was bullet-proof."

"In the simulation," O'Neal countered, "yes, you were bullet-proof. In reality, we're not one-hundred percent sure. Do you really want to test it by getting shot?"

Rich pursed his lips and shook his head. They'd tested their powers over the last two days. Every one of them had performed the same in reality as they had in the simulation. The only thing they didn't want to test was Rich's bullet-proof-ness. They all had hoped that it would hold up in reality. They also hoped they would never have to find out.

"I feel like a tank," Rich grumbled.

"That's ok, big guy," Sandy quipped. "You look like one too."

"I don't know," interjected Stan. "I actually like these better. I feel more protected. That and I never really felt comfortable in the spandex."

"We're glad we don't have to look at you in the spandex, too!" Kat retorted, drawing snickers from Jeremy, Candace and Ranj. Matt, Melanie and Chris were not going on this mission. Matt and Chris because their powers would probably not do much good, and Melanie since her projectile-kenesis was already honed from her days in the military.

The mission, as O'Neal described it, was simple. A small terrorist cell had been positively identified and located outside Houston. They were currently walled up inside a prison, with the inmates. The prison guards were being held as hostages. The police and the army have been unable to get in without sheer brute force, which they did not want to use in case the hostages might get killed.

"The mission will go in two stages," O'Neal had said at the briefing. "First Stretch (Ranj's new name) and Rush will be transported inside the prison. Your job will be to find the hostages. When you do, attempt to make physical contact with them, without endangering them. Once physical contact is achieved, we can transport all of you out.

"Stage two will be Nightlite, Remix, Glacier, Thermal and Kat. Your mission will be to subdue anyone in the prison who is not a hostage. We're not sending you in until after stage one is complete, so there shouldn't be a problem. We've notified the authorities outside to expect something good soon, but, we're not really telling them what yet. We're hoping for a good surprise and some good PR. The press is there too."

Seems simple enough, Ranj was thinking. *I just have to get used to being called Stretch*. He and Jeremy had worked out a method of quick scanning the prison. Ranj would essentially become a belt on Jeremy's body armor. Ranj did not feel entirely comfortable with the idea since his was the only costume that was not body armor. His suit was a nanotech infused spandex that could stretch as he did but kept him covered. It provided some protection, but it wasn't bullet-proof.

Outside the staging area, Ranj had stretched himself around Jeremy's waist and around both shoulders, creating an 'X' pattern on his chest and back. "Is a good ting yo' costume and mine almos' match. Brown an' ahrange. Glad you ain't red. Dat'd be show to say 'shoot me he-ah!'"

"Now there's not a weight problem with this is there?" O'Neal asked. The GNA had given them all some degree of enhanced strength, and Ranj was easily the lightest looking of any of the group. Jeremy seemed to blink out of existence for a moment only to reappear with his new 'belt' stretching a bit upon stopping.

"No problem he-ah," he said reassuringly. "Jus lapped da ho' level and I cain't really tell he dare."

The brown belt around his shoulder mumbled an 'ouch'. "We might want to work on the stops."

"Hey," Jeremy argued. "Dat mean you need to hol' on tighter." This elicited a few chuckles from the group.

"Ok, begin stage one!" O'Neal said, activating the door to the staging area, which obediently slid aside. As 'team one' entered, he reminded them,

"As soon as you've found them-"

"We'll let you know," mumbled Rush's belt.

The door slid shut. The mission had begun.

* * *

The prison looked much like every prison ever seen in almost every movie. Both of them knew roughly what to expect. But both of them were a bit daunted by actually being there.

"I nevah been in one o' deese befo'. Is kinda creepy," Rush said, looking tentatively around the empty hallway they'd been transported to.

"Jer- sorry, Rush. We need to get started," his belt said. The sound momentarily startled him and it took a moment to realize that Stretch was still wrapped around him.

"Right. O'Neal say day all in da other side of dis place. I'm gonna do a quick run true. You ready?" His belt giggled a bit. "I take it das a 'yes'." And he began to run. Not at his full speed. He was a bit afraid that even stretched as tightly as he was, Stretch might fly off.

Getting to the west wing of the prison took, almost literally, no time. He stopped at the main gate to the wing, receiving a small muffled sound from Stretch. "I got an idea. Stretch, can you, like, look around da cornah. Make sho no one dare."

His belt slithered a bit and a smaller version of Ranj's head appeared at the end of a snake-like body. "Remind me to fix your accent when we get back." He peered around the corner near the top of the gate.

The hallway was littered with, well, just about everything. Mattresses and papers burned in the hallway. Cell doors were hanging from their hinges. The smell was the worst as bodily fluids were liberally sprayed almost everywhere. Stretch did notice that some of those fluids were not voluntarily sprayed. There were three bodies about halfway down the hall that had been shish kabobbed on a spike in the middle of the floor.

Stretch quickly returned to Rush around the corner. "There aren't really any guards near the doorway. But I don't think you're going to really be able to run in there. There's too much everything, everywhere."

"So now what?"

"I've got an idea," Stretch said, completely untangling himself from Rush's body armor, but maintaining his snake-like appearance. "You stay here. I think I can sneak around like this and find what we're looking. Then we can just let 'team two' clean up everything."

"Sounds good to me," Rush replied.

"Your accent..."

"I *can* annunciate if you really want me to." Stretch began to slither through the bars. "I jus' chews not to." Stretch moaned slightly as he continued through the bars. He decided that staying on the upper level of the three story prison wing would be best. He slithered up the near wall to the top floor where he froze, using his eyes to scan as much of the wing as he could.

Something was wrong. If there was a terrorist cell here somewhere, where were they? Rush had run through the east wing and the main offices and prison clinic without seeing anything. Stretch had to take his word for it as he saw nothing more than a very vertigo-inducing blur.

The two had assumed that everyone had been moved to this, the higher security, wing. It was, and he hated to think of it this way but, dead quiet. The only visible bodies were the three on a pike in the middle of the hall, but that didn't mean there weren't more. He took this as a bad sign.

An even worse sign appeared when he slithered by the first cell.

The four oddly-shaped lumps in the cell could probably be reassembled into the two men who lived there. Stretch had never seen that much blood in one place, and this was also the closest he'd been to a dead body. The stench was unbearable. The blood was caked on everything in the cell.

And Stretch felt oddly calm.

He adjusted his form from a somewhat-human-headed snake into a noseless, snake-headed snake. He turned back down the catwalk and moved on, trying desperately to make his mind numb to the horrors around him. Every cell contained roughly the same thing: two bodies, each cut in half.

It took several minutes to get to what appeared to be the center of the hallway. Still no voices. Still no signs of life. Still two severed bodies in each cell.

He peered over the edge of the catwalk at the three skewered bodies below. Their pattern from above made almost an asterisk; a body in the east-west position missing. Something else about the bodies seemed wrong.

Being two stories up wasn't going to alleviate the problem of finding what was wrong. As much as he didn't want to, he had to move down. He slithered down one level and discovered two things. One, the pattern of two bodies per cell was the same on this level. And, two, the impaled bodies were wearing prison guard uniforms.

He continued to the first floor. He had to switch girders to slither to avoid the flames of a burning mattress. The amount of bodily fluids was astounding. He clung to the bottom of the girder to avoid actually having to touch the floor. He glanced back up and realized that everything from the top two floors was probably just dripping down through the grated floor.

Dripping?

It wasn't dripping.

If there was dripping, there should be an accompanying sound. There wasn't. The blood on the upper levels had dried on the walls of the lower levels. This did not feel right at all.

He reshaped his head to human, sans nose; to be sure there was no sound. There wasn't. Complete silence.

No.

Not complete. A faint, raspy breathing sound. He looked at the spike and noticed the head of the top-most body was facing him, upside down, and smiling. A wicked, bright-eyed smile made more gruesome from the blood trickling from the corner of her mouth to her forehead.

"He said you would come," the head sputtered small amounts of blood with each word. Stretch almost lost his grip of the scaffold, his eyes grew big. He wanted to cry out in terror... but couldn't find his voice.

"He said you would be the one to find us," the not-quite-dead woman continued. "He told us." The head coughed and the body convulsed, making a horrible squishing sound on the spike. When she convulsed his left arm flung itself over his head. It was holding a small, silver cylinder with a red-button on the top, under his thumb.

"Tell them," she rasped. "Tell them that there will be equality. Tell them nice snakey. Ten."

"Nine."

Stretch's eyes widened. He reformed a hand to tap the communicator in his ear. "Emergency Transport! Get us out of here!!!"

* * *

Ken Reed had been out in the sun too long. He and Kevin had been waiting for this story to break for...

Seven.

Long.

Hours.

GNA: INITIATE

Texas heat was not the best place to be in the summertime. And this was May.

He wanted to go back to Chicago. Chicago was the place to be in the spring. The weather's nice. The Cubs have hope, this year. That would, of course, change in the fall. He even knew the sure sign of spring was for the Cubs to have a pitcher on the disabled list.

But this *was* spring. And the weather was nice... in Chicago. Here, it was just hot.

And he had been assigned to cover some terrorist plot at a prison in Texas. Kevin, his cameraman, had seemingly / wisely decided to take a nap. Police and Military forces had surrounded the prison, but hadn't 'gone in yet'.

There was talk among the reporters, of which Ken and Kevin were only two, that they were holding off on sending people in because a new 'government project' was going to be unveiled here. Some sort of new anti-terrorist group.

And they want all the good press they can get, Ken mused. He picked up the camera. Not as heavy as the ones they used a few years ago. And so much easier to use. Like a mouse, point and click. *May as well get some set-up shots,* he thought. *I can always change tapes before something happens.*

Like anything's going to happen, he thought skeptically.

He raised the lens to get some shots of the outer wall and the west wing of the prison, where they'd been informed that everyone had been moved. They were still almost half a mile away from the prison, since the authorities wouldn't let them get closer, but the lenses on the camera allowed for a beautiful close-up shot of the prison.

He filmed several different parts of the wing and the wall, when the west wing exploded. Not just the left side. Not just the right side. The whole wing. *And I just got that on film.*

Quickly glancing around him at the other press members he realized that he was the only one holding a camera at the time. As horrible as he felt about the people inside who'd died, he also found himself with *an exclusive video of a failed government anti-terrorist group.*

34
NOT AS PLANNED

Every major news channel had picked up the story.
"New Anti-Terrorism Group Blows Up Prison With Hostages Inside"
That was the headline in almost every major newspaper in the country and several from around the planet.

Colonel Schmid stared at two of the papers on her desk. Same headline. Same story. She'd seen the whole thing live through their monitoring system. Stretch had been debriefed and she knew the story. The only two members of the group in the building were not capable of doing that kind of damage. The more she thought about it, really only two members of the group could have made an explosion like that, but Nightlite and Thermal weren't there, Stretch and Rush were.

They had made a press statement, but not revealed any of the particulars of the group, namely the super-human abilities. The statement was a denial of their participation in the destruction, and an apology to the families of the hostages and inmates.

Their specific organization had not been mentioned. The group could still make a positive first public appearance. Hopefully.

* * *

Matt, Ranj, Stan and Rich sat in Rich's quarters watching the fiasco unravel on the television. The media was ripping everything military for this "completely uncalled for use of lethal force".

"I don't know that it was completely uncalled for," Stan complained. "I think there could be some good that comes out of it."

Matt looked skeptically at his friend, "How?"

"Well, terrorists may think twice when they realize we'll blow our own people up just to get them."

"That's pretty thin."

"I know," Stan muttered. "I'm trying to be optimistic."

"Well I'm tired of watching it," Rich said as he picked up the remote to change the channel. As he clicked the button, the view outside changed from a mountain range to a seascape. He sheepishly pointed the remote at the window and changed it back.

Their rooms were almost completely the same as they had been in the VR simulation, right down to the holographic windows. The only real difference was having more than one television channel. Matt tossed Rich a different remote. "Try this one. It actually works the tv."

Rich, obviously a bit embarrassed, took the other remote and began the stereotypically male pastime of channel surfing. Unfortunately the amount of channels didn't actually mean they'd find anything to watch.

Prison *click* Prison *click* Flaming Prison *click* News lady complaining about the government *click* Prison *click* Infomercial *click* Infomercial *click* Talk Show *click* Prison *click* Flaming Prison *click* Prison *click* Golf (most of them enjoyed the sport but agreed that watching it on television was almost as pointless as watching...) *click* Fishing *click* Red banner with a black asterisk *click* Red banner with a black asterisk *click* Red banner with a black asterisk *click* Red banner with a black asterisk...

"Dude, when channel surfing, one must actually change the channel," teased Rich.

"The numbers going up on the screen," Matt noted. "He is changing the channels."

"Thank you," Rich muttered sarcastically casting a derogatory glance at Stan.

"I think we should pay attention to this," Ranj interjected in an almost whispered tone. "That symbol on the banner... that's the way the bodies on the spikes were laid out.

"I don't think it's a coincidence."

The other three looked at the screen in apprehensive anticipation. Rich did change the channel a few more times to find out if another station had the sound to accompany the image. The same image was on every channel, no sound. *This can not be good*, he thought.

"*I hope we have your attention,*" the television said abruptly. "*Your government is deceiving you.*"

"This is definitely not going to go well," Stan muttered only to be shushed by the others.

"*By now you should have seen the footage of the Texas Hostage Massacre. We believe you should be made more aware of the group responsible for the explosion.*"

"I'm guessing it was you?" Ranj quipped.

"*The United States government is conducting experiments in genetic manipulation, and you should know what it can do.*" The image changed from the flag to a stone colored wall with a metal beam vertically bisecting the screen. Soon a small brown snake coiled its way down the beam. Before long, its head had assumed Ranj's noseless form. To most people, he would be rather unrecognizable. To the group in the room, he was unmistakable.

"H-h-how?" Ranj stammered at the screen.

"*This is not doctored footage. This image was transmitted from the Texas Hostage Massacre just before the explosion. This is the kind of program your government is working on,*" the television continued. *Your tax dollars at work. A multi-billion dollar super-human program. This is but one example. But you should be aware that there are more. They may be among you.*

"*Are you comfortable knowing these beings even exist? Knowing they can invade your home with little or no knowledge to you.*

"*If your government really believed in everyone being equal, why are they working on projects like this? We are Equality For Americans. We believe that everyone was born equal and should live equally. We are here to protect you from them.*"

The image of the red banner reappeared. "*We will be here for true Americans.*"

The screen resumed its regular programming while the group simple stared, dumbstruck, at the television. It was a few moments before anyone spoke.

"Are we as screwed as I think we are?" Matt asked.

"Could be," Rich replied.

Stan turned to Ranj with a puzzled look on his face. "Two questions. One, did the guy on the spike that spoke have a camera? And, two," he paused to look at the television momentarily before turning back to Ranj, "where was your nose?" he asked, pointing at the television.

* * *

Less than ten minutes after the global broadcast, the entire group and staff, most of which the group had never seen before, had been assembled in the honeycombed lower chamber. The GNA faction was amazed at the sheer numbers present. The group, in civilian clothes, looked out of place compared to the volume of camouflaged uniforms.

"I guess, we underdressed," Kat muttered to no one in particular.

"We'd probably stand out if we were in uniform," replied Sandy.

"I stand think we're standing out just being here," Rich quipped.

Chris stifled a laugh. "You stand out a bit anyway. You're only, what, two-feet taller than most of the people here." The comment elicited a group chuckle which was joined by some of the camouflaged people within earshot.

"TEN-HUTT!" a voice shouted from the door. All of the camouflaged people stood at attention. The GNAs looked rather uncomfortable as they realized they were the only ones bunched together and not in a straight, gridline formation, except for Mel.

"Suck up," Kat muttered to her at her as the group tried to figure out how to get into a formation that would 'fit-in' with the rest. They eventually gave up as there really wasn't enough room to make the formation work, especially with Rich. They all turned their attention to a platform near the door.

Colonel Schmid and Major O'Neal had, apparently, arrived. The Colonel was taking a position behind a podium, O'Neal flanked her.

"I believe all of you have either witnessed or, at the very least, heard about the broadcast," the Colonel began. "The 'Equality for Americans' group has been on our list of groups to keep an eye on for some time. Unfortunately, our intelligence has been lax in this area. We did not anticipate their group making a move so soon.

"We have dispatched more intelligence agents to find out why the move came so quickly and unexpectedly. But that is almost irrelevant now.

"They have moved. They have exposed one of our own." This comment brought a flush of embarrassment to Ranj's face. "They have made it look as though we were the terrorists. We will make them regret their mistake. We are taking steps to be more proactive. They will not catch us unaware again."

The room seemed alive with electricity. Even standing at attention, the crowd seemed energized, enthusiastic. The Colonel's charisma was unmistakable. *That's probably why she's in charge*, Stan thought.

"Everyone," she continued, "return to your stations. Make sure that everything is running as perfect as possible. GNAs" she addressed the casually dressed section of the audience, "briefing room! Ten Minutes!" With that, she turned and left, O'Neal trailing her.

"AS YOU WERE!" the same voice as earlier shouted.

"Mel," Chris asked after watching the others disperse, "the guy doing the yelling, what did he say when everyone came in?"

"Ten-hutt," she replied with a questioning look. "Why?"

"What does that mean?"

"It used to be 'attention'. But it's gotten a bit lax over the years."

"Ah." For a scholar, Chris was very intelligent in his field but sometimes lacked a bit in other areas.

"While we're asking questions," Sandy piped in, "What are those black honeycomb things?"

"Those are the VR chambers," she answered as most of the group entered the elevator to take them to the briefing room. Rich and Stan were left behind to take the next car. "Each of you was plugged into one of them for a while to do the orientation to the program."

"Why so many?" Candace asked.

"There were a lot of people who got GNA infused. Not just the people at the school. Think about how many people would have seen this guy over his twenty-year career. That's a lot of kids."

"Are they still being used for anything?" Matt questioned.

"Yes," she said with a sigh. "Unfortunately there were a few that could not be turned off and, to be quite honest, were too dangerous to let go."

* * *

It had been twenty minutes since the broadcast when the Colonel and the Major entered the room. It was possible that the room dropped about 20 degrees when they entered. *It's also possible that Sandy's just got gas*, Stan thought with a bizarre amusement.

"The command staff are already aware of the E-four-ay group," the Colonel began as she moved to the head of the conference table. "But we haven't had time to properly brief you on them. They'd been pushed back as they weren't considered a real threat… until now."

She activated the holo-projector which displayed the red banner with asterisk logo they'd all seen on the broadcast. "'Equality For All' began as a religious movement," she continued. "Their symbol is a variant of the Christian cross. From their propaganda, the cross is symbolic of everything that we should *not* be."

O'Neal passed a small brochure to everyone in the room before reading the first paragraph inside, "*Today's society is more concerned with movement up and down the social, political and economic ladders, they have neglected to remember that everyone is equal in the eyes of God. Our cross is a reminder of everything we can not afford to be.*" He tossed the flyer back on the table. "Good idea. Just doesn't work."

Most of the group muttered an assent. *It is a nice idea*, Stan thought. *It's just that the people who make the policies are rich and don't want to lose their power.*

"We suspected they'd come after us when we went public," O'Neal continued. "We were not expecting a preemptive strike with terrorist methods."

"Why should you have expected it?" Matt asked. "They're a church. Why would you have expected someone with high religious standards to act like terrori—" he cut himself off. "Sorry, that sounded much better in my head than out loud."

"No, Matt," the Colonel said sympathetically. "It doesn't make sense. They've always been a 'peaceful protest' group. They've never acted aggressively. We think the church has come under new leadership. This new tactic also has to include some form of espionage," she finished ominously.

"Espy-what?" Jeremy tried to surreptitiously ask his neighbor.

"Spying, you twit," muttered Kat from across the table drawing an abashed look from the Cajun.

"How do we know they've got an espionage... what's the word?. unit?" Sandy asked.

"They knew we'd be there," Ranj answered staring straight through the holo-flag. "Why else have the demonstration? Why have the spiked bodies in their cross pattern? Why have the camera?"

Chris, seated next to Ranj, leaned toward him and put a hand on his shoulder. "You ok?"

"No," he replied. "Not really. That was a really bad place. The bodies. The blood. The look on that guy's face." He turned to Chris. "I'll live. But I don't ever want to go through something like that again."

"That's what we're going to try to prevent," said the Colonel matter-of-factly. "We weren't going to mention it until later, but since this has come up. We have another active GNA who was already cleared for espionage work."

"Calling in Squeak?" Stan quipped, receiving a smack from Rich for his efforts.

"Squeak wasn't real."

"If I may continue," the Colonel admonished. Stan looked appropriately abashed. "The operative was undercover with the FBI when we activated him and, well, the Feds weren't too happy with us taking him. So, we gave him back, turned on.

"If it comes down to it and there is some sort of...war, just remember that Steven Callahan is on your side."

"Slash?" Glacier asked in the surprised tone everyone seemed to feel.

"Yes," O'Neal responded. "I've already talked with the Feds and they want to cooperate with us on this operation. Since he's already trained in covert operations, they're going to try to get him inserted in the church. That information *does not leave this room*."

"Colonel," Melanie piped in, "if you think there's a security leak, why are you announcing it to us? Everyone in the complex has had the clearance check except us, well, them," she motioned to the group with a jerk of her head. "If there's a leak, its most likely in this room."

"Actually," she responded, "the communications everyone in this room has with the outer world is tightly monitored. I can give you transcripts of everyone's conversations for the past several weeks, from Stan's conversation with his mother to what Chris claims he'll do with Martha when they get back together."

Stan's eyes had expressed embarrassment when his name was mentioned. The expression quickly became amusement at the mention of Chris's fiancé. He turned to his friend and asked "So what are you going to do to her, stud puppy?"

"Let's just say he's a bit kinkier that you think and get back to the subject," the Colonel admonished. Chris, for his part, simply sat ramrod straight in his chair and expressed gratitude to his God for having a dark, non-blushing complexion.

"The point in telling you is in case you encounter him, don't blow his cover, and, if one of you is the security leak, I'll be able to narrow it down farther. As far as everyone else in this complex is concerned, Steven was turned off and sent home. They do not know he is still active."

"Is there some way we can strike back at them without causing too much of a fiasco, Colonel?" Matt asked.

"Unfortunately, no. The best we can do is to move forward and be prepared for what they do next.

"The first thing I want to do is set up city patrols. Let the people see you for who you are and what you can do."

35
IN PUBLIC

Kat loved the night. Her new abilities made her actually cat-like. She ran across rooftops with such light feet that she didn't make a sound. She leapt from rooftop to rooftop with an elegance that she doubted anyone has ever felt.

This was a city she could really enjoy. She'd wanted to run across the rooftops forever. She knew she had a job to do, but there was no reason, she figured, that she couldn't enjoy it too.

As she leapt over an alleyway, she saw something job related. A mugging. Two on three, but the two doing the mugging were the one's who were armed. Two muggers against a husband, wife and kid. Time to even things up a bit.

As she landed on the far side of the alleyway, she immediately leapt backwards, adding a half-twist to land properly and a full flip, just for effect. The child, possibly an eight-year-old boy, was the first to see her, pointing up and mumbling, "cool."

She landed perfectly, or so she thought. One foot on each gun, bullet-proof boot heel on the muzzle. Both attackers dropped their guns and stared slack-jawed at *their* assailant. Comparatively speaking, they were both about six-inches taller than Kat. However Kat was armored in her "Kat-suit", and she was armed *with her claws*.

She raked both mugger's faces first bringing their head together with a violent 'clunk' and a second time to send their bodies sailing into opposite walls of the alleyway. Both bodies fell, sufficiently unconscious.

Kat turned to the family to make sure they were undamaged. The boy looked up at her with wide-eyed wonderment. The parents looked apprehensive. "Are you unharmed? Do you require medical attention?"

"Uh, no," the husband stammered. "We're fine." He handed her his wallet shakily. "Take it. Just don't hurt us."

Kat dropped her head into her hands. She realized that rubbing her temples, the reason for dropping her head, wouldn't really work with the head-piece on. "Sir, I don't want your wallet. My job is to make sure people are safe. You're a bit better now that these guys are unconscious. But this is still not the best neighborhood." The husband, still shaking, dropped the wallet.

Kat, her reflexes being what they were, caught it before it hit the ground. His driver's license fell out anyway. She equally snared it before it got to the ground. She glanced at the license before putting it in the wallet to hand to the man. Dr. Thomas Wayne. She put the license in the wallet and handed it to Doctor Wayne. She turned to the child, who was still staring awestruck at her. "You're name's not Bruce is it?"

"No," he replied. "It's Mike."

Good, she thought. *That would have been just too weird.* She closed the Doctor's hand around the wallet as he was apparently still too petrified to actually get a grip on it. "Take your family home Doctor," she said with a smile before pointing an arm at each of the unconscious assailants.

A whooshing sound came from each of her wrists. Both of the mugger's legs were instantly encased in a quick hardening foam, preventing them from running before the authorities arrived. *Randy makes some really wonderful toys*, she mused. She smiled at the family again before bounding back up the wall and out of site.

"When did super heroes become real?" the wife asked.

"I told'ja they were," Mike said proudly as he walked out of the alley.

His parents, still in shock, followed *him* home.

* * *

Paul MacIntyre was a simple man, or, to be more precise, that's how he thought of himself. He liked simple things. Well, things he considered simple.

Paul was someone that very few people actually knew. He made his living in a way that few could.

Paul was an internet scam artist, virus producer for hire and hacker.

His latest idea was to hack into the IRS database and rearrange things so that he would not only never have to pay taxes again, he'd get a six-digit refund check. After all, he'd become accustomed to being surrounded with his simple things.

Ninety-inch HD-TV. Prototype Dolby 9.1 Surround Sound stereo. Picassos on the wall. Leather on the couch.

Simple things...

In *his* mind.

And his computer... several levels beyond state of the art. The processor alone was the equivalent of six linked *Pentium 8* chips. Even Windows couldn't slow *this* system down.

Finding the IRS's IP address wasn't hard (for him). Bypassing the firewalls was a breeze (for him). Finding his particular file in one of the more remote corners of the mainframe took longer than he expected. The IRS had transposed two of his social security numbers. He hadn't counted on that but it didn't delay him for very long.

Something else that he hadn't expected was the monitor suddenly going black. He looked puzzled at the dark monitor. There were no pets or children to trip the power cords. Nothing else in the house was on.

The power supply hadn't gone out. The computer itself was still lit as it had always had been. The light on the 25-inch monitor was still on. It was still getting power. The video card? Had he blown another one?

As he scooted his chair back to get a better look at the CPU, a message appeared on the monitor in plain white text.

You have been very naughty Paul.

"What the hell?" he mumbled. Was *he* getting hacked? Who the hell could be good enough to hack *his* system?

Don't bother getting up. Don't bother looking for a hacker. You've been tagged.

Tagged?

And you're about to be bagged.

Bagged? What was this thing talking about?

That's when he heard the banging on his door, a gruff voice telling him something about the police and opening up, and a loud banging of something heavy crashing through what used to be the door.

He tried to get up and run out the back door.

That was the simplest escape route. He liked simple.

He was almost vertical when two bolts of electricity shot out of his front computer speakers flinging him across the room to land on the couch.

The first of the policemen had seen the bolts strike Paul. Realizing that Paul would be in no shape to put up any resistance, and that the rest of his team which was filing through the door, would cover the stunned hacker, the officer went to the computer.

"That might have been a bit excessive," he said.

Sorry Scott, replied the monitor. **Didn't want him getting away.**

"S'ok, Dot. If you get any more leads…"

I'll let you know.

The screen briefly revealed the face of a dark-skinned man with a Zorro-esque mask who nodded, smiled and blinked out of existence.

God I Love My Work!

* * *

The silent alarm had been triggered. That would be a given. Some smart-ass always triggered the silent alarm. Probably someone in an office overlooking the lobby.

That was all right though. They wouldn't be here long enough for the cops to show up anyway. The guards had been subdued. The patrons of the bank weren't going to be a problem. There were six people in his team. Three to get the money, three to make sure everyone was kept on the floor.

It always amazed him what six ski-masked people wielding fully-automatic rifles could do. Now the only thing was the clean get away. And for that there was a wonderfully armored car out back.

"Time!" he called and his team sprung into action. The three getting the money from the tellers and the safe jump the counter in almost synchronous fashion. *There's an Olympic Sport in the making*, he thought wryly. *Synchronized Bank Robbing*. He shook himself from his brief reverie and followed the group out the back door.

The armored car was just where it was supposed to be. The engine was running. The back doors were open. His group was filing into the back like the well-oiled machine they'd practiced so hard to be.

As soon as he exited the building, he helped push a dumpster in front of the door. That may not stop people for long, but any delay would be helpful. He and his 'dumpster buddy' jumped in the car and slammed the door as the car drove off.

The driver, dressed as a normal armored car driver, opened the small window between the cab and the back. "So, how'd we do Danny-boy?"

Danny pulled off his mask, as most of the passengers in the back were doing. "I think we did just fine," he replied surveying the bags of money laid out on the floor. "Just fine indeed."

Numerous sirens passed their vehicle, presumably attached to police cars responding to the alarm. "And they don't even know what we're drivin', do they?" The bank had been blind to what the robbers had driven to the bank in due to a lack of windows near the back door.

He could hear the traffic outside. They were traveling right down one of the main streets in the town and no one knew that the armored car was really the getaway vehicle. Brilliant!

He looked out the back window knowing its tinting would hide his face even from the car directly behind them. He watched the police cars speed toward the bank. "Seven of them," he announced to the group. "We're improving. The last job got us only five." He received a few chuckles, which is what he made the comment for anyway.

He looked out the window again and saw something odd. A tree had fallen behind them. Not a terribly big tree, but big enough to block traffic. He knocked on the window to the cab, which promptly slid open. "You got a problem back there?" asked the driver, Tony. "If someone sees me talkin' through the slot they may thing somethin's up."

Danny looked through the slot and out the window. No oncoming traffic. He glanced at his watch, three in the afternoon. There should be more traffic than this. There were only a few cars in their lane. Something was wrong.

"Danny!" called one of the other guys from the back. "What the hell is that?" Danny turned to see his colleague pointing out the rear window. About 20-feet behind the car was a man. He appeared to be metallic and... *is he floating behind us?*

The man, who was leaning forward slightly, extended his arms toward the van. A small red light shone on each of his palms. The small light suddenly extended from his hands and through the back door of the car... *through the armor!* Each light was attached to a steel cable grappling hook that opened connecting to each other and effectively attaching the metal man to the car.

The metal man leaned back and it appeared as flames shot from the bottom his feet. The car began to slow. "Punch it!" Danny called out.

"I'm tryin' Danny!" Tony responded. Danny looked out back window. The metal man was still there. The metal man suddenly... clapped his hands, and the cables that had been attached to each of his hands were now both attached to his left wrist. His right hand pointed more toward the ground at the car. A small projectile launched from his wrist.

Its effect was almost immediately felt. The van lurched to the right; obviously the result of a blown tire. The armored car, their getaway vehicle in seven heists so far, was betraying them. Ideally they'd shoot this metal menace, but the back doors were still held in place by the hooks.

"Who is this guy?" Danny muttered.

He wasn't sure if his words triggered something, but at the same moment he spoke, a gas sprayed from the grappling hooks. "And this was turning out to be a good day," he complained to no one in general as he passed out.

* * *

Jay Ward had been a cop for most of his life. He enjoyed it. The pay wasn't as bad as most made it out to be. And every so often, you'd see something that would surprise you.

Today, he saw one of those things.

A tree had fallen in the road about a mile back blocking traffic. The radio had ordered him to check the road ahead as it was only blocking the flow of traffic in one direction. Earlier the radio had informed him of another tree blocking traffic from the other direction leading most people who knew about both trees to think that something was going on between them.

There was only about a two-mile gap between. That wasn't much room to do something terribly big, but it could have something to do with the bank robbery that had just occurred.

He sped from one fallen tree to the other with the siren going and lights flashing. He loved this part of the job too, driving fast with the siren on. He didn't get to do it nearly as much as he'd dreamed about as a kid, but in a sense, that was a good thing.

He hadn't gotten far before the radio announced that some government team was in the process of apprehending the bank robbers somewhere between the two fallen trees and that other cars would be responding from the other direction. Jay was instructed to make sure nothing got past him.

He was prepared to see a car speeding toward him. Possibly a small plane. A tank. Even a cruise ship was more of a possibility than what he saw.

A man in a metal suit was attached to the back door of a lopsided armored car by two steel cables attached to his left wrist. The lopsidedness he attributed from the obviously blown tire on the back passenger side of the car.

The driver, apparently in a state of panic, jumped from the vehicle and attempted to run on foot, right toward the oncoming police cars. *Idiot.*

The man in the metal suit clapped and one of the cables switched to his other hand before both retracted from the armored car. He stretched out his left hand and shot a white substance at the runner. The goop hit him in the back and he fell, but the goop had solidified into… well, he wasn't sure what it was except that it was doing a good job of keeping the former driver from running.

He pulled the car up behind the armored man as the cars from the other direction blocked off the armored cars route from the front. Several officers from the other cars moved to cover the runner; the rest moved to the back of the vehicle.

Some started to point their guns at the armored man. Jay had exited his vehicle and called out to his fellow officers: "He's good! Cover the car!"

The armored man looked to Jay and asked, in a very robotic voice, **"They're unconscious but I still have the door sealed. Ready for me to open it?"**

"Uh, yeah, I think we've got it covered," he replied. *Is this thing a robot of some kind?*

The robot, if that's what it was, turned back to the van and pointed at it. A loud clanking noise sounded from inside. **"You may want to let the air clear a moment first."** The doors swung open and a cloud floated out. It took only a moment to actually clear and when it did the officers entered the armored car and began transferring the bank robbers from their vehicle to one of theirs, handcuffed, of course.

"How did you…?" Jay stammered.

"It's my job," replied the metal man.

"Do you, uh, have a name I can put in my report?"

"GEAR."

"Gear, eh? So you, what, just did this solo?"

"No, Sergeant. I had backup." He pointed at the sky where two figures hung, completely in defiance of the laws of gravity. One was a non-metallic gray; one was half-red and half-blue, divided down the middle. Jay started to ask another question when he realized that 'Gear' was flying toward them. The trio flew off, fittingly, into the sunset.

"Sergeant Ward!" a voice called. He turned to see his supervisor, Captain Burke. "Are you just going to let him fly off like that?"

"Well, sir," he replied as he turned back to watch the trio fade away into the distance, "the guy in that suit just stopped an armored car. By himself. And rendered most of the suspects unconscious, except that guy over there."

He held up his 9mm sidearm. "Do you think this would have stopped him?"

"I am not going to have a damn vigilante force running amok in my town!" he announced. "I don't care what government task force they're with!"

"Well, sir. We should probably get used to it."

"Oh really, Sergeant? And why is that?"

"Welcome to the 21st century, Cap. We've got super heroes!"

36
ROUND TWO

Randy O'Neal removed his helmet and placed it back on the mannequin head he kept it on. "I think that went even better than most of the sims I've been running."

Matt and Sandy, also removing their costumed headpieces, were simply awestruck. "You actually built that?" Sandy asked, regaining some of his composure.

"That's what I do," he replied. "Well, mainly what I do. I made several of the gadgets that are built into the suits, like the night vision, the communicators and the goop-guns."

"What is that stuff anyway?" Matt queried.

"I call it 'goop'. It's essentially a compressed and liquefied but quick drying calk. It'll slow down most people, but I wouldn't want to try using it on Rich. I thought it would be a good addition to the suits since having all of us carrying handcuffs wouldn't be terribly practical."

"I'd probably melt mine."

"True," he moved into a cubical in the changing room and began removing his armor. "You guys should get changed. The colonel expects us to debrief her on the bank heist as soon as possible."

The pair moved to their own cubicles. The room was, for all intents and purposes, a locker-room. Their quarters weren't really a sensible place to store their armored costumes. Especially with O'Neal wanting to add gadgetry to them as often as he did.

"Hey O'Neal," Matt called from his cubicle, "did you create that sim we were in when we first got here?"

"Yes, why?"

"I've got a couple questions about it. Like the shadow thing. What was that?"

"You saw it too?"

"I guess I should explain that one," O'Neal replied. "Part of it was to prepare you to expect the unexpected. Having a wandering shadow is something most people wouldn't expect, so, there it is.

"The other part is that he's actually wandering around here."

"A wandering shadow?"

"Yep. It's part of one of the GNAs that didn't quite go right."

Sandy, who'd finished changing into his 'civvies' stepped back into the room and leaned against the entrance of his cubicle, asked, "What do you mean 'didn't quite go right'?"

O'Neal sighed. While foiling the heist hadn't taken that long as he'd planned, removing his suit was taking longer. "I'm not authorized to tell you about it unless you specifically ask about that person. And even then, I'd probably lose my job over it. So, please, don't ask."

Matt, who'd also finished changing, did not like having secrets kept from him. He'd always tried to be honest and open with everyone. That was probably why he'd been burned so badly by his ex-girlfriends. "Does this have anything to do with the dreams I had in there?"

"You remember having dreams?" O'Neal asked, finally dressed, as he left his cubicle and led the others to the elevator. "You shouldn't have had any dreams. You were supposed to just have one day blur into the next."

"I had a couple dreams too," Sandy added. "Something about the briefing room and three... shadowy people."

"That was mine, too."

O'Neal regarded the two as they entered the elevator. "I didn't program anything about that. Shadowy figures?"

"They mentioned things like, planning out what would happen next and progress reports.

"They felt... ominous," Sandy added

The elevator doors parted to reveal the rest of the GNA group in the hall. Most of them were leaning against walls or sitting on the floor.

"What are you all doing out here?" O'Neal asked.

"The Colonel said she wanted to talk with the whole group," Melanie answered. "So, here we are."

"Not sure I like the sound of that," O'Neal said more to himself than anyone else. He absent-mindedly kissed her on the forehead. "Our mission went fine and I think we'll get some good press out of it."

"Anything's better than what we've been getting," Matt quipped. "I haven't seen that many people protesting since we did that march on the Capitol."

"You marched on the Capitol?" Ranj asked, clearly surprised.

"Yeah, we were protesting the way the whole Middle East thing was being handled."

"We're not coming off *that* bad are we?" O'Neal asked.

"I don't think so," Candace answered. "But we are more recent so we're drawing attention from the problems over there."

"Wonderful," Stan muttered. "As if gas prices weren't bad enough."

"True."

"Why is it called the Middle East?" Rich asked.

"What do you mean?" O'Neal countered.

"Well, New York is in the East. L.A. is in the West. Chicago is in the Midwest. How the hell did Baghdad get to be in the Middle East?" His comment, as absurd as it was, did make most of the group chuckle and seemed to lighten the somber mood. Rich's expression, however, looked as impassive as the rest of him. "Seriously. How does that work?"

Whoever was going to answer was saved by the opening of the briefing room door. They entered and took their seats, with Colonel Schmid already sitting in her spot at the head of the table. "Guys," Rich pleaded as he sat in his oversized chair, "anyone? How did that happen?"

"How did what happen?" the Colonel asked.

"Nothing Ma'am," O'Neal answered giving Rich a 'now-would-be-the-time-to-shut-up' stare. "Our mission was successful and there were no problems with the suit. I think it even went better than the simulations."

"That's good to hear, Major," she answered. "But as much as I'd like your report, something has come up that requires our attention. It may require all of you to be sent on a mission.

"The situation in the Middle East has become more of a problem than the Military had anticipated. There is a terrorist cell calling itself e-four-ay. We are uncertain at this time if they are related to the E4A we are dealing with here. What we do know is that they have very advanced weaponry and have already destroyed two units outside of Baghdad.

"We have been asked to deal with the situation." She flipped a switch on the desk to activate the hologram system, which promptly sprung to life displaying some sort of combat robot.

O'Neal stared intensely at the image. "That's one of mine!" he exclaimed, almost jumping out of his chair. "Those bastards got one of my designs!"

"I had suspected as much," the Colonel replied. "Not many people would design a three-legged battle droid. The reports indicate that they are not as fully armed as some of the other… toys Major O'Neal has designed, but they are still capable of destroying tanks and repelling heavy artillery. Major, in your designs, are these things remote piloted or do they require actual human interfacing?"

O'Neal's brow furrowed. "For this design, they need three pilots. Not so much one for each leg, but there are numerous systems that would need monitoring."

"Colonel," Matt interjected, "Is there a way we can get a better scale for the image? This hologram made me think they were small. But if there's three people in them…"

She made an adjustment to the holographic controls and while the image shrank, it added a second component. An Abrahams Tank. The tank was about as wide as the battle 'bot, but only as tall as the lower part of one leg. "And they've got three of them."

Sandy let out a low whistle. "That's big."

"Yeah," O'Neal sighed. "And if they used my design, there are very few weak spots. I've compensated for almost every kind of attack. Even Chris's electrokenesis shouldn't be able to take over its computer systems. These things would have to be hit hard."

"Conveniently," Rich said proudly, "I'm pretty good at that."

Stan patted his big friend's chest. "Easy big fellah. So when do we leave?"

The Colonel shuffled a few papers on her desk as if looking for the answer. "That's the problem with this mission. We don't know where they currently are. So, I need all of you to get suited up. You'll need to be ready to go at a moments notice."

37
TOYS IN THE SANDBOX

The group had been donned their costumes and were waiting in the staging area. O'Neal had added a new aspect to the room. In case of extreme temperatures, the room had been equipped with a holographic weather system so they could have a chance to get used to the general weather.

That meant the room looked like a giant sand box and it was really hot.

They were standing, sitting, or lying on the floor of the staging area, but the circular platform was surrounded by sand except for a walkway that led to an open door that revealed a hallway in a building that didn't appear to be there. Most of them had removed their headpieces after ten minutes.

They'd been waiting for over two hours.

"Hey, O'Neal," Stan called from across the circle, "is there a reason we don't just wait until they appear and then leave. I mean, there have to be better things for us to do than just wait here."

O'Neal's answer was cut off by a young, camouflaged man who ran into the room and right up to O'Neal, who was on the far side of the room. "They've been sighted sir! The most recent intel is being uploaded to your system now. Two minutes until transport!" he announced as he ran out of the room.

"Thank you Mitchem!" O'Neal called as the young man left. "Everyone suit up. We go in two!"

"You should have said something about two hours ago," Rich quietly jibed.

Unable to come up with his own retort, Stan just mumbled a quick "Shut up."

"Ooh, I got an ay-de-uh," Jeremy exclaimed.

"It's a bit late," O'Neal commented. "Make it quick."

"Why don' we jus' transport dem 'bots into space?"

"Because they're not tagged like you are," Chris answered. "I've been studying the system. Randy's suit—"

"GEAR."

"Sorry, GEAR, has some of the same properties as our GNA. That's what they lock on to. So to transport something we'd have to be physically touching it."

"So as ah run up to one, ah'll touch it, you 'port it, and—"

"Won't work," Chris interrupted. "You want to be transported into space, or a mountain, or whatever too?"

"Uh, no."

"Good," O'Neal declared. "Nice try Rush. Codenames only people."

A disembodied voice announced "*Initiate*," and the only change apparent in the room was that the circle, walkway and door had disappeared.

"O'Neal, shouldn't there be something here other than sand?" Remix asked. Instead of receiving an answer, Glacier picked his friend up, turned him around and set him back down. "Oh."

The holographic model did not do these things justice. They were huge. Their legs were set up in a tripod manner with a knee joint about half way up, thus O'Neal's name for them: Tripods. Each leg was connected to what could be a large pie-pan shaped control center. Each leg appeared to be armed with multiple missile launchers. The torso appeared to be heavily armed with assorted guns.

And this was what they could make out from a distance. They had been transported in about a click away. "Bigger than advertised."

"Cut the chatter Remix," Gear said as his suit began to hover. "Recoil, try to take out some of its weapons systems from here and work post-cap. Stretch and Kat, cover her. There may be other groups nearby. Rush, quick recon. Don't try to engage them. Thermal, take Nightlite. I've got Remix."

"There's no way in hell I'm gonna' be able to carry him!" Breeze exclaimed, jerking a thumb at Glacier.

"Glacier, can you jump that far?" Gear asked, receiving a shrug in response. "Well, catch up when you can. Let's move people!" With that he flew straight up, flipped into a loop coming down over Remix who reached up to grab Gear's arms as he flew by.

"Show off," Sandy muttered. He offered a hand to Nightlite, who accepted, and the two flew after Gear with Breeze and Glacier following close behind. Kat and Stretch took up flanking positions to Recoil who set up her large rifle at the top of a dune.

"Hope you've got some big bullets in that thing," Stretch commented.

"Very big," she replied. "Just keep me covered."

"Ooh, got an idea," Stretch said with an obvious sound of delight. He rearranged himself to serve as an arc shaped tent over Recoil. His costume, almost sand colored anyway, made a wonderful blind for the huntress. Kat joined Recoil under the Stretch-tent.

"Ok, so no one can see us, and he's got his head on the outside. That makes me feel so useful."

"It's ok Kat," Recoil said in an odd tone. "It could be worse."

True, she thought. She would be good backup in case someone saw through Stretch's disguise.

But something was nagging at her. Something she couldn't quite put a finger on. It wasn't just her feelings of inadequacy concerning the mission. It was something small. Something missing. Something—*click*.

"Where's Dot?"

* * *

Rush was not moving as fast as he felt he could. *Probably the lack of good traction*, he thought. The Tripods were not moving terribly fast. Their traction was no better than his, but he had considerably more speed than his tri-legged adversaries.

They were traveling in a mostly straight line, point a to point b—wherever those points were. He ran ahead of them for a mile. Nothing there. Nothing visible for miles except more sand. He ran back and arrived before Gear and the others. *Where are these things going?*

He noticed Remix and Nightlite being dropped off on dunes behind the trio of tripods, freeing the hands of the flyers to launch their own attacks.

All of their combined were attacks launched almost simultaneously. Remix liquefied one of the tripod legs toppling it to the sand, making it an excellent landing pad for Glacier, whose impact turned the Tripod into a crater of scrap.

An intense beam of orange light shot from a black sphere bisecting another tripod.

Two down.

While Thermal distracted the third with alternating heat and cold blasts, Gear fired a grappling hook at the front leg of the Tripod and began to quickly orbit the tri-legged beast. The controllers of the monstrosity obviously caught on to his plan and shot him. With what? Rush couldn't tell. Gear crashed to the ground in a heap.

Rush ran to their leaders side and without much further thought removed Gear's grappling gun and resumed his laps around the Tripod. Even at his sand reduced speeds, it took less than two seconds to exhaust the amount of cable in the gun and sufficiently tie up the Tripod's legs.

Rush retuned to Gear's side and removed Gear's helmet. O'Neal appeared dazed but was able to focus enough to see the tangled Tripod fall.

He glanced at the other fallen Tripods and noticed two of the Tripod pilots attempt to flee on foot. Although he couldn't think of where they could possibly run to, there wasn't anything for miles in any direction. Their escape was cut short as they became encased in O'Neal's goop.

"Where'd the goop come from?" Rush asked.

"Recoil," he hoarsely replied. "She's that good a shot."

"Sorry boss," Rush returned his concerned look. "What happened?"

"I'm not sure. The suit just gave out."

Remix's panicked voice came over the communicator, *"Glacier's not here!"*

O'Neal surveyed the battlefield. The Tripods were disabled. Remix was standing near one of them looking through the wreckage. "Where's Nightlite?"

"Recoil to Gear. Kat just vanished."

Gear cursed himself for not realizing what was happening. "O'Neal Override Alpha Point Two! Emergency Transport!"

38
MY TOYS

The desert-scape dissolved into the familiar dark circular room. This should have made the group feel more comfortable, but it didn't. Several of them were missing.

Nightlite, Glacier and Dot weren't the only members missing. Kat, Thermal and Breeze didn't appear in the room either. The remaining members dusted themselves off and left the staging area.

"What the hell is going on Randy?" Stan demanded. "Where is..." he looked up and down the hallway, "everybody?"

Ranj and Jeremy also examined the hallway. "He's got a point Major," Melanie added. "Even the staff is gone."

O'Neal said nothing; he continued to lead them to his work area. Upon entering his office, he detached something from his suit, presumably the power pack, and plugged it into, presumably, the recharger. He moved to his desk / workbench and turned on the computer monitor, grabbed the keyboard and began furiously typing.

"Randy?" Melanie implored. "What's going on?"

"One moment." He flurry of typing continued for almost a minute before ceasing. He abruptly went to a panel in the wall, opened it, and removed a large computer board.

He dropped his head and sighed before turning to the remainder of the group. "Someone has gotten into our system," he explained. "My guess is that someone from E4A got into the system and took our transporter hostage." He tossed the computer board on his desk. "Of course they'll have trouble working it now."

"So, what? That ting in da' dessert was a distraction?"

"I think so. We started disappearing one at a time, not as a group. There must be a reason, but I can't even find the transporter log. Someone's wiped it."

"So what do we do now?" Stan's obvious frustration mirroring the emotions they felt. "The staff is gone. Our friends are gone. We don't have a transporter. Now what?"

Very Clever.

The words appeared on his monitor and were echoed through the small speakers flanking it. The sound startled most of the group. Melanie almost shot the monitor.

It won't stop me. I already have the rest. You are the ones that matter least.

"Who is this?" Randy typed into the keyboard.

I'm in the honeycomb room if you want to find out so badly.

That stunned the group. "Well, that was unexpected," Stan deadpanned.

"Edwards," Melanie said suddenly. "Can you access one of the Edwards to see what happened?"

"Worth a shot," O'Neal said turning to another computer. A moment of furious typing yielded unfortunate results. "According to this, they're all offline."

"I guess we're going honeycombing," Stan announced and headed toward the door with Jeremy and Ranj in tow.

O'Neal slapped a panel on his desk and the door slid shut. "No."

Remix turned to O'Neal. "Look. I know that we're basically just lab rats to you. We're an excuse for you to play with your toys. But those are my friends down there and I'm going to help them. I don't care about your military hierarchy. You can't order me around. I'm a human being damn it! And I'm going after my friends!" Remix turned back to the door which liquefied at his mere gesture.

"Stan!" Melanie had forced herself between Remix and the door. She glanced over his shoulder at her husband. "I have an idea, but I need Randy to stay here and help me with it." She inhaled sharply and pointed a finger at his chest. "Watch out for the security system. It's probably engaged on that level. Take the stairs, not the elevators. And for God's sake," she kissed him on the cheek, "be careful."

* * *

Stretch, Rush and Remix exited the stairwell on the honeycomb level. The closest entrance to the honeycombed chamber was blocked by debris. Remix believed that it was probably Glacier putting up a fight, *if Glacier is actually here. We're walking blind into a situation we know nothing about.*

The hallway was almost 200-yards long and paralleled most of the honeycomb room, and it was only lit by the emergency light about halfway down the hall. Considering the subterranean nature of the complex, it was really dark.

"I'm going to go scan the hallway to make sure it's clean," Rush declared.

He was gone before Stretch or Remix could stop him. Less than a second after his seemingly instant disappearance, a section of the hallway, only about 50 feet away, seemed to strobe briefly, followed by a somewhat maniacal laugh with a Cajun accent. "Dat was easy!"

"Rush! Stop!" Remix called. "We don't know what else is down there."

There was no reply.

Ranj began to walk down the hallway. Remix grabbed his friend's shoulder to stop him. "We're going, but we need to go slow. He obviously set something off, but he might not have set *everything* off." He tapped his communicator to activate it. "O'Neal, can you give us more info on the security in the hall?"

"*Not really,*" O'Neal replied. "*I designed most of the weaponry used, but I didn't do the installation. That would have been Micah's job,*" referring to the friendlier of the Edwards units.

"Wonderful," he replied snidely. "I don't suppose you know which one of your toys would make a strobe light effect?"

O'Neal muttered a curse. "*That would probably be a plasma repeater rifle. Try to stay away from it.*"

Remix and Stretch had progressed far enough down the hall to reach a small, smoldering pile of debris. "Actually I think Rush already took it out."

"*He's not running down that hall is he?*"

"I can't tell anymore. He was."

O'Neal cursed again. "What is it Randy? What's down there?"

"*A laser mesh netting.*" O'Neal sounded despondent. "*If he runs through that thing, it will shred him.*"

Remix bit back a snide, bitter remark. "O'Neal, next time you tell us about these things before we run off to fight them."

"*Maybe next time you'll wait for me to do it before you run off.*"

"Touché." Remix and Stretch continued down the hall cautiously.

"Got an idea," Stretch said suddenly. He turned and stretched one arm back to the pile of debris, grabbing a handful of small metal parts. "If we toss these down the hall, maybe we'll set off the rest of the traps."

"Maybe if you'd taken a flashlight you could see them. Hang on a minute." A moment later the lights in the corridor relit.

"You could have done that sooner!" Remix complained to the ceiling.

"Actually I've been trying to."

"Uh, Stan," Stretch muttered. Remix glanced at his friend noticing that he was pointing down the hall; his pallor becoming a rather pale shade of green.

Remix turned down the hall again and realized what Stretch saw. Small cubes of smoldering flesh stretched down the hallway. Rush had found the laser mesh net. The site was enough to turn both their stomachs.

"I never even knew his last name," Remix whispered.

"Wagner," Ranj answered quietly. "Jeremy Wagner."

Remix closed his eyes and took a deep breath. He'd dealt with friends dying before, just not in person or this violently. "We need to keep going."

"I know," Stretch answered wiping a tear from his eye. "Just try not to step on him."

The pair moved slowly down the hallway making an effort not to step on anything that could have been their friend. Remix was subtly using his powers to create a sonar effect to try to discover more traps.

Surprisingly, there were only the two.

As they reached the doorway at the end of the hall, Remix notice Stretch still had tears in his eyes. "We can grieve for him later. I know that sounds cold of me but we need to find out what's going on in there." He jerked a thumb at the doorway. "Are you going to be ok?"

Stretch inhaled deeply and exhaled slowly. "Yeah," he answered unconvincingly. "Want me to peek inside and see what's in there?" he asked contorting his body to where his head had become small and his neck very long. "I'm good at peeking around corners."

Remix smiled at his friend and shrugged. "That's ok. I thought we'd just walk in."

Stretch resumed his normal human form and asked, "What? Like we own the place or something?"

"We do." Remix turned and stood tall and proudly and, essentially, marched into the room. Stretch attempted to mimic his friend's confident form and followed, trailed by an unusually long shadow.

39
UNPLUGGED

The honeycomb room had changed. The honeycombed capsules were still along the wall next to the doorway they'd passed through.

Along the wall to the left was a large pile of O'Neal's solidified goop that appeared to have been discarded. It still held the shape of a person but there was no person inside any of the disposed pieces. Remix figured a lot of people had been recently 'gooped', released and probably placed in capsules.

In the middle of the chamber was what appeared to be a transmitter. It was a short flat cylinder resting on a tripod of legs with a massive dish on the top. Next to it was a single capsule, which appeared to be plugged into the transmitter of some sort.

Between the capsule and the transmitter, there as a man with a very familiar face. He spread his hands in a mock-bowing manner. "Welcome."

His voice had deepened a bit but it was still the same person. It was just a matter of which of him he was.

"Edwards?" Stretch exclaimed. "What the hell? I thought you were all deactivated."

"They are," he smiled. "I'm not. I also know that most humans in this situation want an explanation. And I hate to disappoint you, but you're not getting one from me."

Stretch was taken aback at the politeness of the android. "Micah?"

The android scrunched his face in an effort to look exasperated. "Yes?"

Stretch looked to his partner. "Well don't just stand there! Blast him!"

Remix did not move. He did not blink. He didn't even appear to breathe.

"He can't move dear boy. I've seen to that. Of the two of you, you're not really the one who's a threat to me.

"You have two choices now," the android continued. "You can simply surrender. You won't be harmed. You'll just be capsuled like the rest of them. Or you can resist and most likely die like poor little Jeremy."

Stretch felt his ire rising. This thing just killed his friend and now was almost gloating about it. "I guess you don't really have the Asimov laws programmed in there do you?"

"Oh they're still here. And I am acting in the best interest of humanity. Equality For All. You are *not* equal or human. You do not apply."

"I may not fit the category of human any more... but I am going to apply to you!" Stretch took the mass from his left arm and added it to the right which he transformed into a large hammer. He charged and swung an overhead blow at the android. If Micah had been human, the blow would have crushed him.

However, Micah was not human. And he was behind a force field.

The hammer blow never connected and Stretch was thrown back almost fifty-feet. Stretch recovered from the shock in the air and landed on his feet. His expression of determination was slowly fading into desperation.

He couldn't get through the force field. Now that he looked for it he could see the field stretching across the entire room. There was no way to reach the android. His mind raced over the possibilities, but ultimately he felt his resolve slipping. There was nothing he could really do.

A small tingling sound near the door caught his attention. Recoil had appeared out of nowhere. She was already aiming a large rifle at the android.

"And what do you think that will accomplish, my dear?" The android's tone filled with amusement. *And he has a point*, Stretch thought. *There's a force field.*

Recoil's aim didn't need to be perfect; Stretch knew that. Her ability to alter projectiles in mid-flight was extraordinary. What Stretch didn't know was that this ability apparently included energy weapons.

Two green beams lanced from the gun penetrating the shield. The beams took an abrupt turn, one severing the connection between the satellite and one carving a slice in the top of the capsule itself.

Micah looked in horror at the capsule. "Do you have any idea what you've done?!" he cried.

A dark cloud appeared over the capsule and entered through the crevice.

Remix shook his head, grabbing it with both hands. He quickly focused on the Edwards unit and screamed at it. Micah's torso shattered into millions of pieces.

"I know exactly what I've done." Recoil's voice was icy calm.

Micah's head landed near the honeycombed wall with a smile on its face.

It spoke four final words in a mechanically distorted voice. "Exactly what we wanted."

A hand appeared in the crevice of the capsule and a muted voice called out. "Would someone mind getting me out of here?"

40
A NEW HOME

Recoil, Remix, Stretch and the newly rescued Eric Duffy searched the honeycomb room and found their teammates unconscious in separate capsules. The bottom row contained three extra large capsules, one containing Glacier. The others had been found in standard sized capsules on higher levels.

Upon their release, they were told about what had happened to Micah and his attempt at stopping the program.

Eric explained his ability to travel in a shadow form and possess people. He explained that he had not actually been in his body for several months. His shadow form was unable to penetrate the capsules so once he realized he was able to possess people, he couldn't get to his real body to repossess it.

The staff had been found on the campus above the complex. Recently promoted Lieutenant Mitchem had gathered them and had been attempting to reenter the compound since mass transport.

The Edwards units had been found with their positronic brains missing.

Colonel Schmid was *not* found. Some of the staff believed she was involved. Some didn't. O'Neal decided to hold judgment until she was found.

* * *

Major Randall O'Neal had gathered the GNAs in the briefing room. "Until Colonel Schmid is found, I've been told that I'm in charge of the complex. And I know that a lot of you have questions about what happened. I'll see what I can do about answers.

"For starters, when the dessert mission to get the Tripods began, Micah rerouted the transport signals to get Chris, whom he placed in a capsule. Chris was the biggest and most obvious threat to him.

"From there he started taking us individually. Apparently he did have some trouble with some of you," he nodded at Glacier.

"How did he subdue them?" Stan asked.

"That would have been Eric, actually."

"Me?" Eric sounded as confused as the rest of the group felt. "Uh, Randy, I didn't get down there until Stan and Ranj got there."

"Sorry," O'Neal apologized, "I should say it was your body that did it. Let me continue before you bombard me with questions. We knew about Eric's condition, basically being trapped outside his own body. The Edwards found out that if the body was capsuled and connected to the main capsule system, we could use his body's GNA ability to telepathically paralyze or manipulate people.

"In some cases that was a necessary thing. There were some whose GNA abilities were uncontrollable. We'd kept them in stasis in a capsule with Eric's body monitoring and somewhat controlling the process.

"Eric was even an essential part of the sim program you all encountered when you first got here."

"Oh I'm good," Eric said in a sarcastic manner, after a pause, adding, "apparently."

"So, are there any more questions?"

"Yes," Matt answered, "Are we going to be staying here in our compromised complex or…"

"No, the first is that we should move the complex from here."

"Where is here anyway?" Glacier queried.

"Well, we're just outside of Boise."

"Idaho?" Sandy asked.

Oh, no. They wouldn't.

"No," quipped Candace jerking a thumb at Stan, "he's 'da" her mouth continued the verbal jab but no sound escaped her lips.

Stan cast her a smug look. "Ha ha." He loved creating sound vacuums at times like these.

O'Neal looked puzzled. "He's the what?"

"Da Ho!" the group, save Candace and Stan, answered.

Stan, tongue firmly planted in cheek, dropped his head. "Damn."

* * *

Jeremy Wagner's body had been gathered as best as possible. A funeral service had been held for him with all of the GNAs present. Jeremy's family was apparently so estranged that they didn't even attend.

Ranj Serikahn knelt at the tombstone. "I guess you were kinda like me. I don't know that my family would be that interested in my funeral either. I know Karen wouldn't."

"Yeah, I know. You didn't know Karen. We were together for about six years. I come home one night and find her in bed with… damn; she was in bed with a blow up doll. Do you have any idea what that does to someone who doesn't have much of an ego to begin with?"

He composed himself and wiped at his eyes with the back of his hand, not even sure when the tears had started. "I had assumed that you had this perfect life. You were always so cheerful and… perky. I never suspected it was a cover."

"It might not have been. But judging from the crowd here, or lack thereof, I'm guessing you didn't have anyone either."

"And then you go and give your life for us. Trying to rescue people that you didn't even know two months before. You were a good man, Jeremy."

"I'm really going to miss you."

* * *

The reception was bigger than anticipated. A big band played a wide assortment of tunes, almost every genre except country. Chris couldn't stand country. It was one of his two requests. No country. Martha's family acquiesced. He felt he should ask them since they were traditionally bound to pay for the wedding.

This was fine with him since they were loaded. Not quite Bill Gates loaded, but loaded enough.

His other request was to add a few people to the guest list. The active GNAs were mingling with the family members and friends. It had taken a while, but they even found a suit that would fit Rich. He looked ridiculous, but the children seemed to love climbing on him and he didn't mind.

Martha had never looked better. Her long flowing white wedding dress was hugging her in all of the right places making him look forward to the honeymoon suite where *he* could hug her in all those places.

He had told Martha that he would be working with the GNA group. He'd even told her about his abilities. He trusted her to keep it a secret.

Gigi had brought the husband and the kids. Mike Wood seemed like a nice man. It was his idea to name the kids. Fraternal twins, one girl and one boy: Persia and Tiger Wood. "Who the hell would name their kids Persia and Tiger?" Stan had asked the group to which Ranj had replied "Mike Wood," drawing groans from everyone in earshot.

Despite her marriage, she still kissed Eric when she discovered he was still alive. They had decided to keep the information as a surprise. O'Neal said they'd used Eric's ability to wipe her mind of the events of the past several months. "What would be the point of keeping her active?" O'Neal had said. "She'd already turned everybody on." Laughter had, of course, ensued.

Erica Danube's arrival had surprised most of the group, including Chris. It turned out that Erica had gone to college with Martha. Odd coincidence, but it could happen.

Life was looking pretty good to him. Chris had helped O'Neal set up the new computer system in the new, above-ground complex outside Lebanon, Kansas; the geographic center of the United States. They had a new house, which he had paid for, near Kansas City.

The only dark spot was Stan, who was at the bar rapidly becoming inebriated. His stupor allegedly caused by the appearance of Melanie O'Neal, in an absolutely stunning dress, attached to Randall O'Neal, in a similarly stunning tuxedo.

He'd noticed Stan had trouble looking at her since their revival from the sim. And he never found out what happened in the hallway. He wasn't sure O'Neal did either. He did notice O'Neal excuse himself to take a cell phone call a few moments ago.

When O'Neal reentered the room he looked distressed. He'd be damned if someone was distressed at his party, other than Stan, so Chris made a bee-line for his boss. "You ok Randy?"

"The other capsules were empty," said in a hushed tone.

"Yeah, I know that. Once they got me out I helped open the others."

"I just got a call from Lieutenant Mitchem. The computer records for the transporter show Edwards used them to make one mass transport before he was deactivated. The 'uncontrollables' aren't in stasis any more.

"Look, I'm going to have to grab the rest of the group. We need to find them before something terrible happens. This is your wedding, you stay here. Enjoy yourself." O'Neal weaved his way into the crowd to gather the GNAs.

*　*　*

Erica Danube stood near the stage and simply observed the party. She wasn't much of one for this kind of thing. She did get a kick out of the bizarre expression Melanie had shown when Gigi was talking about *initiating* a new program for the twins.

Mostly her upbringing taught her to be unobtrusive, invisible. It was proving to be a valuable lesson. No one seemed to notice her while she noticed everyone.

One of the things she noticed was Randall O'Neal gathering her old classmates and heading for the door. Soon the only people from the old school were Gigi, Chris and herself.

Good, she thought, *just as it should be.*

TO BE CONTINUED

Printed in the United States
64068LVS00004B/85-87